The Krewe
House of Lazuliè

A Novel

E. Lane Redmond

CLASSIC XVII PUBLISHING
Imagination Ignited
New Orleans • Louisiana

Second edition: April 2026
ISBN: 978-0-9983261-3-9
Library of Congress Control Number: 2026902361

Cover design, interior design, and copyediting by
E. Lane Redmond

Printed in the United States of America
Softcover edition, 5.5 × 8.5 trim size

Classic XVII Publishing LLC
New Orleans, Louisiana

DEDICATION

To my elders,
whose wisdom anchors me.
To my ancestors,
whose spirits guide me forward.
Your blood runs through my ink, and your voices echo in these pages. Thank you for your sacrifices, your strength, and your stories. May this work honor the path you paved.
And to the next generation: may you never be afraid to follow your calling, even when the world says it's too strange, too much, or too loud.

"For nothing is hidden that will not be made manifest, nor is anything secret that will not be known and come to light."

— Luke 8:17

PROLOGUE

Mardi Gras Evening – February 27th, 1906

The Creole manor loomed behind its wrought-iron gate, white columns rising two stories into the late-afternoon light. Black shutters sealed the tall windows. Brick chimneys streaked with soot crowned the roof. Oaks leaned close, their branches netting together high above, shadows striping the pale façade.

From somewhere deep inside, a woman's voice rang out, "Georgianna!"

The child trotted over, her feet pattering fast. "Yes, ma'am?"

"Chil', now what I done told ya 'bout runnin'? Want the Madames to hear ya?"

"No, ma'am." The words came soft, her eyes fixed low, her mouth pulling down at the corners.

Elizabeth hooked a knuckle under her chin and lifted. "Wanna help ya maw out?"

The child gave a quick nod. Elizabeth reached into the pocket of her apron, drew out a dingy cloth, then bent to take one of Georgianna's hands and placed the rag into her palm. "Take this here rag and give them baseboards a good ol' wipe down while I finish gettin' supper ready."

The brightness left Georgianna's face. "Yes, ma'am," she muttered, her feet dragging as she left the kitchen.

She dropped to her knees just outside the door and set

to wiping the baseboards, just as her mother had told her. Grime spread across the cloth as she crept up the wall, small strokes trailing her down the length of the grand room.

The space felt larger when she was alone in it, the scuffed floor stretching wide around her.

Sometimes traces lingered. Perfume worked into the curtains, laughter tucked into the corners. On other days, the space was alive with voices and footsteps, trays of her mother's carefully crafted hors d'oeuvres and little samplers of her rich Creole fare passing from hand to hand, glasses of wine balanced in clusters. At carnival parties and charity socials, she and her siblings moved through the crowd, serving those who rarely looked their way.

It felt different now. Hollow. Echoes waited for the next time they'd be woken up.

She kept her head down and worked her way toward the far side, the sliding door behind her closing the kitchen off.

By the time she reached the far wall, her knees ached against the boards. She shifted the cloth in her hand and pushed on, turning into the narrow hall. Bedrooms and bathrooms lined both sides, with a coat closet tucked to her right, just before the stairwell. Beneath the first run, a low, narrow door stood ajar, a door usually kept shut.

She stopped, hand hovering at her side. The half-open door held her in its stare.

From beyond the door came the old whispers: that it led to a place that smelled of death, that the sight alone could sour the stomach. Other young house workers swore they'd been inside what they called the burning room, insisting the place reeked of meat left to rot.

Georgianna eased the door open wider and peered in. A narrow staircase wound downward into dimness, the first few steps hemmed in by cold, stone walls. She stepped onto one stair, then another, the dark pulling her down with patient invitation.

Halfway down, the wall to her left broke away, replaced by a run of wrought iron railing. Its black bars twisted into curling shapes. Candlelight from below licked up between the scrolls, throwing shifting patterns across the opposite wall.

A steady drumbeat rose, thrumming through the metal under her fingertips. She crouched at the bend of the staircase, her face pressed close to the cold iron curls of the railing. Between its swirls, she caught the room below.

Geneviève, the eldest sister, stood in her knickers by the gramophone spinning its bright, feverish tune. A foot or so away, a woman sat motionless in a rough-hewn wooden throne. A ring of tall ivory block candles encircled her, every single one burning.

The other two sisters, Désirée and Adelaide, slipped into the circle, also stripped to their underthings.

In union, the three yielded to the melody. The drum bent their spines, rolled their shoulders, and moved their hips in measured accord. Désirée's hands rose, fingers curled. Adelaide's bare feet struck the concrete, the cold surface answering each slap with a deadened echo, a counter-rhythm to the drum's pulse. Geneviève's head tipped back, lips parted, her arms spreading wide in the candlelight.

The fine strands at the back of Georgianna's neck bristled. She had seen enough.

Without a sound, she backed up the steps one careful inch at a time, making sure her shoes didn't creak against the wood. When she reached the top, she broke into a run.

"Mama!" she whispered, but the word still came out loudly as she skidded back into the kitchen. "Mama, they doin' somethin' down there. Somethin' bad."

Elizabeth looked up from the pot she was stirring, brow furrowing deeply. "Who chil'? And whatcha mean 'bad'?"

"The Madames, mama. In the burning room! They was all standin' 'round some woman in a chair with nothing but their britches on and a bunch of candles all over!"

Elizabeth wiped her hands on her apron. "This why I tell you 'bout pokin' where you don't belong," she muttered, more to herself than to the child. "Them eyes ain't even learned how to see right yet."

"I know what I saw," she said softly, her little heart pounding rapidly.

Elizabeth's head snapped toward her.

"I know what I saw, Mama," she repeated, louder this

time, voice still shaking. "And it warn't nothin' good." She clung tight to her mother's arm.

"Alright, alright. Lower that voice. Just settle down, you hear?"

"Yes, ma'am." Georgianna tried hard to still her trembling hands.

Elizabeth's tone softened as she slid out of her daughter's grasp. "Now… you said they down there in the burning room?"

The little girl nodded, quick and frantic.

Elizabeth sighed long, gathering herself before she moved. "Alright then," she muttered, heading toward the hallway.

"I'll come with—"

"No. You stay put. I'll go and take a look. Just go'on and take that pot off the stove and get the rice started for me. I'll be right back."

Georgianna hesitated, biting her lip so hard it nearly quivered. Elizabeth waved her off with a flick of the wrist.

"I swear," she mumbled as she walked, shaking her head. "Don't even know the difference between mischief and mess."

Her muttering continued as she crossed the hallway. "Probably done caught 'em foolin' with that wine they keep tucked in the pantry… always carryin' on, them three."

Elizabeth spotted the cracked door at the stairwell and stepped through.

Stone walls pressed close. She placed a palm on the wall and descended one slow step at a time.

She went just far enough for the candlelight to reach her. Her knees gave a hard pop, then another, echoing faintly against the stone as she lowered, one hand braced on the rail, peering through the ironwork where she could see without being seen.

Her nerves stilled, her sight fixed through the narrow curls of iron, while everything else faded away.

At first, she caught only restless shadows and stray flares of light off the circle of candles. Then Désirée emerged from the dark, sinking into a squat near the candles.

She watched as she snatched one and held it out. Geneviève stepped forward to retrieve it, and Désirée picked up two more as she rose to her feet. Then both women stepped back.

Adelaide knelt, tilting a shallow brass bowl to let the fine, gritty powder spill in careful streams. Bit by bit, a heart formed on the floor, its sides widening before narrowing to a blunt point. Through its center ran a single straight line, fleur-de-lis blossoming from either end, curlicues curling loose but balanced enough to hold the design. When the last curve closed, Adelaide rose, clapping the dust from her palms as Désirée placed a candle in her hands. Then, without warning, they began chanting in Haitian Creole.

"Nou twa nou bay. Souf ak doulè, chak baryè nou louvri. Nan zo ak sann, dèt nou siyen. Baron Samedi, fè chemen an parèt. Papa Legba, soti nan fèmen ak lapriyè… pa manda san, lage Lazuliè lib!

—We three have given. Breath and sorrow at each gate, risen. In bone and ash, our debt is sealed. Baron Samedi, let the path be revealed. Papa Legba, from lock and plea… by blood's decree, set Lazuliè free!—

The flames of the candles in their hands began to flicker violently. They chanted again. Then once more. Then stillness. Each flame burned unnervingly calm, its wick glowing with a thin red core.

"The gate has been opened! Mèsi Baron Samedi! Mèsi Papa Legba!" Geneviève sang, stepping toward the sleeping woman. Right in front of the powder-drawn heart, she called out, *"Maitrès Lazuliè, ou bèl, ou jantiy, e ou plen ak lanmou. Rèn tout-pwisan nan lanmou, liks, jènès, ak bote. Tanpri sòti vin ranmase ofrann ou yo. Bèl gason ou ap tann ou."*

—Mistress Lazuliè, you are so beautiful, kind, and full of love. Queen all-powerful in love, luxury, youth, and beauty. Please come out to collect your offerings. Your handsome man awaits you.—

After the last sentence was spoken, the flame on Geneviève's candle sputtered… then died. Désirée and Adelaide's candles went out as well. Then, one by one, each flame of the ring of candles blew itself out. Now, only the torches that hung in each corner were left to illuminate the room. Next, an unfamiliar voice spoke. *"Ki kote li ye?"*

—Where is he?—

A low voice rolled through the room, and the candles the Madames were holding relit themselves all at once.

"Ki kote bèl gason an?"

—Where is the handsome man?—

The once-unconscious woman stood and stepped through the circle of unlit candles.

Geneviève dropped her candle and fell to her knees. "Ayibobo! Mistress Lazuliè, we are so thankful that you have come forth!" Désirée and Adelaide carefully set their candles down, then followed their big sister's lead.

While bowing, they shouted in unison, "Ayibobo!"

"O pa! Ranmanse chandèl la kounye a, timoun! Ou dwe kenbe yon kay pwòp!"

—No! Pick up the candle now, child! You must keep a clean house!—

The woman scolded.

Geneviève immediately picked up her candle again. Somehow it was still lit.

As she gawked at the candle, she forced herself to say, "My apologies, Mistress Lazuliè."

The woman then took a moment to survey her surroundings before noticing a man lying in a bed across from her. His hands and legs were tied to the bedposts.

She lingered, a smile bending her mouth as he writhed, every frantic snap of his body a performance for her eyes. He thrashed, but the knots held tight.

Without uttering a word, Mistress Lazuliè gracefully moved past the sisters.

Before reaching the bed, the woman's reflection in the floor-length mirror caught Elizabeth's eye. The smile in the glass wavered. Too wide. Then it eased itself back into beauty. Elizabeth gripped the railing tighter to steady her nerves.

With admiration, the Mistress eyed herself as she slowly ran her hands down the voluptuous curves of the body she was in. She then moved closer to the mirror to ogle the vintage gold necklace that dangled from her slightly elongated neck. The royal blue diamond-encrusted pendant attached was in the exact shape of the doodle Adelaide had drawn on the floor. When she lifted her hand to touch the pendant, she noticed the blue and white flowers that were fashioned into a bracelet around her wrist. She lifted the corsage to her nose to get a whiff of the flowers and smiled when the sweet scent of jasmine oil filled her nostrils.

As the deity continued to admire herself in the mirror, the Madames approached her.

Geneviève held out a tray with a single champagne flute filled with the manor's most expensive bubbly. "Are you thirsty, Mistress Lazuliè?"

Before she could answer, Adelaide stepped forward with a tray of assorted blue and white petit fours. "Here are some sweets for you, Mistress Lazuliè."

The woman turned around to face the sisters and threw her hands out at them to clear her path as she slunk over to the bed.

Once she made it to the bed where her offering lay bound, she exclaimed,

"O wi! Nonm sa a se bèl tout bon!"

—Oh yes! This man is truly handsome!—

Her nightgown slipped from her shoulders, pooling in pale folds at her waist. She straddled him with the gravity of a queen claiming a throne, the low glow sketching the curves of her body.

While the Madames crept nearer, she spoke English for the first time. Turning to them, she purred, "I am pleased with your offerings, my children. Now… speak your desires, and if they delight me, I shall carve them into fate." Her gaze drifted downward to the man sprawled beneath her. "But only after I have known my Bèl Garson and tasted the wine of his devotion."

"Mèsi, Mistress Lazuliè. My sisters and I are well into our fifties. Our beauty is fading and our strength is thinning. Marriage has passed us by. We ask that you restore our youth, that we might have a second chance to be chosen." Geneviève bowed low as Désirée stood beside her, holding up a gold-plated tray. On it lay a dagger curved into a crescent, its jagged blade etched with markings worn by time. The hilt flared wide at each end, and at the center rested a lapis lazuli stone, deep blue veined with gold.

From the shadows, Elizabeth mumbled to herself, "Lord… what kind of conjure is this?" Her fingers locked around the iron bars. Her hands tightened on the railing until the iron trembled.

"Lè sa a, li pral fè!"

—Then it shall be done.—

Lazuliè shouted before taking the dagger into her hand.

The man lay rigid as she leaned over him, lowering her face close to his. Her palm brushed the rough stubble along his jaw, then gently drew the knife in a line across his cheek.

"Will you surrender to me?" she crooned, withdrawing the blade.

His eyes locked on hers, dazed, transfixed. His pupils widened; a faint hum slipped from him. His head dipped in surrender.

"Bon… ou chwazi jan ou te dwe."

—Good… you've chosen as you should.—

She let her nightgown slip away, baring herself.

With one hand, she loosened the ball gag and let it drop to the floor. Then she took the dagger, bending forward to slit the bindings at his wrists before returning it to the tray Désirée held out at her side.

The instant his hands were unbound, he reached for her face. She seized his instead.

Their mouths collided, frantic and consuming.

His body surged beneath hers.

She broke from his mouth to nip at his ear. The sound he made was rough, something between a moan and a yielding cry.

She lowered her mouth to his chest, tracing slow circles with her tongue, savoring each twitch beneath her.

Another jolt ran through him, and without hesitation, she sank onto him, her hips moving in a steady grind. His thrusts met hers, each one an offering, each one drenched in desire.

The Madames hovered at the end of the bed, mouths slightly open.

Moved by the sight, Geneviève snatched the dagger and leaned in, slicing through one rope at his ankle, then the next. She lingered only a heartbeat, biting her lip in anticipation before returning the blade to Désirée's tray, her composure slipping just enough to betray the pull of the moment.

The man gripped Lazuliè's waist and flipped her with rough force.

Now he was on top.

Their bodies shifted once more, his weight pressing her into the mattress as his hips drove forward. She arched to meet him, one hand knotting the sheet, the other raking slowly along his spine.

He caught her wrists and pinned them gently above her head.

"Mine," he breathed, his voice trembling.

"Yes… show me your devotion."

The tribal drumbeat banged louder and louder in the background, matching the frantic pace of their bodies.

The torches' flames stretched tall, throwing monstrous shadows against the walls.

He tensed. One final thrust. A shudder. Then stillness.

"I love you," he moaned. And for a heartbeat, everything froze.

The torches stopped dancing. The drums dropped dead.

"O, Bèl Garson mwen… pawòl ou yo… yo konsole mwen.

—Oh, my Bèl Garson… your words… they console me.—

Her face glowed as she raised her hands.

"Let this moment be written amongst the stars! Our souls shall be tethered together until the heavens themselves fall away," the Mistress declared before sliding from beneath the man and rising to her feet.

Panic flashed in his eyes. Lazuliè saw it before he even knew it had arrived. "Wait!" he blurted out.

"What is it, lanmou mwen?" she said weakly, her lips quivering on the words.

"I-I'm not sure of what I just said," he stumbled over his words, glancing around. "Can't we… can't we slow down a bit? Maybe get to know each other proper?"

Her expression collapsed.

She stared at him, as if she could not quite comprehend the words he had spoken.

The fire in her eyes dimmed and the man saw it.

He reached for her, voice shaking.

"I just need a chance to make sense of this… of you."

"Enough!" Lazuliè's voice sliced through the air.

She raised a trembling hand between them, commanding the very air to take his voice.

Tears streaked her face. The sound that followed was a chorus of weeping, soft and shrill, until it filled the room.

He scanned the room frantically until the staircase at the far end came into focus.

It was a good distance away, but it was his only hope.

While the woman wept uncontrollably, her face buried in her hands, he seized the opportunity, snatching up his pants and bolting toward the exit.

He was halfway to freedom when the dagger flashed through the air, sinking deep into his back with a sickening thud. He froze, his legs buckling, and collapsed to his knees.

From the bed, the ethereal beauty drew herself up, her face a portrait of grief turned rage.

She stalked toward him with the pace of a predator, then crouched and settled the dagger into her palm. With one slow pull, she dragged it downward, slicing through skin and sinew.

He collapsed backward, wheezing, bleeding out fast.

She loomed over him and hissed,

"Ou se jis tankou rès la!"

—You are just like the rest!—

Then she sank onto him and drove the dagger into his chest.

He convulsed, choking on blood as wet gargles spilled from his mouth.

When it was done, she rose and stood sovereign above him.

Turning to the three sisters still gathered by the bed, she commanded, "Come, you must bathe in the blood whilst it is still fresh!"

Eagerly, the sisters scrambled to obey.

Quickly, they slithered across the bloodstained floor, scooping handfuls of the man's blood and coating their bodies with it.

Under the candlelight, their bodies shone. Slick. Red.

Their laughter echoed hollow and high.

The drum Elizabeth had followed into the dark was now beating within her.

Up the staircase, in the shadowed dark, Elizabeth crept.

One hand gripped the railing to steady her shaking legs, the other pressed tightly over her mouth to keep from making a sound. Tears stung her eyes, but she blinked them back. The wood groaned faintly beneath her heel as she took a step.

She froze, heart pounding almost loud enough to give her away.

She moved again.

Not daring to breathe too deeply, she clung to the shadows. She fell into the wall's embrace, hiding her as she crept back toward the hush that waited above.

CHAPTER 1

Mardi Gras Season – Present Day

"Alright, nah!" a few people in the traveling crowd shouted as they watched Alexis dance to the cadence of the highly syncopated jazz tune. Alexis let the horns pull her forward, shoulders rolling loose, her spine carried by the pulse of the street. She was the newest girl in the Krewe of Lazuliè, but already out front, high-stepping with the best of them. She'd meant to keep her steps small, but once the trumpets blared, she couldn't dial it down. The melody caught her, and she was gone with it.

Following the brass band, Alexis skipped forward. Her waist-length braids tumbled loose from the neat high bun she'd fastened them into as she crossed her legs and spun around. Then she dropped into a squat, sweeping the ground with her festive-colored handkerchief.

Even though the heat hadn't peaked yet, Alexis still broke a sweat. Humidity gathered on her skin like dew on midnight cane, gleaming with every step down Bourbon Street.

"Heyyyyy!" the crowd kept hyping her up as her petite frame popped back upright. One of the straps of her faded denim overalls came unbuckled, swinging loose. Her knee-high socks worked overtime to keep up with her footwork, shuffling like she was caught in a game of Double Dutch.

It was the first major second line of the season and Alexis was enjoying every minute of it.

Even as the rhythm pulled her forward, she kept a watchful eye.

She scanned the crowd and sidelines.

It was a habit she couldn't shake.

There was always somebody lurking. Watching.

Nevi skipped backward just behind Alexis, her sequined umbrella spinning above her head. A whistle cut through the music. Hers. The line behind her responded instantly, narrowing in. She flashed a smirk at Rae, who just grinned back and twirled her own umbrella.

Della clapped once, then again, syncing the tempo of her steps to the beat of the snare drum as she moved in time beside them. Her voice rose over the horns, shouting out a chant that the girls behind them picked up fast.

The three women moved in matching jumpsuits, their sequins flashing like flint striking metal. They moved with the kind of ease that made everyone else fall in line. All around them, heads turned, and bodies shifted to make room.

Trailing behind came the rest of the girls, the final initiates, moving as one bright current of energy, color, and hunger. Eleven young women strong, moving with the reckless joy of youth… and something quieter beneath it.

Some moved with polished precision, flowing smoothly and hypnotically like a slow current. Others burst forward, their movements spilling across the cracked pavement. Some came fresh from college campuses. Others were from around the way, tired of the same cycles, craving something different.

But all of them carried the same invisible weight, the need to matter. True Blue Hearts.

After Alexis wrapped up her solo, the rest of the Krewe broke into their own routines.

As the parade rolled on, more bystanders joined the current.

By the time they rounded the next corner, the second line stretched over a block long, a rolling wave of bodies moving as one. Sensing the rising energy, the band slid effortlessly into a fresh tune. This one was heavier. Rowdier. The bass rolled through the pavement, and the crowd answered on instinct, shouting, twirling, and dancing.

From balconies and doorways, more people spilled out, drawn in by the sound, the movement, the magic.

Then a low sound cut under the brass.

Alexis slowed, squinting ahead as the music blurred into the background. It was a voice coming through a beat-up speaker in an old wagon, tugged by a man walking alone just behind the tail of the band.

"You walk these streets, dressed in your Sunday best, thinking your good deeds will shield you…"

He held a wireless mic in one hand, his words steady and unshaken as he moved. "Remember Job, who was upright, yet faced trials beyond measure. Remember Paul, who spread the word, yet was beaten and imprisoned…"

Alexis edged closer to the sidewalk, not fully stepping out of the celebration, but just far enough for the sermon to come in clearer. Her eyes didn't follow him at first.

"It's not enough to mean well. The path to suffering isn't always paved with wrongdoing."

Her hand twitched at her side, instinct itching to move, yet something in his voice pinned her in place. The sound pulled at her.

"The righteous who walk blind with guilt may step straight into damnation." The speech carried on.

Her eyes followed him now, watching the way he moved steadily through the crowd, not stopping for anyone, not looking to be praised or fought with.

"Lex!" A voice snapped her out of it. A hand caught hers. "There you go again, zoning out!" Jade teased, laughing as she pulled her through the line of faces.

"I wasn't zoning out," Alexis uttered, still halfway turned toward the preacher's fading voice.

"Yeah, alright, girl. Just c'mon!"

They weaved their way back into the second line, where Raven and Jennifer were already dancing near the center.

They'd slowed into more of an amble now, letting the second line carry them. The brass band blared ahead, but the girls drifted toward the sidewalk's edge, pausing to steady themselves in the haze of celebration.

"Wait, hold on." Raven reached into her small

crossbody slung from shoulder to hip, its strap glittering purple, green, and gold like parade spoils. "We've got to commemorate this moment, y'all!"

Alexis perked up fast, smiling too big. "Yes, let's!"

Alexis fought the urge to cringe, knowing her response came off weird, but the others rolled right along with it.

Jennifer turned, beaming. "You read my mind, girl. Come on, group up."

The three of them gathered without hesitation. Alexis slid an arm around Jennifer's waist.

"Okay. On three." Raven's grin spread as she angled her phone.

Jennifer held a peace sign up to her cheek, smiling widely. Alexis leaned in, eyes bright, lips parted in an open grin. Raven stuck out her tongue and winked one eye, a picture of reckless joy.

Click.

Then Raven turned to Jade, waving her over. "Girl, bring your ass over here and get in this damn picture."

"Uh-uh!" Jade waved her off. "I'm a sweaty mess."

Raven rolled her eyes and shoved the phone into Jennifer's hand. "And? We all look a mess."

She stepped in and grabbed Jade by the wrist.

Jade laughed but dug in her heels. "I'm good, y'all, deadass." She held out her free hand. "Jen, hand it over. I'll play photographer."

Jennifer didn't move. "Say cheese!" she called, already angling the phone toward them.

Alexis stepped closer, smiling softly. "Come on, girl. It's just a little picture."

Then Raven added, "Shit, ain't like nobody else is gonna see it, anyways. You know how the Madames feel about posting krewe-related content. I done come too far to get kicked out over something small like that, boo."

Jade narrowed her eyes at Raven, sighed, then caved. "Alright, y'all hoes come on then."

Raven let out a little squeal, dropped Jade's hand, and bounced back into place. Jade eased in, sweeping her locs over her shoulders before dropping her arms to her sides. Alexis slid between them; one arm wrapped around each girl's waist.

Click.

Jennifer handed Raven her phone. "Make sure you drop these in the group chat."

"Will do." Raven slid it into her purse.

They lingered a second longer, then eased back into their walk with the foot parade, bouncing a little, laughing again, hips loose and spirits lighter.

"Y'all, we really made it!" Jennifer shouted. "It is exciting, huh?"

"Bitch, exciting?" Raven cut in. "We started with almost twenty girls, and only twelve of us made the cut. Shit was like the Hunger Games! I didn't even think all four of us was gon' make it."

"Nah, but listen though," Jade sang. "From what I heard, this is only the beginning. The real challenge starts tomorrow." She threw a glance at Alexis and looked away before the moment could settle. "But anyway. This? This is our moment. We earned it."

Alexis shifted her stance. She almost pressed Jade on the comment but let it go.

"Yeah… exactly. We've got to hype ourselves up. We made the Krewe."

"We *definitely* have to hype ourselves up!" Jennifer nudged her. "Especially you, Miss High-Stepper."

That pulled the smile back to Alexis's face. "Please. I've *been* carrying y'all!" She tossed a few braids over her shoulder.

"Hold on, how you hit that li'l move again?" Raven asked, already trying to mimic her two-step.

Instead of answering, Alexis decided to bless her with a proper demonstration. A few tight steps, a quick turn, just enough to light up their little circle as the parade thundered past.

"Ayyyyeee!" Raven shouted, doubling over with laughter.

They were still giggling when Alexis felt a gentle tap on her shoulder.

Her body went still. Instinct had her shoulders brace before she made herself ease back.

Before she could fully turn around and register who had

touched her, the unfamiliar girl blurted out, "Hey! You went to Dillard, huh?"

Alexis blinked, taken aback. Unease slithered up her spine. She didn't know who this girl was, or what she was about to say next.

"Yeah…" A hint of skepticism was evident in her tone.

The girl's grin widened, sly. "I knew it was you. We had psych together, remember?" She gave Alexis a quick once-over but didn't wait for a response. "I thought you was one of them dicks. But look at you, out here cutting up in the middle of the street. What happened? Don't tell me they let you go!"

Instead of answering the question, Alexis offered one of her own. "I'm sorry, do I know you?" The question came out cold.

"Well damn, bitch. I was just speaking to you. You don't have to be so rude." The girl stomped off without giving Alexis a chance to reply.

Alexis stood there, irritation crawling up her neck.

"Wait, Lex. What she said? You want me to pop that hoe?"

"No, girl. Chill out." Alexis rolled her eyes.

Jade stepped up beside Alexis. "You know ol' girl?"

Alexis shook her head. "I don't know who that was. But she obviously had me mistaken for someone else."

The words came out smooth, practiced, but her throat tightened halfway through.

She forced a thin smile. "Let's go before the Madames notice we're not in the line anymore."

Alexis took off, needing the movement to shake off the sting of that exchange.

"Wait up!" Jennifer called, jogging to close the gap.

Raven and Jade fell in behind them.

By the time the girls reached the front again, the music had rolled on without them, the second line carrying itself down the block. They stopped a few feet from the Madames.

"Blue Hearts!" Nevi's voice carried through the street. "Gather, please."

Alexis watched as the girls moved without hesitation, gathering into a tight huddle. Then she stepped forward.

"The narrowing has been meticulous… at times, tedious," Nevi went on. "But still delightful, nonetheless." She glanced across the girls, appraising them one by one. "And we believe the next Crowned Heart stands before us."

The girls shifted. A few exchanged quick glances.

"We now enter the next phase," Nevi continued. "Preparation. It begins at our manor."

Before she could go on, Alexis spotted a dark bruise on Rae's forearm.

"Madame Rae, you alright?" she asked, brow furrowing.

"She is perfectly fine, dear," Della interjected, waving her off.

"Yes," Rae added, her smile stretched thin. "Just caught an elbow in that second line shuffle. Della gets a little too spirited when the horns get going." She moved her sequined umbrella to the other hand, tucking the injured arm closer to her side.

Alexis nodded, but the unease held, tight as a fist.

Leaning in, Raven murmured, "One little tap and she's out here looking like she got jumped. Must suck getting old."

Alexis swatted Raven's bicep, whispering, "Shut up, girl!"

The girls laughed softly, but Nevi heard it.

"What's so amusing, ladies?"

"Apologies, Madame Nevi," Alexis spoke up quickly. "We didn't mean to interrupt."

"Thank you," Nevi replied, her tone clipped, though her jaw loosened just enough to pass as composed.

"Now, as I was saying." Her voice softened but held. "Tomorrow evening marks your entry into something sacred. From that moment until Sunday, the House of Lazuliè will hold you. Use the time you have left wisely. Make peace with the outside world. Pack only what you need."

After a brief pause, she added, "Because once you cross those gates Thursday evening… you will not leave until your stay is complete."

A few scattered "okays" and murmurs of agreement followed.

Then Della offered the closing word.

"We'll see you ladies tomorrow."

As the rest of the girls made their departure, Alexis's circle lingered a little longer.

"You ready for Preparation?" Jennifer bumped Alexis's shoulder.

"Yeah, I guess so," Alexis said. "I've heard so many things about the place, so it'll be nice to finally see it for myself." She let out a small sigh. "But at the same time, I don't know. It's probably crawling with spiders and… whatever else comes with a house that old."

"Shit, I know I'm ready!" Raven scrunched her face. "You tripping, Lexi. Talking 'bout the damn house."

"She must not know what's gon' go down," Jade added.

"Okay, what the hell are y'all talking about?" Alexis squinted at them.

Jennifer grinned. "We're gonna get sponsored!"

"Sponsored?" Alexis frowned.

"Alexis, girl… bless your heart," Jade chuckled.

"Girl, we 'posed to be getting hooked up!" Raven looked at her like it was obvious.

"Hooked up? With who?" Alexis asked.

"I don't know," Raven responded. "Probably with some dudes from another krewe. Like a matchmaking thing."

"I heard it's supposed to be some rich old dudes." Jade shook her head.

"Well shoot, somebody's grandpaw finna be paying my rent then," Raven shot back.

"I didn't hear none of that. Who told y'all that, the Madames?" Alexis wanted to know.

"No, but that's been a rumor about this krewe," Raven told her.

"Right!" Jennifer jumped in. "You never heard about that, Alexis?"

"No, I haven't."

"Well, I guess we're about to find out if the rumors are true," Jade said.

Alexis stopped and eyed the three of them. "Well, I'll see y'all tomorrow. My bus stop's just up the street."

"Girl, you not catching no damn bus. One of us can

give you a ride," Raven told her.

"I can bring you. I live uptown, too." Jennifer volunteered.

"No, I'm good. I'm not going straight home, and I don't want anybody going out of their way."

"You sure?" Jade double-checked.

"Mhm."

"Alright then," Jade responded.

"See you tomorrow then, girl." That was Raven.

"See y'all tomorrow." Alexis hugged each girl and watched as they disappeared around the corner.

The music still blared in the distance, bodies bouncing and swaying beneath the pinkish dusk settling over the city. But at this point, Alexis was over all of it.

A flicker of memory stirred.

The righteous who walk blind with guilt… may step straight into damnation.

She walked faster, the words hooked into her, pulling her out of the music's sway.

CHAPTER 2

"Dammit, I know I'm forgetting something," Alexis muttered, pacing the room as her mind raced. The sienna suitcase toppled off the bed and hit the floor. The zipper gave way, spilling a week's worth of chaos onto the carpet.

"Dammit," she hissed, dropping to her knees and scooping everything up fast. Pants. Shirts. Underwear. Her anti-itch hair oil. A pack of hot pink hair ties. She shoved it all back in.

Then she climbed on top, pressing her weight down until the zipper caught.

Tomorrow, she'd be locked away at the House of Lazuliè. No leaving until the Krewe's next phase wraps.

Still perched there, she paused and scanned the room.

Her attention landed on two books stacked neatly on the desk.

The Cost of Keeping Us Safe. Beneath the Black and Blue.

Heavy reads. Personal ones.

Her throat pinched.

We ain't cut from the same cloth, bitch…

They ain't never gon' see you as nothing more than a pawn…

She shook the voice from her head. In the motion, her gaze caught on the piece of metal resting on the nightstand.

Crescent moon wrapped around a gold star. *Lieutenant 199* stamped clean across the middle. Still polished, even after all these years.

Without wasting another second, she grabbed the badge and tucked it into the small inner compartment of her suitcase.

Wiping the back of her hand across damp eyes, she trudged into the living room.

"Hey, my baby." Alexis smiled when she saw her cat lounging on the sofa.

Taking a seat next to the pudgy black furball, she stroked her back and said, "Now, Mama's gotta go away for a few days... but don't worry. Auntie Toni's got you."

Dusty turned her head and glared.

"Don't look at me like that," Alexis sighed. "I'll be home before you know it."

She stood, gave the modest apartment one last scan, then headed outside to haul both her and Dusty's bags to the banged-up white Impala. After loading the trunk, she went back up, secured Dusty in her kennel, and carried her down.

"Let's buckle you up," she muttered, snapping the seatbelt across the carrier.

Then she slid behind the wheel, clicked in her own belt, and pulled off.

Antoinette flung open the door with a scowl. "Lexi, why you always banging like the damn police? You're gonna give Maw Maw a heart attack!"

"Hey to you too," Alexis smirked, brushing past her big sister.

Cornbread and lemon cleaner met her at the door. A fan purred against the heat, while the TV muttered low in the background.

"Where's Teedy's baby at?" Alexis wondered aloud, setting down Dusty's kennel and cracking open the door. The cat slipped out slowly, spine curling high in a stretch.

"With his pappy. It's his week." Antoinette's voice was dry as bone.

Alexis's mouth twitched. "Right. My bad." She cleared her throat. "How's Maw Maw?"

"Resting. Just finished her dialysis."

Alexis started toward the back, but Antoinette caught her arm. "No. Let her sleep."

Alexis let herself be steered to the couch. "You really went through with it."

"I wasn't about to leave our grandma rotting in that nursing home."

"But how are you going to juggle everything?"

"Morning shift. Center in Kenner while I'm working. Joshy said he'll help too."

Alexis snorted. "We'll see about that."

Before Antoinette could clap back, a soft weight landed on Alexis's thigh. Dusty. Tail flicking in slow arcs. Alexis rubbed behind the cat's ears, her hand moving without thought.

Then the TV's drone filled the room.

"You've been different," Antoinette said finally. "Distant."

"Busy," Alexis answered, too rushed, and winced. "After this case, I'll have more time."

"Gabrielle Alexis Rochon!" Antoinette leaned in. "You really still on that mess?"

Alexis rubbed her temple. "Nothing's changed."

"Well, I told Maw Maw."

Alexis sighed. "What'd she say?"

"She said you better watch them people, 'cause they do voodoo."

"Girl, I doubt it. Those ladies are some hard-up Catholics."

"Them be the main ones," Antoinette muttered with a crooked smile.

"You need to stop listening to old, senile women," Alexis giggled, scratching Dusty under the chin. "Anyway, I'll be at the House of Lazuliè for—"

Suddenly, pain flared between her thumb and forefinger. "Ahhh!" Alexis jerked her hand back, staring at the bead of red welling where Dusty's teeth had sunk in.

The cat didn't budge. Her body went tight, crouching,

tail whipping in arcs. Her pupils devoured her irises until her eyes looked all black, two pits boring through Alexis. A hiss unspooled slowly, then broke into something closer to a growl.

Alexis froze. For a moment, Dusty seemed more like a stranger than her pet.

Then she sprang, claws skittering against the floor as she vanished down the hall.

Antoinette's brow rose. "Well. Guess I'm in for a treat with this wild beast in my house."

"Sorry." Alexis rubbed the sting from her hand. "I don't know what got into her."

"Don't tell me Miss Thang's got separation anxiety." Antoinette shook her head. "You said she wasn't gonna be any trouble."

"She won't, I promise. I probably just startled her; she wasn't paying attention."

"Mmm hmm." She leaned back against the couch, tucking one leg under herself. "Anyways… how long you 'posed to be posted up at that place for?"

"Just four days."

"Just four days?" Antoinette's face twisted.

Alexis dipped her chin. "Mhm. It's something they've got the Krewe's official members doing. They call it Preparation."

"Preparation?" She couldn't hide the concern on her face. "Lexi, you know you don't have to do this, right? I'm sure there are plenty of other missions you can go on."

"Yeah, I know, but—"

"I just don't want you to lose yourself trying to prove yourself," Antoinette rested a hand on her little sister's knee.

Alexis dropped her head. "I'll be fine."

Time held its breath.

Her eyes drifted. Landed on a photo perched on the narrow wall shelf. The frame was worn and sun-faded. All four of them crammed on the couch. Mama in the middle, arms wrapped tight. Baby Joshy in her lap, laughing.

Her mouth moved toward a smile, but it stopped short.

Her gaze slid to the next frame. It was a formal portrait. Hands folded. Uniform pressed, collar snug, tie clipped firm. A single gold bar on each shoulder board. The badge on her chest, steady as a vow. *Lieutenant 199.*

"Mama would be proud of you."

Alexis dipped her chin, blinking fast, caging the tears before they could fall.

The words struck deep.

A speck of light flared on the frame, spilling across her vision, washing everything white.

Then she closed her eyes and, in her mind, she was back in uniform.

Starched stiff, collar biting at her neck. Early morning sun burned straight through her eyes. She stood in a row of recruits, bodies locked in formation. Shoulders squared, chins up; statues under the heat, ready to finally be sworn in.

At the podium, her mother stepped forward.

Her gaze moved down the line and stopped when it found Alexis, their eyes locking.

"You've always had a big heart," her mother said. "This city needs that heart."

The words ripped loose and fluttered away.

She tried to swallow the small knot that had formed in her throat.

"Now why y'all in here hootin' like a pack of wild hens?" a raspy voice cut close.

Alexis wiped at her eye and turned to see their grandmother standing in the hallway, one hand braced against the wall.

Antoinette jumped up. "Maw Maw! What are you doing without your cane, woman?! You gon' mess around and bust that hip again."

"I don't need no damn cane," she huffed, wobbling into the room. "Just came to see if it was really my favorite grandbaby makin' all that noise."

Alexis stood, moving to help, but the old woman waved her off with a flick of the wrist and all the stubborn pride that came with it. She settled into her recliner with a soft grunt, eyes never leaving Alexis.

"So, it *is* you," she murmured. "Knew I felt somethin' stir… You done carried somethin' up in here with you?"

"Maw Maw, what?" Alexis's brow furrowed.

"Don't 'what' me, girl!" the old woman snapped.

"I told your 'favorite grandbaby' what you said about the voodoo stuff," Antoinette muttered, tossing her little sister under the bus.

Maw Maw caught the subtle shade aimed her way but didn't bother to dignify it. "Chil', I ain't say nothin' about no voodoo. What them folks do… is twisted conjure. Rootwork gone bad!" She looked at Alexis as she pinched at the hem of her faded house dress, thumb working the thin cotton gently before she spoke again. "You need to stay away from them folks, baby. That land is cursed. And this family tree has been tangled up in their wickedness from the root."

"Ugh," Alexis groaned. "Ma'am, I don't have time to decode your riddles right now." She waved a hand, but her voice lacked its usual bite. "You don't really believe in all that, do you?"

"Belief ain't got nothin' to do with it," Maw Maw spoke in a hushed tone. "Rootwork don't need your permission to take ahold."

No one spoke. To her ears, the TV even seemed to hush. Alexis felt it under her skin.

The spell broke with a sudden burst of sound, the news anchor's voice cutting through. "Family and friends of nineteen-year-old Jennifer Wright are urging anyone with information to come forward…" Antoinette's eyes jumped to the screen. "Wait… is this the girl you told me about?"

Alexis turned to look. A woman was sobbing into her hands. It was Jennifer's mother.

"Yeah," she sighed.

"Damn. That's like the fourth one, huh?"

"Fifth," Alexis corrected while rising stiffly.

Maw Maw's eyes never left the screen. Her fingers found the hem of her faded house dress again. "One by one," she muttered. "Just like before."

Alexis cast her a sideways glance, then looked away. Her phone buzzed hard against the cushion beside her.

She grabbed it without thinking. "Shit," she muttered.

"Where the hell are you, Rochon?" barked Captain

Landry on the other end.

"Still at my sister's."

"You didn't hear the all-units call forty-five minutes ago?"

"…Must've left my radio in the car."

"Get your ass to St. Louis Cemetery. Now!"

"Which one?"

"Basin Street."

Alexis let out a dry, nervous laugh. "What, another grave desecration?"

"Thirty-C."

The words hit her like a fist. Her smile dropped.

"What happened?" she rasped.

"You'll want to see it for yourself. Move your ass."

Click.

The line went dead.

Alexis shoved the phone in her pocket.

Antoinette stared.

Alexis didn't speak.

She opened the door…

And left.

CHAPTER 3

Alexis double-parked her Impala along the cracked curb outside the cemetery, her heart hammering.

The battered stone walls rose like crooked teeth. Only a few struggling streetlights buzzed overhead, casting jittery shadows across the rusted gate.

The humid night pressed in.

She sat still for a moment, breathing in deeply. Then she stepped out, her sneakers pressing into the gritty crunch of crushed shells and gravel.

Walking through the gate, a chill licked the back of her neck. Ahead, a few officers stood behind the yellow crime scene tape, their faces washed pale by the stuttering pulse of red and blue lights.

The farther she trekked into the cemetery, the paths narrowed. Stone tombs pressed close on either side, their cracked faces worn by wind, rain, and the weight of forgotten names.

Sergeant Simmons gave a small wave, already turning toward the scene. "She's over here."

He wore his usual. Plain slacks, sleeves rolled, badge clipped to his belt. Nothing special. But he still carried his calm like a weapon. The sharp line of his jaw, the shadow carved into his brow… every time she saw him, it struck something she couldn't seem to shake. She tried anyway.

Alexis hesitated, exhaling slowly before falling into step behind him.

Simmons slowed just enough to fall in beside her.

"You know… You really don't *have* to be here," he murmured, low and rough. "I could have just relayed the details."

Alexis didn't break stride. "Cap told me to come. I'm fine."

"'I'm fine,'" he echoed her words. "You always say that."

She kept her sight straight ahead, pretending she hadn't heard him.

He didn't push.

They rounded the final bend, and the smell hit. Sick and bitter… unmistakable. Alexis swallowed hard.

At the base of a cracked tomb, beneath a flickering streetlight that caught just right through the trees, lay the body. A young woman. No more than twenty-one.

She wore a cotton white nightgown, torn and bloodstained. Her ankles were bound with rope. Her wrists lashed together around a crude cross. Two splintered pieces of wood tied into an X with bloody fabric ripped from her gown.

Dark bruises bloomed across her arms and legs. The light caught her face. It was angled just enough for recognition to strike her.

Alexis froze, the recognition hitting her so hard it paralyzed her.

"That's Milan," she said low. "From the Krewe."

The words hung.

Simmons stepped forward, concern flashing across his face. "You sure?"

"Positive."

No hesitation.

The girl had gone missing right after not being accepted into the Krewe after the first round of cuts. The reason they gave for cutting her was that she didn't have the poise they were looking for. Too rough, not refined enough.

But Alexis remembered her differently. That smile. The spark in her voice. Milan had energy and heart. Maybe she needed polish, sure… but she had potential.

Now, all that light was gone.

"What's the time of death?" Alexis inquired, crouching and sliding on latex gloves.

Vargas, the forensic tech beside Simmons, crouched with her. "Lividity's fully fixed. Judging by temp and stiffness, I'd say she's been dead eight to twelve hours. Throat was cut. Clean slice across the carotid. Minimal blood around the facial wounds compared to the neck, which means everything else happened after death."

Alexis's gaze caught the girl's face, and her stomach turned before she could steady it. The mouth had been carved wide, deep cuts running from each corner of the lips to the ears, as if someone wanted to stretch a smile she never wanted to give. The eyes were stabbed into pulp. The whole region collapsed into a wet ruin.

What chilled Alexis most were the streaks of red running from the corners of Milan's eyes. Someone had dragged them down, leaving two neat trails on each cheek like bloody tears pulled by fingers.

Slowly, Alexis freed the wooden X from the girl's wrists. The wood was rough and partly blackened with blood, gritty to the touch. Singed into the grain were four short lines.

She read them aloud, her voice just slightly above a whisper. "Seven moons… seven boons…seven gates… seven tombs."

She stood, the X dangling from her fingers.

"What does that even mean?" Simmons wondered aloud rhetorically.

She answered him anyway, "I have no clue."

"Out of all the girls who went missing, she's the first one to turn up?"

The voice came from behind her, loud and clipped.

Alexis didn't need to look to know who it was.

Still, she turned.

Detective Stewart stood across from her, arms crossed. Her weight shifted onto one heel, waiting to be seen.

Alexis met her eyes, calm on the outside. "First one to be found… like this," Alexis replied evenly. "No movement on the others so far."

"Only three have verified connections to the Krewe," Simmons added, stepping in beside Alexis, almost instinctively. Too close.

Stewart's eyes jumped to him, then back to Alexis, fast but noticeable. Her lips pressed into a line.

"We should revisit the case files on the other two. Make sure *nothing* slips through the cracks." She looked at Alexis when she said the last part.

Captain Landry joined the group, glancing down at the evidence bag in Alexis's hand. Short, solid, and somewhere in her mid-fifties, she carried the stance of someone who didn't need height to own a room. Her ruddy skin glistened with a light sheen of sweat. She looked at the bag, then at Alexis.

"Well, this changes everything."

"And the media's gonna eat this up," Stewart muttered, still watching Alexis instead of the body.

Alexis drew a slow breath through her nose but remained silent.

"Not if we lock it down," Landry cut in. "No leaks. I want this airtight before anyone else gets a word out."

Alexis slipped the wooden X into the evidence bag, her hand trembling slightly.

"She was strangled first," Vargas added, cutting into the tension, "before her throat was slit."

A vivid flash surged through Alexis's mind. She saw someone cloaked in darkness, kneeling in the dirt, their hands locked tight around Milan's throat.

Vargas lifted Milan's lifeless hand, turning it slightly to reveal blood beneath her fingernails. "Looks like she tried to fight back."

Alexis got another flash. Milan clawing desperately at the stranger's arms, her nails raking against skin as she fought to break free.

Tears welled in Alexis's eyes, burning hot and blurring her vision. She blinked fast and hard, forcing the emotion down. She couldn't fall apart. Not here. Not now.

"You getting a sample from under her nails?" she asked.

Vargas gave a short nod. "Already bagged it. Should tell us something."

"Where exactly are we with this investigation, Rochon?" Stewart's pitch was a little too high for Alexis's liking.

Alexis stood tall. She had to lift her chin to meet Stewart's gaze. The moonlight brushed over her caramel skin, muting its warmth into a dusty blue. "Still pulling it all together."

"You pushed to lead this. If *this* is your idea of leadership…" She raised both hands up like she was surrendering.

Alexis opened her mouth, but Simmons beat her to it.

"She just got back," he snapped. "Ease up."

That made Alexis roll her eyes.

That was the wrong thing to say.

Stewart stared at Simmons, taking him in from the ground up. "Cute," she muttered.

Not bothering to utter another word, she excused herself from the huddle.

Alexis didn't look at Simmons. She didn't have to.

"We need answers, not excuses." Landry was firm. "Now we have a body."

Alexis felt the graveyard close in on her as she watched the techs finish up.

One girl dead.

Four still missing.

Something dark was at work.

Landry called to her. "Walk with me."

They moved away from the scene, flashlights fading behind them.

"You sure you're up for this, Rochon?" Landry checked.

"Yes, ma'am."

A long pause hung between them. Landry looked at her for a moment too long, her mouth tightening as if she were deciding whether to say more.

Finally, she did.

"You know you didn't really have much of a choice that day, right?"

"That's what everyone keeps saying… like if I hear it enough times, I'll finally start to accept it as the truth."

"It *is* the truth."

Alexis held Landry's gaze for a second longer, but something within her fractured.

Before Landry could say anything else, the night around Alexis blurred.

She closed her eyes to clear her vision, but when she opened them, the fluorescent lights overhead caught her off guard. Her heartbeat pounded in the rhythm of fear it had come to memorize. Her hands were already raised.

"Stay the fuck back or, I swear to God, I'll kill this bitch!"

The man holding the woman hostage was wide-eyed, sweating through a stained white button-up Dickies shirt. One hand was locked around the back of her neck; the other had a steel-gray pistol pressed lightly to her temple. She was crying, her legs visibly shaking.

"Okay, now." With both hands still raised, Alexis took a few steps backward. "All I want to do is talk to—"

"You think I'm playing?!"

The man lifted the pistol and fired once into the ceiling.

Debris rained down. Chaos exploded behind him. People screaming, ducking, and begging to be let go.

But he was unmoved.

He turned the gun back to the crying woman's head.

"I'm gon' light this bitch up if you don't get out my fucking way."

"Rochon!"

A deep exhale left Alexis before she realized she hadn't been breathing.

She blinked hard, snapping herself back to the present.

"I-I'm sorry, Cap. I just—"

"Look, Rochon," Landry cut in. "You don't have to explain a damn thing to me. I just want to know if you're okay."

Alexis gave a slight nod, forcing herself into the now, shoving the rest into a locked corner of her mind.

"Yes… I'm fine." She cleared her throat and turned back to the matter at hand like she hadn't just traveled back in time. Like she hadn't just relived the worst day of her life.

"This isn't random. But whether the Krewe is being targeted or involved somehow… I'm not sure of just yet."

"Either way, it's getting bad," Captain Landry sighed. "And you're in the middle of it."

She shifted her weight, glancing to the side, in search of the right words. Then she stepped closer and laid a firm hand on Alexis's shoulder. Her fingers gave a slight squeeze as a silent check-in.

"If you need out… say it now."

"I'm good," Alexis replied. Dry. Resolute.

Landry searched her face. She didn't find what she wanted, but let it go.

"Nobody is to be trusted at this point. Not the girls… and especially not the heads of that organization."

She turned without another word and disappeared.

Alexis stood alone in the dark. Her thoughts twisted up like vines of guilt, rage, doubt, and bad memories.

She walked to her car, the night breaking apart again… right back to that day.

"Okay, everybody, calm down!" Alexis shouted, trying to gain control of the room.

"SWAT's already outside. You can surrender peacefully… or take your chances and get yourself killed."

"Fuck!" The man's broad shoulders dropped an inch. His knees buckled slightly, and the woman he was holding took an infinitesimal step to the right.

Hearing the panic in his voice, Alexis decided to try her luck.

"Listen… you don't have to do this," she said gently. "Let's just talk. What's your name?"

Ignoring her, he hollered, "I ain't tryna die today. This ain't how it was supposed to go."

At a snail's pace, she took a step forward. "I know where you're coming from, brother."

"Brother?" He squinted. "You saying that like you one of mines."

"I mean, we might not be blood, but we're still family."

"Maybe at one time you was." He eyed her badge, and his face twisted. "But not no more. You traded your skin for that badge."

Now feeling defensive herself, Alexis replied, "I became an officer to protect people like us."

"Us? We ain't cut from the same cloth, bitch. And the sad part? They ain't never gon' see you as nothing more than a pawn."

"Look." She shook off the sting, steadying her voice. "I'm trying to help you, but we don't have much time before they move in."

He chuckled dryly; something in his brain already popped loose.

"Oh, nah. We got all the time in the world. I'm gon' figure something out. Believe that."

His fingers flexed.

Tap. Tap.

Alexis jolted out of her mind and back into her body.

The standoff dissolved into the night, leaving only Simmons outside her car, his fist knocking gently on the window.

She rolled it down.

"Look," he spoke gently, dipping his head to look her in the eyes, "we're eventually going to have to—"

"I… I don't have time for this. Not right now," she cut in, harsher than she meant. Her voice cracked just slightly. "I'll get back to you when I have more details on the case."

She didn't meet his eyes, but she could feel his stare.

He didn't respond.

Just stood there looking like he had more to say.

She almost said something herself.

And almost let those words fall.

But she swallowed them instead.

Simmons let out a short, humorless laugh.

"Stubborn," he mumbled.

"What?" she snapped.

"You'll come to me when you need me. You always do." He slapped the roof of her car, then turned away, heading back to his own ride.

Slouching in her seat, she watched him walk off.

Didn't call out.

Didn't move.

And still… she felt the absence more than the man.

CHAPTER 4

Alexis paced across the worn wooden floor, studying the place. Every detail of the house demanded her attention. Pristine dove-gray walls rose to the high ceiling. Tall arched windows looked out on the front lawn and the wrought-iron porch, its black curves wrapping the house like a cage. This was the House of Lazuliè, both the Madames' home and the Krewe's headquarters.

She'd made it a point to be the first to arrive, allowing her to count the others as they filtered in. One by one, the girls had come.

Alexis had expected ten girls to be there by now, but only eight had arrived.

Raven had been the last to arrive so far, slipping in nearly thirty minutes ago.

Kayla and Jade were still running late.

Jennifer's absence hung over the room.

The girls lingered instead of settling. Two of the girls leaned against the curve of the staircase banister. Another pair stood near the front windows. One perched on the arm of a velvet settee. The rest were scattered in clusters across the room.

Alexis kept her pace measured, careful not to make it obvious she was listening. She slowed near a cluster by the staircase.

"...it's sad."

"I just saw that girl."

"I just hope she's okay."

"You think they found her yet?"

Alexis kept her face still, eyes on a nearby portrait.

"That's so crazy."

"You think the Madames will say something about it?"

That was it. Nothing she could use.

She drifted on, crossing toward the windows now, pretending interest in the front lawn.

Another cluster stood a few feet away, their voices pitched even lower. She caught Jennifer's name again and angled herself a little closer without fully joining them, but there was still nothing to grab onto. Just the same fear, passing from one mouth to the next.

She was about to give up on hearing anything worthwhile when her ears perked up.

"Trafficking ring?" Natalia shook her head. "Some people, they just talk to talk. No saben nada."

"Wait. What trafficking ring?" Alexis stepped closer to Markeysha, the girl Natalia had been whispering to.

Markeysha leaned in. "I was saying, people have been saying this place is like a brothel... or trafficking ring."

Alexis lowered her voice and looked from Markeysha to Natalia. "Where'd you hear that?"

Markeysha shrugged. "It's a whole thing on my campus." She tossed her braids across her face, clearing her view. "I told some girls on my dance team that I'd be staying here for a few nights, and one of them said, 'They gon' have y'all in that house hoeing!'" She pitched her voice up for the impression.

"Hoeing? Shit, that sounds like my kind of party, lowkey." Raven shrugged, a crooked smile pulling at her mouth.

That pulled a small chuckle out of Markeysha, but she caught herself quick.

"Chill out, I'm just playing." Raven side-eyed her. "Damn, it wasn't *that* funny."

"Uh-uh! Don't act like you're not about that life now!" Markeysha teased.

Now both Markeysha and Natalia were trying not to laugh.

Alexis gave a faint shake of her head, the corners of her mouth tugging into a reluctant smile. She didn't know what bothered her more, the rumor or how casually it was being tossed around.

"It's… just the same old bullshit rumors," Natalia added after realizing Alexis wasn't laughing.

Jade burst through the door just as Nevi and her sisters entered the room. "Hey y'all, sorry I'm late… had to take an Uber. My car decided to quit on me today," she grinned nervously.

Nevi's eyes flicked toward her. "Well, aren't you a last-minute miracle?" Her voice oozed sarcasm. "You missed the preamble, but I suppose better late than never."

She turned with a graceful wave of her hand. "Well. I suppose we should get on with the show, hmm?"

Just as she pivoted, Alexis spoke up. "Kayla still hasn't made it yet. We're not going to wait for her?"

Nevi's smile didn't falter, but her tone cooled. "We were kind enough to wait as long as we did. I think we've extended more grace than necessary." Her eyes swept over the room. "There are always one or two who back out at the last minute. Happens every time."

Then Della and Rae slipped into the room, falling into place beside Nevi.

Rae's eyes moved like a pendulum as she began the roll, clipboard in hand, pen tapping once before each name.

"Raven Fontenot?" She glanced to the left.

"Check." A neat stroke on the page.

"Imani Pierre."

"Check." Another smooth mark.

"Markeysha Long." A small nod.

"Check."

"Kayla Evans." Rae's full lips pressed into a thin line. She paused, then drew a sharp X beside the name and moved on.

"Natalia Santiago." She looked up from the clipboard.

"Check."

"Olivia Reeves."

"Check."

"Brielle Robbins."

"Check."

"Nia Jordan."

"Check."

"Destiny Williams?"

"Here." Destiny raised her hand when she noticed Rae nearly passed her.

"Check."

"Jade Green."

"Check."

"And… Alexis Brown." Rae looked directly at her, holding the gaze just a second longer than necessary. Then she made a mark next to her name.

"Check."

Della gave two quick claps. Just enough to slice through the chatter.

The girls straightened all at once, a ripple passing through the group.

"And with that," Della announced, her voice calm but firm, "we are now officially down to ten initiates."

"Let's begin the tour, shall we?" Rae gestured toward the long hallway behind her.

But Nevi raised a hand. "One quick thing before we get started. We'll need your phones."

The room fell silent.

Alexis blinked. Several girls shifted and traded looks.

"Wait… we've got to give up our phones?" Nia didn't bother hiding her disbelief.

Nevi dipped her chin. "For the duration of your stay, yes. No recording, no texting, no distractions. This experience requires full presence. It's non-negotiable." She held their eyes, letting the message settle. "So, let's not waste any more time. Phones off. In the basket. Thank you."

Grumbling sparked immediately. Olivia scoffed. Raven shook her head. "Man… y'all tripping. I ain't sign up for all this."

Natalia folded her arms, eyebrows up. "What if there's an emergency? I need my phone."

Then Della and Rae stepped forward, each carrying a wide wicker basket in their arms. They didn't say a word. Just held them out like it was the most natural thing in the world.

Raven leaned toward Alexis, whispering, "I don't like this shit already."

Alexis kept her eyes forward. "Chill."

Each in sequence, the girls started surrendering their devices. Some stalled. Others tossed them in with a roll of the eyes and a muttered curse.

"Y'all got a landline or something in case my mama needs to reach me?" Destiny asked as she dropped her phone in the basket with a sigh.

Rae only smiled.

Alexis hesitated, then let it go. The phone landed in the basket with a dull clatter.

Once the last phone was collected, Nevi smiled wider.

"Wonderful! Now we can begin properly."

They started down the hallway.

And just like that, the house swallowed them whole.

Alexis wanted to say something, but the words scattered before they could reach her lips.

She tried to ground herself, but her thoughts kept drifting.

Something felt… off. And still, she said nothing.

Finally catching up with Alexis and Raven, Jade slipped in between them. "Hey, y'all."

Alexis gave her a quick hug. "I was beginning to worry about you, chick!"

"'Bout time you showed up." Raven pulled Jade into her arms next. "I was ready to send a search party."

"My bad," Jade sighed. "Shit's been so hectic today."

Raven wasn't buying it. "Mmm-hmm. You expect us to fall for that story you told the Madames too or are you gonna tell us the real tea?"

"Ain't no tea, fool. That's what really happened." Jade rolled her eyes. "Anyway, what did I miss?"

"Not a damn thing," Raven said, letting it go.

Alexis added, "We've just been sitting in this room waiting for everyone to show up."

"Oh shit, I held y'all up. My bad." She winced.

"You're good," Alexis assured. "I just can't believe Kayla flaked on us like that."

"You don't think she's just running late like I was?"

Alexis shook her head. "The Madames warned us beaucoup times about being late, and even with that, they still waited an extra forty-five minutes. Kayla kept going on about how much this meant to her, how serious she was about earning her spot. Then she just… doesn't show? That doesn't make sense to me, for real."

"Yeah, when you put it like that, it's kind of wild," Jade admitted. "All that talk, but she wasn't really about that action." She paused, her tone cooling. "Anyway… y'all heard about Jennifer, right?"

"Yep. It's been all over the news… damn near every hour."

"Which is wild because you know they wouldn't be broadcasting it like that for a regular-degular Black girl."

Raven's voice thinned. "Y'all, I'm so torn up behind that shit. When I saw her mama crying on the news…" She shook her head. "It's just so crazy because we was just with her. I hope she's okay. I hope they find her."

"Right," Jade said quietly.

Alexis glanced between them. "So, what happened after we split up?"

Raven answered first. "Jen and Jade walked me to my car first."

Jade cut in, "Then Jennifer walked me to my car."

Raven sucked her teeth. "And you ain't bring her to her car? That's too damn stupid!"

"Well bitch, you didn't drive us to our cars…" Jade defended herself.

"That's different, Jade. You should have—"

"Come on, y'all. This is serious," Alexis cut in.

"I am serious!" Raven snapped.

"Look, y'all, I offered to give her a ride. I swear I did, but Jen kept saying her car was only a few blocks away and she'd be good."

Alexis noticed the way Jade's face fell and let it go. "Did y'all hear anything about it at school or anything?"

Jade shook her head. "No. Just what they been saying on the news."

Raven nodded. "There's this rumor floating around campus… somebody said they saw her get snatched up by two dudes wearing all black. Said it happened in that parking garage off Decatur."

While they whispered, the Madames led the girls through the mansion. Every so often, Alexis, Raven, and Jade glanced up, catching pieces of the tour, but they mostly moved on autopilot, eyes cutting back to each other, too wrapped up in the conversation to take much else in.

"Did y'all tell the police that?"

"I don't know about anyone else, but I didn't."

Alexis looked at her. "Why not, Raven?"

"Well, for one, I don't believe the shit. And two, I don't even know who the original person was that said it. What I look like calling them dicks over a rumor?"

"Shit, I hope so." Alexis chewed on the exchange, then changed the subject. "Jade… did you ever tell ol' boy you're sorry?"

"Who, Jalen?" Jade feigned forgetfulness.

"Yes! I mean… unless you got another one on the roster…"

"Don't play with me like I'm out there like that. I don't have a damn roster," Jade laughed.

Raven snorted beside them. "You sure about that?"

"Raven, girl, shut up before I air you all the way out." She mushed Raven's shoulder. Then she mushed Alexis's. "And while you're trying to clock my tea, are you going to tell us about Tahir finally?"

Alexis's smile dropped. The room felt fifteen degrees hotter. "How do you know about Tahir?" she posed, tilting her head.

"I see you texting the dude all the time. How could I miss seeing his name flash across your phone's screen?" she stated sardonically.

"Yup, I've seen that name too." Raven cosigned.

"Oh!" Alexis exhaled in relief as the tension in the room dropped a few notches. Playing along, she added, "Y'all so damn nosey… But I'ma tell y'all about him later."

They all snickered.

That's when Della stopped mid-step, forcing everyone else to come to a clumsy halt behind her. She turned just slightly, raising a brow. "Is there something you girls want to share?"

"Oh, umm… we were just trying to figure—" Jade started, her voice small.

"Save it, Jade," Nevi cut in, her tone clipped and tired. "I've grown weary of hearing your excuses already. Just keep it down."

"Will do, Madame Nevi," Alexis answered quickly.

As they resumed the tour, Jade leaned toward Alexis and muttered, "These old hoes really think they're teachers or something."

Raven choked on a laugh. "Girl, hush, before they send us home."

The giggles hit the three of them at once. Jade hid hers behind a fake throat-clear, Alexis bit down on a smile until it shook, and Raven covered her mouth, her shoulders trembling.

After passing a row of bedrooms, the line stopped at an open room.

Alexis, Raven, and Jade fell silent, their eyes widening in unison as the space revealed itself.

To the left sat a mahogany-stained basswood harpsichord, its lid propped just enough to tease the gleam of ivory keys. Across from it, a solid wood armoire desk held a gold-plated candlestick and a miniature grandfather clock.

Alexis's eyes stopped there. Between the two stood a small porcelain figure of a woman draped in blue and white. In its hands rested a heart ringed in thorns, pierced through with seven silver blades. She found herself staring, the seconds stretching before she forced herself to look away.

Rae stepped to the end of the room and wrapped her hands around the brass handles. She slid the doors apart in one smooth pull, the track releasing a low, satisfying groan. Light poured in from the next space, landing on polished wood, glinting glass, and flashes of gold.

To the left, a chandelier hung over a long dining table.

To the right was the kitchen. Dark espresso cabinets framed the walls, their gold handles precisely placed. The pale marble counters shone brilliantly, interrupted only by a deep farmhouse sink and a curved brass faucet. A matching center island stood in the middle, its surface bare except for a neat row of glass canisters and a bowl of green apples.

"Straight ahead is the door to the backyard where we have an impressive garden," Rae's voice snapped the girls out of the trance they were in. "But I'm sure you young ladies would rather see something more interesting."

"I'd rather see what's upstairs." Olivia's voice carried a thread of nerves she didn't bother to hide.

"As you wish, my dear." Nevi's smile didn't falter as she gracefully pivoted. Her short stride set the pace, and without a single glance back, she started toward the front of the house. Della and Rae fell in beside her without a word. The others followed.

When they reached the staircase, Alexis's gaze snagged on a narrow door tucked right under it. Barely noticeable, its paint the exact shade of the wall. Something about it seized her attention.

"Where does this door lead?" she tilted her head toward it.

"Oh, sweetheart, don't worry about that door." Nevi's hand lifted in an airy wave. "It leads down to an old crematorium, but no one's set foot down there in decades. We had it painted to match the walls. Less of an eyesore that way."

"Oh… okay," was all Alexis could say.

She bit the inside of her cheek. Something about that answer tugged at her nerves, but she kept walking.

Once they reached the second level, they passed through another hall lined with bedrooms and closed doors. At the very end, a dark room waited, its thick drapes swallowing every sliver of light, sealing the space off from time itself.

While Della moved to draw the curtains, Rae flicked the switch on the wall.

The antique ceiling fixture sputtered overhead, casting more shadow than glow.

As sunlight finally spilled across the room, Alexis shielded her eyes from the sudden brightness. Then she froze.

The room stretched wide beneath a vaulted skylight, the light angling just right to catch the gleam of varnish and glass. Each wall told a different story.

To the left were large portraits, photographs hung neatly on the wall, their gloss dulled by time.

The wall to the right mirrored it, but these portraits were painted. Fewer, yet louder.

Straight ahead, the back wall held the photography setup. Two antique cameras, each perched on tall tripods, formed massive, creature-like silhouettes against a moon-and-stars backdrop. One wore a wine-colored hood. A stool sat centered beneath a theatrical lighting rig. Behind it, an old mirror leaned crooked, cracked, with no business still standing.

"Go on. Explore as you please. We'll be nearby."

The girls spread out across the room, their murmurs fading. Somewhere near the back, Raven gave a soft gasp.

At the center of the room, a single painting sat on an easel. Sunlight spilled from the window above, touching only her.

A woman stood framed from the waist up, shoulders squared beneath a gown of lace the color of lapis lazuli. The fabric clung in careful structure, revealing a narrow sweep of skin at the collarbone before curving into a modest plunge. The lace turned opaque where it crossed her face, a veil drawn low enough to cover her eyes completely.

Beneath it, thick trails of black seeped from hidden eyes and ran clean down both cheeks, drying against skin the shade of deep bronze. Her mouth was cut open at each corner, the wounds raw and unhealed, the skin torn in a way that left deep lines: a permanent half-smile carved into flesh. Neither joy nor sorrow lived there.

The hair beneath the veil was gathered smooth and regal. Her neck, long and bare, rose from the lace like a column meant to bear weight.

Behind her, a wall gave way to an expanse of ornate crests. Each one was an intricate heart of deep royal blue crossed with a golden lattice. A vertical golden rod pierced through every heart's center, fleur-de-lis blooming at both ends. Spirals of gold curled outward from each side in perfect symmetry. Row after row, the design stretched beyond the frame.

She tilted her head. "Isn't that our krewe's symbol behind her?"

Della's stare bore down on her until she stilled. "No, that is *her* symbol. It's called a veve."

"A veve?"

"Yes. It's a calling card of sorts," Della said. "Something you draw when you want something old and powerful to take notice."

"She's… impossible to look away from," Jade stepped up.

Before a reply could form, Della's silky-smooth tone returned. "She has that effect." She approached without hurry, hands folded at her waist. "Isn't she striking?"

"The painting's beautiful." Alexis's sight stayed fixed on the veiled face. "But unsettling."

"Mhm," Della replied. "You know it in your bones 'fore your mouth can call it."

She stepped closer, her fingertips tracing the black streaks down the woman's cheeks.

Alexis blinked. Milan's mutilated face flashed across her mind; mouth carved open, eyes stabbed out, blood dragged down her cheeks.

She swallowed and looked back at the painting. "But why cover her eyes?"

Della's voice softened. "A woman like her doesn't show everything at once. Some things take time."

"Who is she?" Alexis had to know.

"By the end of Preparation… you'll know."

Della then crossed over to the far wall lined with framed portraits. The girls trailed after her, curiosity pulling them in.

"They're so pretty," Jade whispered once they stopped.

"Well, can you tell us who *they* are?" Alexis asked, eyes drifting over the faces.

Della chuckled low. "Now these," she gestured toward the wall, "are specimens of perfection. Crowned Hearts of years past."

Four portraits in total, each dated in looping script along the bottom edge. The earliest read 1906, followed by 1936, 1966, and finally 1996.

Alexis moved from one frame to the next. All of them were beautiful. Mesmerizing, even. But it was something else—something in their expressions—that held her.

"Damn, girl!" Raven came up behind her. "You don't hear me calling your name?"

Alexis flinched before catching herself. She turned, brows drawn slightly, the corner of her mouth lifting into a half smile. "Huh?" was all she managed.

With her arms folded, Jade added, "This girl is always spacing out. I swear, her body's in the room, but her mind's three blocks away."

"Leave my girl alone. You know she's a deep thinker." Raven nudged Jade. "You heard Della say she's the one who painted those paintings over there?"

"No, I didn't hear that. Really?" Alexis turned back toward the wall.

"Yeah! She fire with it, huh?"

"Madame Della, you're a very talented lady," Jade said. "All these paintings are beautiful… but that one", she pointed across the room, "is gorgeous. Mad realistic."

Before Della could speak, Rae slid in, smile already set, steps quick.

"She *wishes* that one were hers. But nope, that one's been watching this house for over a hundred years."

"Wait… so that's not y'all in the painting?" Raven squinted.

"No," Rae said. "But we are descendants of those women."

"Shoot, I thought that was a throwback of y'all before the wrinkles set in," Raven blurted out.

The girls laughed, but the mood changed.

"Shut up," Jade muttered, nudging her. "Just be saying *whatever* comes to your mind."

Della lingered, her eyes on the portrait. Her voice softened. "Youth *is* a privilege. Beauty without effort, that's the gift. But the curse of it is ignorance. Naivety leaves scars, and sooner or later, they show."

Her gaze slid toward Raven.

"Aging is a privilege, too. To endure. To outlast. To gather enough wisdom so that no one can fool you again. But that wisdom comes at a price. The years beat it into you, and they don't spare your body in the process."

She smoothed her sleeve before continuing.

"Youth has its shine and age has its weight, but the rarest thing is when they both meet in the same body. Effortless beauty sharpened by knowledge and experience… that's real power. And with it… you can take whatever you want."

Della crossed the room in measured steps, gliding past Raven so close their sleeves brushed. She didn't spare Raven a glance, only lifted her chin higher.

A hush lingered in her wake. No one risked another laugh.

Nevi's voice floated in, gathering the girls back to her. "Those three women founded the Krewe of Lazuliè. Geneviève, Désirée and Adelaide."

Three figures regarded her from the frame. The first, on the left, wore her locs in a high knot, her warm brown complexion glowing against a simple blouse. Her expression unwavering. In the center, a bronze-skinned woman in rust silk and a matching wrap looked down with subdued authority, her smile tempered with something colder. To the right, a cocoa-skinned beauty in finger waves held her body in perfect posture.

They couldn't have been more than in their mid-twenties. Captured in their prime. Preserved. Eternal in a way youth never truly is… at least not naturally.

Alexis studied the painting, noting how uncannily the women resembled the Madames.

"Wait," Olivia blurted out, excitement brightening her whole face. Giddily, she posed, "Is that Nicolas Trevigne? Was he a part of the Krewe, too?"

Alexis followed her finger until his image stared back at her: olive-toned skin, white coils brushed neatly back. His black suit gave him an air of power and reverence.

A chill ran up the back of Alexis's neck. Nevi's brow lifted, but her pause lasted a breath too long, as if the name brushed against something she'd buried. "Why, yes. You've heard of him?"

Olivia nodded quickly. "I read about him once. It was just a mention, but I remember this portrait from the book. It's the same one."

Nevi blinked once, slow, before leaning in slightly, her curiosity tempered with caution. "Well, go on and tell us what you've learned about the man."

"Well…" Olivia hesitated, her eyes darting to the others. "It mentioned that he was a Black man who owned slaves."

Suddenly, the atmosphere changed. Nevi's mouth twitched, almost a wince, but she held her poise.

"'Owned' is the word they like to use. In truth, he bought people to free them. Some stayed on afterward, worked the land, tended the house, and helped raise the children. Not because they were bound to him, but because there were only so many ways to survive out there. He gave them food, shelter, and a place that could call home." She turned back to the portrait. "History's never as it truly was, dear. It's written by people with ink in one hand and blood on the other."

The hush stretched thin as glass. Raven spoke first, loud enough to shatter it.

"That man's Black?" she asked rhetorically. "Could've fooled me."

Nevi's mouth curved faintly. "Yes, people did mistake him for being White. Used that when he needed to, too. A mask that opened doors his name alone couldn't. Built his empire with it."

Olivia leaned in again, eager. "Passe blanc. Some lived their whole lives pretending to be White just to get ahead. I find stuff like that so… fascinating, the lengths people will go to get the things they want."

"Indeed." Nevi inclined her head as she stepped aside.

"And so, she's Black too?" Alexis pointed at the portrait of the fair-skinned lady next to the one of the three sisters.

Suzette's likeness looked down at her, painted in careful strokes that caught both softness and severity. Her skin was light against the dark waves of a glossy bob, the contrast making her features stand out. There was a calculated precision in her posture. A subtle command in her eyes. The paint seemed almost wet. Alexis paid close attention to its shimmer.

A shadow slipped across the frame; Rae had moved in beside her. Alexis's pulse tripped. For a second, the shadow felt detached from its source.

Rae tipped her chin. "Their mama." She briefly cleared her throat before going on. "At twenty, Suzette left her daddy's plantation and came to New Orleans. By twenty-three, she had married Louis Meaux.

"Now, Mister Meaux didn't come from the kind of family she was raised to expect, but he made his own standing.

"He ran one of the most respected preparation houses in town, handling embalming and cremations. Folks trusted him to make the dead presentable... same way certain folks take pride in making the living presentable."

She gestured to the painting on the other side of Suzette's.

The portrait depicted him from the waist up, with a composed posture. His skin was rich chocolate, smooth as polished stone. A dark jacket framed him. His expression was composed, almost gentle.

"She helped him in the crematory when she could," Nevi cut in. "Kept the books and such, but she cared far more for her domestic duties.

"She had a gift for making a place feel tended to and proper. And she valued elegance, not just in appearance, but in conduct.

"At the table, the girls sat with straight backs and napkins folded neatly in their laps. Suzette could correct posture with nothing more than a tap or a look. She made them sound out every word until even the Queen herself could understand them. Said clear speech opened doors that manners alone could not.

"She also taught them their great-grandfather's tongue, though they took more naturally to Creole, having picked it up from Louis's people.

"Suzette hated that. Said folks mistook it for ignorance and looked down on those who spoke it, and to her, that was the ugliest thing of all."

Rae's mouth curved faintly. "And when she did take time for herself, she went to the salon owned by one of the city's finest conjure women."

"She went there more for the gossip than to get her hair done," Nevi smirked. "And over time, she and the Rootworker got close. Good friends. Then Louis got sick. Really sick. The doctor told her he couldn't do anything. Suzette begged the woman to help, but the woman hesitated. Eventually, Suzette brought her to the house. When the woman saw how bad it was, she made him a gris-gris bag and told Suzette to slip it under his pillow."

"Did it work?" Natalia asked.

Nevi shook her head. "No. After a week, he was barely conscious. Suzette got desperate. She begged to meet the woman's teacher, the one who taught her everything she knew. He visited the Meaux house several times, but by then, it was too late. Louis died at just thirty-seven."

"But if her daddy was rich… why didn't he help them out? Could've gotten that man the best care in the city!" Raven looked incredulous.

"Because Suzette defied him," Nevi stated plainly.

Rae added, "Her father had arranged for her to marry into another wealthy family. They grew rice, and he figured if their land joined with his cane fields, the two names could corner half the parish in crops. But Suzette didn't want to marry for money. She just wanted to be with the person she truly loved. And ol' Poppa Nick couldn't bring himself to forgive her for that."

Della's tone was smooth, but her jaw flexed. Her grip cinched, the pressure blanching her skin. "Didn't even come to the funeral," she added. "Far as he was concerned, she chose her path. So everything after that was on her." Her smile came too late and stayed too long.

"And that wasn't even the worst of it," Nevi cut in. "After he passed, folks took to talking. Said Suzette had been fooling with the 'voodoo man' and put roots on her own husband. The same mouths that once called her a lady were the first to call her a whore."

"She tried to keep going. Tried turning the house into a bed-and-breakfast. Called it The Meaux House. Tourists loved it. Ten bedrooms, near the streetcar, and close to downtown."

"But bitter hearts don't let peace settle," Della muttered.

"Indeed," Nevi agreed. "Someone kept painting a big ol' H over the M on her sign. Turned 'Meaux' into 'Heaux.' She'd clean it, and the next day, it'd be back. Eventually… she just stopped fighting."

"She even stopped leaving the house," Rae chimed in again. Her arms folded tight, eyes distant.

"And it got so bad that, eventually, she rarely got out of bed."

Her voice thinned. "Some folks don't ever come back from shame."

"Now them people know they're wrong for that!" Destiny burst out, disbelief cutting through her voice. Markeysha jumped in. "So, is that why they started calling this place the Heaux House? All because of rumors and lies?"

Nevi lifted her chin. "And yet… the sisters reclaimed the insult. In 1880, they founded the Krewe of Heaux and turned pain into power. That's legacy."

"Started humble," Della pursed her lips before continuing. "Small soirées and patron affairs… Then Mistress Lazuliè showed them what beauty could purchase, and in return, the Krewe took her name."

Alexis glanced back at the portraits. Their painted faces seemed to hold more than the room gave away.

"I'm glad the Krewe eventually rebranded," Olivia sighed. "I get the whole 'reclaim what was meant to tear you down' thing, but the connotations of that… I mean, people still talk about this place being for that kind of business, even now."

"Oh, we're well aware of the city's whisperings." Della's smile bent. "So, just to keep from disappointing them, we laced a little harlotry into the brand."

Nevi rolled her eyes. "Figuratively speaking, of course."

Raven folded her arms. "Well, figurative or not, when do we get to that part?"

"For real," Imani chimed in. "All we've been doing is community service."

Della grinned. "That's what the Plaçage Ceremony is for."

Before any of the girls could even ask what that meant, Nevi raised her hands.

"We'll talk more of it on the morrow, Blue Hearts. Now, before dinner, let's get you all settled in. Your belongings are still in the foyer, but you can grab them once you're assigned your bed."

With a graceful pivot, she led the girls down the corridor.

The Madames opened each door and showed the girls to their rooms.

From the moment she found out they would be staying at the Krewe's headquarters, Alexis had imagined the place as a creepy, old mansion. In places, the house met those expectations. But when she stepped into the bedrooms, everything changed.

Each room had its own flair. The furniture was still antique, its polish dulled by age, but the beds were dressed in lively colors that made them feel less worn. Old bones in new skin.

Her eye caught on the far-left bed, draped in a rose-colored comforter.

On the nightstand, a silver-trimmed glass tray held a pale blue ceramic dish shaped like a crescent moon. Beside it sat a tall, pink candle. And in the corner, lay a sprig of dried forget-me-nots. Delicate touches.

"Okay, this is definitely my bed!" Alexis threw herself onto the bed.

"We had a feeling this room would speak to you," Della beamed.

"Ooooh, this is cute!" Raven chirped, already flopping onto the center bed and peeling back the embroidered throw blanket. A turquoise candle rested on the nightstand beside her bed.

Jade strolled to the bed on the right, her eyes sweeping across the pillows and folded linens. A forest-green candle stood in a glass jar by her bedside.

She smirked. "Okay, not y'all giving me my favorite color!"

The girls drifted through the room, admiring their spaces with soft gasps and little squeals of delight. Alexis offered them a quick smile, but kept scanning the room.

Then she stepped into the hallway.

"Where are you headed?" came a whisper behind her.

She turned to see Raven right on her heels.

Alexis gave a casual shrug. "Just want to see how the other girls' rooms are set up."

She hadn't expected Raven to follow, but she didn't want to make a fuss about it.

She kept walking.

Destiny's door was already cracked. Smoke drifted into the hallway. Alexis gave the door a gentle push.

Inside, the scent was herbal and sweet. Destiny stood barefoot on a velvet rug, sage burning low in her hand. She moved in slow, fluid steps, and the smoke answered. It coiled around her wrists and waist, clung to her ankles, and curved through the air in tight loops behind her.

She circled the space, sweeping through the doorframe, past the windows, around the furniture.

Markeysha and Natalia were stretched across the chaise and floor cushion, laughing.

Raven stepped in behind Alexis, waved her hand in front of her face, and broke into a dramatic coughing fit, already laughing through it.

"You sure the Madames won't have a problem with you smoking the room out?"

Destiny didn't pause. She brushed smoke across the window as she spoke, her tone soft and melodic. "Oh, I'm sure the fairy godmothers cleanse their spaces, too. They won't mind." She turned without looking up, drawing the smoke into the corner behind Raven.

Raven glanced at Alexis, her shoulders lifted like she was holding in a comment. Instead, she cleared her throat.

"Ohhh, this room got a vibe to it," Raven said between coughs and giggles.

"And the beds are so comfy," Markeysha added. "I don't know about the other rooms, but ours is decorated all cute. Red, orange, and yellow. And with matching candles. I love it!"

"Our room's pink, teal, and green," Raven stated. "It might sound like a mess, but it works. Huh, Lexi?"

"Yeah, ours is nice too," Alexis responded. "Which was a surprise. I thought the rooms were gonna be old and dusty."

Natalia scoffed. "Right? I was expecting some—"

WHAP.

"Wha—girl, what the hell?!" Raven jerked back, coughing for real this time.

Destiny stood in front of her, a damp cloth in hand, already moving on like nothing had happened.

SMACK. Markeysha blinked as the cloth popped her forehead next.

"Ugh! What is that?!"

TAP.

"Ay, qué carajo?!" Natalia snapped, rubbing her forehead.

Before Alexis could protest, Destiny stepped in and pressed the cloth gently between her brows.

Cupping her forehead, Raven squawked. "Wait, did this bitch just baptize us?!"

"It's for protection. You're welcome."

She moved back to her bed and sat cross-legged. From her bag, she pulled a velvet pouch and opened it. A deck of cards rested in her lap. She began shuffling, calm as ever.

Raven's eyes lit up. She dropped her hand from her forehead and flopped beside Destiny on the bed, folding her legs. "Ooooh, are you about to do our readings? Because I need to know if I'm gon' find me a rich baby daddy when things really start to pop off here."

Markeysha looked over from the chaise. "Figures you'd be into tarot."

Destiny kept shuffling, not even bothering to throw a glance her way. "What's that supposed to mean?"

Markeysha just kept watching. Saying nothing.

Natalia stepped back slowly. "Yeah… no, I'm good on that."

She pressed her fingers to her forehead, then to her chest, left shoulder, right shoulder. "That's y'all vibe, not mine. I'm gonna grab my luggage and see what the other girls are getting into."

She gave Destiny a side glance before turning and walking out.

Raven leaned in, ready.

Destiny lifted her chin. "Alright. Start with your birthday."

"Yeah, I'ma head out too. Y'all have fun though." Alexis had seen enough.

The door clicked shut behind her.

She halted. Touched her brow. Rubbed her fingers together. Sniffed.

The smell was faint. Floral. Clean.

She kept walking.

From the third suite across the hall, soft voices spilled into the corridor.

Olivia stood near the dresser, folding clothes into neat stacks. Nia crouched by her open suitcase on the floor, smoothing out a long, silken scarf. The room around them glowed in soft purples and muted golds. Warm tones threaded through cool grays. A woven mustard throw was draped across the foot of one bed. On the far wall, three delicate prints hung in a perfect row: abstract florals, inked in violet and ash, framed in brushed brass.

A tiny glass vase of fresh lavender sat on the nightstand, next to a slate-colored candle in a jar.

Then her eyes landed on the third bed.

Neatly made. No sign of a girl settling in. Just a flat, untouched comforter in pale gray linen.

She slipped out of the room unnoticed, not even uttering a single word.

Last, she peeked into the fourth room. Only Brielle and Imani were inside. Imani was already sprawled across her bed like she owned it, arm thrown over her head. Brielle sat upright against the headboard, flipping through a small hardcover book.

"Y'all good?" Alexis hung out near the doorway.

"Yeah, we're okay," Brielle replied. "I mean… a little creeped out, but I'm straight."

"What's creeping you out?"

Brielle shrugged. "It's just a feeling. Hard to explain, though."

"The vibe's off, huh?"

"Yeah. It's the vibe."

Alexis bobbed her head. "I've been picking up the same thing."

"It's the house," a soft voice chimed in, right behind her.

Alexis turned slightly, caught off guard. Olivia stood there, eyes bright, a soft flush rising in her cheeks.

"Old mansions like this hold many memories inside them," she continued. "So many ghosts."

Alexis stepped aside, letting Olivia move past her into the room.

Olivia turned toward Brielle, smiling. "Hey, Nia and I have a bed free in our room. Wanted to see if you'd maybe want to stay with us. Totally up to you, no pressure."

Before Brielle could answer, Imani shouted, "Oh, please go!" She sat up. "I'd love to have the room to myself."

Brielle laughed under her breath and closed her book. "Okay, I'll let the queen have her space." She rose from the bed.

Olivia beamed and threw her arms around her. "Yay!"

Grabbing Brielle's hand, she tugged her toward the door. "Come on, I think you'll like our room better. It's got a better vibe."

Alexis didn't say anything, letting the moment unfold. She stepped aside as the girls slipped past her, their laughter trailing off into the hall.

Imani reached over, grabbed the eye mask from the nightstand, slipped it on, and lay back down like nothing had changed.

Alexis glanced around the room one last time.

Two empty beds now.

On the walk back to her own room, the math clicked into place.

Four rooms.

Two in the first. Three, if I counted myself.

Three in the second.

Three in the third.

One in the last, with two empty beds.

One meant for Kayla.

And the other… Jennifer's.

CHAPTER 5

"Stay the fuck back or, I swear to God, I'll kill this bitch."

The words echoed, rippling through the room in warped layers. The floor trembled beneath Alexis's feet. The man's voice stretched like it was coming through a tunnel, then snapped back.

The fluorescent lights overhead blinked. The tile beneath her boots shimmered, just for a second, coated in blood. The walls behind the man flickered.

One blink, and the peeling wallpaper of the bank became blackness. Deep. Endless. Etched with a single symbol glowing bright blue. A heart, pierced through by a rod, fleur-de-lis unfurling from each end. Its tendrils curled outward, spiraling across the wall. Another blink, and the wallpaper returned.

Alexis raised both hands. "Okay, now. All I want to do is talk to—"

"Bitch, you think I'm playing?!"

He cut her off and fired into the ceiling.

The sound echoed through her before the muzzle even flashed.

"I'm gon' light this bitch up if you don't get the fuck out my way."

Alexis squinted. The woman he was holding kept changing. One second, she had jet-black straight hair and rich dark-brown skin. The next, reddish-brown curls and a golden complexion. Only her swollen eyes stayed the same.

"Jennifer?" Alexis's voice had a mind of its own.

"Why did you let this happen?" Her mouth moved, but the words dragged themselves forward in broken delay.

Before Alexis could respond, the bystanders behind the man erupted in screams.

"Okay, I need everyone to calm down!" Alexis shouted over them.

But they weren't crying anymore.

They were laughing.

Hysterically.

Their heads snapped back. Mouths stretched too wide. Some too long.

The setting fractured; the bank dissolved into a vast, hollow chamber carved of stone. The ceiling loomed far above, lost in darkness.

A circle of candles sparked to life around the man and the girl. Each one ignited on its own, flaring with a hiss.

Alexis backed away, hands still raised.

Behind them, near the far wall, cloaked in shadow, lay another girl. Bound at the wrists and ankles and dressed in white. A golden nameplate necklace rested in the hollow between her collarbones. Pamela.

"Please, Alexis. Please!" she sobbed, her voice rising to a pitch that broke.

Alexis heard the sound of metal scraping next and her heart dropped when she saw the long blade in the shadowed figure's hand.

The girl thrashed, her cry turning raw.

"Please, please don't—"

A wet, ripping tear followed, each fiber surrendering with a squelch. Then a burst of gurgling, frantic and wet, as her scream broke off mid-breath.

The blade opened her throat clean across, skin parting as blood erupted in chaotic spurts, painting the air.

A hush fell over the room.

Then everything changed.

The figure now sat on a throne that looked carved from a massive tree stump, its roots still planted deep in the earth.

Alexis stilled as its form began to bleed through. First, she noticed the curve of its mouth, then the veil hanging low enough to conceal the eyes beneath it.

It was her, the woman from the painting, only darker.

Blood slipped from her fingers. She raised one and pointed it at Alexis.

The man looked up at her.

Then he looked back at Alexis. His voice warped again.

"I'ma show you what type of shit I'm on."

He raised the gun.

The girl's head slowly turned to face him. Her tears had stopped.

In the second before he pulled the trigger, she changed again. Her skin faded to porcelain. Her eyes glazed over, then vanished, leaving dark sockets behind. Her mouth was sealed shut.

Alexis didn't notice the man moving his aim.

By the time she turned toward him, it was too late.

He took the shot.

The bullet slammed into her chest, sending her flying backward with brutal force.

She hit the ground hard.

Her hand reached up, searching her body.

No blood.

Just a deep, expanding heat behind her sternum.

Laughter echoed. But it wasn't coming from anyone she could see.

Then the veiled woman moved.

She glided across the candlelit circle without a sound. Her gown slithered behind her.

She stopped at the man's side. He stood frozen, weapon still half-raised. His eyes stretched wide.

Swiftly, she raised her hand, then brought it down.

The man dropped, every bone turning to rubber in an instant.

Then she turned to Alexis, moving as if gravity forgot her.

Her steps left no sound. Candle flames bowed in prayer as she passed.

She knelt.

Alexis couldn't move.

The veiled woman tilted her head. Leaned close. Her eyes still hidden.

Her lips didn't move.

But her voice bellowed all around her, splitting into seven distinct tones that overlapped.

"Surrender.

Or die.

Surrender.

Or die.

Surrender.

Or die.

Surrender…

…or die."

Alexis's hand shot to her hip and drew her gun. She fired.

The bullet struck the woman, and she screamed.

The sound coming from her was no longer human.

It shattered the room into pieces of light and sound.

Her voice became a siren, ripping through Alexis's skull.

BRRRIIINNGG!

Alexis jumped up from the bed.

Before she could make sense of anything, someone shouted, "What the fuck?! What is that sound?!"

Jade's voice. That's when Alexis realized she'd been dreaming.

"Bitch, I don't know! But whatever it is, somebody needs to make it stop!" Raven hollered.

Alexis groaned, pressing her palms over her ears. Then she spotted the old-fashioned, metal twin-bell alarm clock chiming away on the vintage chifforobe across from the beds.

She got up, walked over, and picked it up, turning the thing over in her hands. It didn't look like any clock she was used to. No buttons or switches.

"Turn the fucking thing off, Alexis!"

"I don't know how!" She tossed it to Jade. And just like that, it went silent.

"Bitch! I thought that was a fire alarm at first," Raven huffed, sitting up.

Jade stared at the clock in her hands. "Damn… It's only six-something."

"Alright, Blue Hearts! Time to get up!" Nevi's voice floated in through the crack of the bedroom door.

"Sometimes I'm convinced all three of 'em got a few screws loose," Jade muttered with a laugh, kicking the covers off.

Raven smoothed the edge of her blanket. "Right? They act like this is a damn sorority or something. They can play if they want to… but I know who they not about to haze in this bitch."

Alexis made her bed, still fussing over the comforter even after it was perfectly fixed.

"You good, Alexis? Over there, all quiet and shit."

"Y-yeah. I'm fine," she lied, sliding into her slippers. "Come on. Let's go before they come in here looking for us."

She stepped into the hallway, and the sound of Jade and Raven's footsteps followed close behind. The rest of the girls were spilling out of their rooms, too. Robes on. Bonnets twisted. Voices low and groggy. Some yawned. A few others muttered complaints, eyes squinting against the hallway lights.

As they lined up behind Nevi at the far end of the hall, Della stood near a window with a porcelain mug in hand. She turned and gave a sly little smile.

"Good morning, ladies. I do hope sleep found you well."

Destiny gave a long, languid stretch, arms reaching toward the ceiling. "Oh, I slept like a baby."

"Before waking up to those loud-ass alarms," Raven muttered.

"Right, I thought the house was on fire." Imani rubbed her face. "Damn near had a heart attack."

Low murmurs of agreement followed, tired and annoyed.

Nevi turned to face the group, one brow lifting slightly. "Well, I do apologize if our alarm clocks startled you. I suppose those little things can stir up quite the ruckus."

She paced slowly in front of them, heels clicking, eyes sweeping over each girl, searching beneath the surface. Then she stopped.

"Now that everyone's shaken off their dreams," Nevi remarked, "go ahead and get dressed. Something comfortable, but respectful. You'll be joining us in the grand room shortly."

"For what?" Raven stifled a yawn.

Della sipped from her cup. "A few things to help shape the woman you're meant to be."

"Think of it as… reflection," Nevi added. "A little guided soul work."

Destiny gave her a look. "So like what… yoga or group therapy?"

Nevi smiled. "Not quite."

"Oh, and my precious Blue Hearts," Rae called out gently from the end of the hallway, "there's a light spread waiting for y'all in the main dining room near the kitchen. Go on and help yourselves."

Nevi nodded softly in Rae's direction before turning to where the girls stood. "You've got three hours." Then she angled toward the stairs. "And this time," she added over her shoulder, "I expect everyone to be punctual." Then she sauntered off down the hall, silk hem dancing across the floor behind her.

After another sip from her mug, Della fell in step without a word. Rae lingered long enough to offer a faint smile, then followed.

Then the sisters were gone.

Alexis watched the girls scatter like sleepwalking soldiers, slippers scuffing against the hardwood as they drifted down the hall, still half-draped in dreams.

She fell in step behind them.

At the far end of the house, the dining room waited.

The table was set with gold-trimmed porcelain, folded napkins, and rows of empty flutes beside the pitchers and champagne bottles. Along the marble sideboard sat a simple breakfast spread of eggs, sausage, toast, fruit, and a few other sides.

Some girls hesitated. Others moved with purpose, making their way to the sideboard to fix their plates. Raven grabbed two pieces of toast and piled on fruit like she was building a tower. Imani carefully scooped eggs onto her plate and passed the tongs to Destiny, who reached for them with a little grin.

A few girls took it further. Brielle twisted open a champagne bottle with a pop, poured a generous splash into one of the flutes, then topped it with juice. Nia did the same, but more sparingly. The bubbles rose in delicate ribbons.

Alexis fixed herself a quick plate of eggs, toast, and fruit before taking a seat near the middle.

Raven and Jade sat beside Alexis. The three clustered together, as usual.

Olivia settled beside them, wide-eyed and taking everything in. Her gaze traced the molding, the wainscoting, the carved ceiling medallions.

"I hope they let us back in the photo room. I barely had time to take it all in. That kind of history? It's… I don't know, it feels special." Olivia flushed, unsure how it sounded out loud.

Across the table, the others found their own tempos. Nia, Brielle, and Olivia drifted close but kept a little distance.

Brielle offered Alexis a nod. Nia stayed alert.

Markeysha and Natalia claimed the far-right corner. Natalia bowed her head slightly, fingers threading together beneath the table. Her lips moved in soundless prayer.

When she looked up again, she reached for her plate and picked at the food.

Destiny moved beside Imani, who sat near the end. When she settled in, Imani leaned close and whispered something that made her smile. The two of them filled their plates with fruit, toast, and cheese. As they ate, their voices sank to a murmur between bites.

After a while, the lull that had settled over the room started to deepen.

"Damn." Raven looked around. "Y'all hear how quiet it just got? Somebody say something before this starts feeling like a repass."

Nia cleared her throat. "Maybe we should have a group discussion."

"About what?" Brielle questioned.

Natalia cocked her head. "What do you think, Jade?"

Jade looked around. "Shit, I don't know."

Alexis leaned forward slightly, chin resting in her palm. "How about we all say why we decided to join the Krewe? You first, Jade."

"Oh. Um... yeah. Alright." She let out a small laugh before continuing. "I mean... I've always known how to play it smart." She picked up her champagne flute and twirled it between her fingers. "Instead of waiting for doors to open for you, sometimes you gotta make your own opportunities. And when the moment comes, you make sure people know they need you. The Krewe of Lazuliè puts me right where I need to be."

Make sure people know they need you...

"The ten thousand." Nia's voice snapped Alexis out of her head. She murmured it with her eyes lowered to her plate, her fork moving without thought, pushing the eggs to one side, rationing them. "That's a semester's worth of tuition."

"Right," Natalia replied, chopping her sausage into small pieces and folding them into her eggs, trying to make the plate stretch. She took a bite, swallowed, and added, "La plata is definitely my motive too."

"Well, I want the ten thousand." Imani reached for a flute in the center of the table. She filled it halfway with orange juice, then tipped in champagne. She sipped, set it down with a soft clink. "But I want that damn crown too. I want the whole thing."

Markeysha leaned in next. "It's really not about the money for me."

"Okay... so what is it about then?" Imani pressed, not letting her off the hook.

"I've always wanted to be in a parade." She buttered her toast in calm, even strokes, covering every inch. "Tried out to be a majorette in high school, but them counts were tearing me up." Her shoulders lifted in a slight shrug, half-laughing. "Guess this is the next best thing."

Brielle was nudging her eggs with the side of her fork. "I'm here for my mom." Her hand froze on the fork as the room turned awkward.

Destiny wasn't affected by it. Lifting a few grapes to her mouth, she told them between bites, "I had a vision before I came. There was a path that led to this manor. Seven small gates. I watched them open, one by one, and light poured out of each one… echoes stirring in the ancestor realm." She reached for her mimosa, took a slow sip. "After I woke up, I looked into this place and found out it sits on a ley line where old energy runs deep. Felt like I was meant to come here. Tap into that current. Let it change me."

A few girls adjusted in their seats.

"But like… how do you even know it's real? The energy?" Olivia wanted to know.

"I feel it. There's a lot of it." Destiny voiced. "But it's not what I expected. It's darker."

Natalia looked uneasy. "Is that… bad?"

"Not necessarily." Destiny's tone stayed gentle. "You just have to know how to handle it."

"For me?" Olivia's eyes lifted to the chandelier, then drifted along the carved ceiling. "I joined because… this krewe is different. It's the only one I found that still honors its old traditions: the gowns, the etiquette, the procession. Everything feels like it's been passed down untouched." She glanced around the room, fingers curling together in her lap. "It's like we're staying in a museum! This kind of stuff gives me chills."

Alexis's eyes were fixed on her plate, but she was still listening, analyzing more than just their words.

When the voices thinned around her, she looked up. All eyes were on her.

"Oh, uh…" Alexis stammered. "I guess I joined because girls like us don't always get seen. I figured maybe this was a way to stop waiting on somebody else to notice and start showing up myself. For us."

A beat passed. Then Raven broke it with a grin.

She rolled her eyes. "Damn. I was going to say I came to find me a rich baby daddy." She fanned herself. "But Sister Mary Clarence over here wants to start talking 'bout saving ourselves. Girl, I'm trying to save my credit score."

Markeysha chuckled. Olivia tried to hold back a giggle. Even Nia cracked a smile.

Laughter trickled down the table, taking the edge off.

Nia rose, murmured "excuse me," and stepped toward the napkins. As she passed behind Imani, her hip brushed the back of her chair just enough to jolt it forward.

"Hoe, watch where you're going!" Imani snapped, rising out of her seat, chair scraping across the marbled floor. "You probably did that shit on purpose."

Nia froze mid-step, glanced over. "I didn't. My bad, seriously. Chill."

Her tone stayed calm.

Imani let out a dry laugh as she muttered to herself, "Oh, she wants me to *chill*." She took a step closer. Close enough for Nia to feel the heat off her words. "You think you can just run up on people and then play it off with a weak ass sorry?"

"It wasn't like that."

Brielle slid between them. "It was an accident. Take a breath, cool down."

"Girl, shut up. Ain't nobody even talking to you," Imani snapped, still locked on Nia. "Now, back to you." Imani jabbed a finger toward Nia's face. "You bump me like that again and I'll beat your ass."

Nia didn't flinch. Her fists tightened at her sides. "Move that finger, or I'll bite that son of a bitch off and spit it back at you. Now I said I was sorry, damn it."

Imani's mouth twitched. "You trying to act tough?"

"I'm trying to eat my breakfast," Nia replied. "But your messy ass just loves drama."

Chairs scraped. Heads turned.

"Say it again," Imani dared.

Brielle tried one more time. "Y'all, seriously—"

Neither of them listened.

Imani squared her stance. "You got one more time."

"I'm supposed to be scared?" Nia tightened her fists.

Alexis saw Nia's toes angle like she was coiling to lunge. She moved before anything else could happen, stepping tight between them and catching Nia's wrist as it rose.

"Alright!" she barked. "Y'all are doing way too much now."

Imani held her stance a moment longer, nostrils flaring, then stepped back without a word.

"We're not doing this," Alexis spoke up. "She said sorry. Let it go."

Stillness settled over the room.

Raven leaned back and whooped softly. "Whew. Lex, you should've let 'em fight. Get it over with. They're gonna be beefing this whole stay."

Jade sipped her juice. "Right? They'll definitely be throwing hands before all this is over."

"Exactly." Raven pointed her fork. "I was about to ask you if you wanted to bet on who'd win."

They laughed, dragging knuckles across the table in a playful handshake.

Slowly, the room erupted in laughter.

Alexis didn't find anything funny.

She sank back into her seat, arms crossed loosely. It felt like she was back at the precinct.

It shouldn't have grated her nerves so much, but it did.

A comment pressed behind her teeth, something they were too young to even really understand. She decided to let it go and focused elsewhere.

She swept the room, taking mental notes.

That's when something moved in the warped reflection of the antique coffee urn atop the sideboard.

Wait.

Someone.

Nevi.

Just beyond the archway, caught in the curve of the urn's belly.

Standing there.

Watching.

Alexis blinked; she was gone.

Then the ceiling let out a low, reluctant whine. A faint thump followed.

Brielle stiffened. Then, slightly above a whisper, "Wait, did y'all hear that?"

Alexis stayed silent.

"Girl, hear what?" Raven was confused.

"It's coming from upstairs," Brielle told her.

"I ain't hear nothing," Jade mumbled through a sip.

"No, I heard it too… I think," Natalia said, her voice low.

"Y'all are tripping," Markeysha said with the tiniest little shake in her voice.

"Everybody just shut up," Brielle snapped, standing halfway. "Just listen!"

A hush rolled through the room.

It only took a few seconds for the moment to pass.

But for Alexis, it left something behind.

It didn't hiss.

Nor did it stir.

It just coiled in her blood…

and waited.

CHAPTER 6

The grand room grumbled when the girls entered, its floorboards sighing beneath their steps.

Yesterday, the room had been arranged differently. Now the long tufted sofa, high-backed velvet chairs, and low coffee table had been pushed back against the walls, leaving space for a wide circle of velvet pillows spread across the center, each one positioned around a small brass tray. On every tray sat a folded notecard, a capped pen, and an ivory envelope.

The room swallowed its voice.

Alexis peeped over at Raven. Her shoulders were stiff. Her lips parted, but the words stayed put.

Even she didn't want to be the first to break the silence.

Nevi stood near the hearth. Della sat beside her on a low stool with her hands folded neatly in her lap atop a small, lacquered box.

"Come in, Blue Hearts," Nevi said finally. "Find a seat wherever you feel led."

The girls hesitated. In slow procession, they trickled in and took their places.

Olivia was the first to sit, settling cross-legged near one of the trays. She adjusted her skirt, smoothing its fabric.

Brielle moved next, dropping onto the pillow to Olivia's right. Nia sat on her left, arms folded, eyes jumping to each corner of the room.

Destiny joined them, taking the spot beside Nia with a soft sigh. Natalia slid in next to Destiny, stretching her legs out briefly before folding them under. Markeysha followed close behind, claiming the space next to Natalia with a glance but no words.

On the other side, Raven dropped onto the pillow beside Brielle with a grunt, like she wasn't in the mood for ceremony. Jade flopped down next to Raven, kicking her feet out and rolling her shoulders like she was trying to shake something off.

Finally, Alexis sat between Imani, who had taken the space after Markeysha, and Jade. The circle was complete. She drew her knees in and rested her arms across them, eyes lowered but watchful.

Della rose, lifting the small, lacquered box. She moved slowly around the circle, giving each girl a once-over.

When she reached Brielle, the girl gave a weak smile, fingers playing with something on her wrist.

Alexis glanced. It was a silver charm bracelet. She stared at it, trying to make out its shapes. Stars… and maybe a moon.

Nevi began to speak.

"This morning is about release," she stepped into the center.

"We spend our lives absorbing what does not belong to us. Expectations. Labels. Wounds. Things we mistake for truth."

Della followed. Her voice was cooler. Still steady. "Today is a journey inward. You'll complete four exercises. Each one is meant to help you see something. Feel something. Let go of something."

She paused, then added, "This first offering… is the offering to yourself."

A few girls looked around. One cleared her throat. Another coughed.

Nevi gave a small dip of her chin, taking them in with the focus of someone measuring more than just posture.

"The first exercise begins now."

She gestured toward the trays. "Write down a truth about yourself. Something you know in your spirit, even if the world has never seen it." Her eyes drifted past Alexis. Just brushing by. "Seal it in the envelope and place it back on the tray once you are done."

No one moved. Then Jade reached for her pen. The others followed.

Ink scratched paper. Natalia tapped the tray with her pen, as if she were waiting for something. Brielle didn't write anything. She just picked up the notecard, folded it, and slipped it into the envelope.

She set it carefully back onto the brass tray in front of her.

One by one, the others did the same. Sealed envelopes returned to their trays, palms lingering a moment before pulling away.

Alexis hesitated. Her fingers hovered above the card. And then the words came.

When she finished, she placed her envelope back onto the tray, aligning it with the others.

The floor creaked once. Then went still again.

Della stepped into the center of the circle, the small lacquered box cradled against her side.

She stopped before the first tray and bent at the waist, a shallow bow.

With her free hand, she lifted the envelope from the tray and placed it into the box.

"Thank you."

She moved to the next tray and repeated the motion. Bowing. Lifting the envelope. Depositing it into the box. Nodding once.

"Thank you."

She moved around the circle, her movements unhurried, her bow precise, each envelope carefully taken and placed in the box like delicate offerings.

By the time she reached the last tray, the box was nearly filled to the brim.

Della had a brief struggle with the box but managed to close its lid. Then she returned to her place without a word.

From her place by the closed sliding doors, Rae watched. Hands loosely clasped.

Somewhere behind the girls, a faint creak broke the stillness.

Nevi stepped forward. "Thank you, Blue Hearts. I appreciate how seriously you're taking this." She looked toward the back of the room, voice softening. "The house has heard you."

A hush followed.

"Now let us let the fire do its part." She turned, calm as ever. "Follow me to the garden."

Rae slid the doors open, the track groaning low and familiar.

The girls began to file through, unhurried, shoes sliding across the threshold. Toward the back of the group, Alexis fell into step as she took in the space.

They followed Nevi through the sliding doors, past the gleaming dining set and spotless kitchen, and out the glass-paned doors to the backyard. Morning sun spilled over the manicured garden. Deep red camellias. Ivory gardenias. White lilies stood among sprigs of rosemary. Lavender in full bloom. The air was floral and earthy, touched with a hint of smoke.

In the center sat a round stone fire pit, blackened at the base from past use. A circular stone bench surrounded it, already warmed by the sun. Bees drifted lazily about, and the faint sound of trumpets and bass carried in from somewhere down the street, the carnival spirit winding its way into even this tucked-away corner of the city.

Della stood by the fire pit, laying bundles of dried herbs and setting a stack of fresh cards beside a brass bowl. A silver lighter glinted in her hand. Nearby, a ceramic vessel of water and a few polished stones rested in careful order.

Rae took her seat first, folding her hands in her lap. Della finished her preparations and then joined her. Nevi remained standing a moment longer, watching the girls settle in along the bench.

When the last of them sat, Nevi began. "This is the offering for yourself. A chance to release what was never yours to hold and make space for what's still becoming."

She knelt beside the fire pit, the hem of her dress brushing the stone, and flicked the lighter until it sparked. The flame touched a bundle of oil-soaked rosemary and bay leaves nestled among the ash. It caught with a soft hiss, the herbs crackling as their scent lifted into the air.

"We carry stories that were never ours. Expectations, lies, roles we didn't choose. And somehow, we start calling them our truths. We wear them. We shape our lives around them. We let them decide how worthy we are."

A crackle burst from the flame as the herbs burned.

"This time," she eased down beside her sisters, "you'll write one of those stories down. A fear. A lie. Something you've outgrown but can't seem to let go of. Write it down."

Della rose again, moving between the girls and placing a card and a pen into each of their hands.

Nevi's eyes swept across them once more. "When you're ready, stand and read it aloud. Then… let it burn."

The fire popped once. Then waited.

No one moved.

Cards sat in laps. Pens untouched.

Then the flames lunged upward, swelling broad and bright, licking at the air as if it could taste what it wanted.

Olivia slowly rose to her feet.

She didn't look around. She only unfolded her card and took one step forward.

Her voice trembled at first. She cleared her throat and tried again. "If I ever stop being useful to people…" A pause. She swallowed. "…they'll realize they never actually liked me."

Her lips trembled at the end. She blinked fast, pressing her card into the fire before the tear could fall.

"Damn," Raven whispered.

Nevi didn't move, but her face lit with approval. "Oh, yes! This is exactly the kind of release I want from all of you."

From their places beside Nevi, Della and Rae began to clap in unison before she followed, the sound spreading through the circle. The girls followed with their own scattered applause, the sound rising faintly above the crackle of the fire.

That made Olivia's frown subside as she sat back down.

Several seconds passed before Raven stood next.

"I'm always broke," she assumed the most serious tone she could muster. Then she balled up the card and tossed it into the fire pit.

"Release that lie, girl," Jade muttered. The others chuckled, then clapped.

The rest joined in.

"I am disposable."

"I destroy everything I touch."

"I'm undesirable."

"I don't deserve to be loved."

And with each release came another wave of applause.

The girls started to look at one another again instead of down at their laps. A few chuckles slipped out between confessions, and they didn't appear as guarded as before.

Alexis still had her guard up, though. But as she watched the words burn and heard the applause swell behind each girl, it was as if something in her eased.

A small piece of the weight she carried cracked loose and fell into the fire, too.

When it was Natalia's turn, she strolled, arms folded, trying to hold herself together.

She stared at the card. Looked at the others. Back down again.

A tear slid from her chin before she spoke. "I am not enough."

She set the card into the fire so gently that it didn't catch at first. Then it flared fast, gone in seconds.

Alexis lowered her head. Her card still sat untouched in her lap.

She weighed her options: scribble something harmless to play along or write the thing that actually lived in her.

A beat passed. Then another.

She set pen to card, the words spilling in a single, flat line of ink.

Rising, she stepped to the pit without hesitation.

"I don't belong anywhere."

She let it fall.

The fire wrapped around the card as if it had been waiting for it and gobbled it up. Those painful words disappeared in a fiery haze before her eyes.

After the last round of applause, Della stepped forward with a round iron lid. She lowered it over the pit in one smooth motion, the metal dropping into place with a muted clank. Something beneath it hissed, then fell silent. The scent of charred paper seeped through the seams, hanging behind like something that didn't want to be let go.

Rae stepped forward and clapped once. "Alright, Blue Hearts. Follow us."

They followed Rae, Della, and Nevi toward the side of the house, where the veranda opened wide, partially shaded by draped linens and latticed wood crawling with vines.

Several of the girls caught the lingering scent. Noses wrinkled in near unison, each one trying not to react.

Alexis could smell it too. Her brow furrowed, but she didn't say anything.

From one end of the veranda, a long strip had been laid. Blackened rice, crushed charcoal, and scorched herbs packed into a dense line across the wooden planks, stretching nearly the full length of the platform.

To the side of the rice path, a small round table held a stack of thick hardcover books. Della stood beside it, waiting with an expectant smile.

At the far end, just beyond the final line of blackened rice, stood Rae, positioned beside a single upright chair. A shallow metal basin rested at its feet, steam rising from the jasmine-scented water. Beside it, a table held a neat triangle of rolled white towels. Rae rested her hands lightly on the top of the stack, ready to receive the walkers when they arrived.

Off to the side of the path, Nevi waited, walking stick in hand. It was made of wood, stained deep mahogany, and finished with a silver cap at its base, worn smooth by years of use.

"Remove your shoes and socks," Della instructed. "Place them at the end of the veranda. You'll walk the path barefoot."

Olivia had taken off her shoes before Della finished speaking.

She was already at Della's side. "Ooh, can I go first?"

Della looked pleasantly amused. "Of course. This kind of initiative is beautiful. The rest of you Blue Hearts should take notes. Olivia has been a star today."

Della gave a short nod. "Hold out your hands."

Olivia obeyed, arms shooting up higher than needed.

"Palms flat. Elbows locked," Della corrected, adjusting her wrists until they were just so. She loaded two heavy books into each hand, their weight pulling instantly at Olivia's shoulders.

The weight sank immediately through her arms, causing a slight shift in her stance. A tremble in the knees, she tried to hide with a smile.

Della reached for a blindfold, its outer layer trimmed in delicate gold lace over thick, midnight-blue cloth. The fabric was dense enough to drink in the light, leaving nothing to see through. She tied it firmly at the back of Olivia's head, then placed a guiding hand at the small of her back, steering her toward the right, where the rice path began.

Nevi stepped closer to the path's edge, silver-tipped walking stick resting lightly in her palm.

"Beautiful posture! Now… roll those shoulders back just a bit more. Elongate the spine. Perfect."

She gave a light nod. "You'll walk the path once. Straight across. When you're finished, sit and soak your feet in the foot pan there. Use a towel to dry off. This… is the offering of yourself."

Olivia nodded quickly, her breath snagging, but her smile stayed.

"Oh my god! It's like we're reenacting history, y'all!" Her smile widened as she adjusted her balance against the books' weight. "In the early 1900s, women used to—"

She stepped onto the rice path.

"SHIT!"

The word punched out of her. Her whole body jolted. The books nearly toppled.

"Language, young lady!" Nevi scolded.

"It's hot!"

Rae's voice was calm. "The path was extinguished several minutes ago," she said. "You'll be fine." She waved her off.

Della added, "Just like beauty, Preparation is pain."

"Wait, how hot is it, Olivia?" Markeysha wanted to know.

Before Olivia could answer, Imani jumped in. "Now, how are you gonna give us a whole history lesson and forget the most important part?"

Olivia winced. Her voice came out lower this time. "I've never read anything about the rice path being set on fire."

Olivia said nothing after that and kept walking.

Each step left a thicker coat of black on her soles. The soot clung heavily, like ink. Her arms began to shake.

By the halfway point, the weight of the books had her shoulders curling in, the strain pulling at her arms. A light tap from Nevi's walking stick cut the curve, nudging her spine tall again. Olivia gave the slightest nod, as if to say she understood the silent instruction, and pushed her chest forward like she was back on a runway she'd never actually walked.

Her smile faltered just once. Another tap brushed her wrist, warning her to keep her arms locked. She swallowed the urge to grimace, willing her stride to hold.

By the time she reached Rae, Olivia's face was flushed, the books trembling in her grip. Rae took them from her hands, guided her into the chair, and slipped the blindfold away. Olivia wasted no time plopping down and sinking her feet into the water. The pan of water, once clear and oil-coated, turned dark instantly. Ash swirling through the liquid.

The cool water returned her smile.

"Lovely job, Olivia. As usual." Nevi affirmed.

Della grabbed a push broom from where it leaned against the side of the house and swept the path clean again.

"Now, who's next?" Nevi asked once the rice path had been reset.

When no one responded, Rae asked, "How about you, Destiny?"

Destiny didn't move at first. She just stared at the path, then at Rae, then back at the path again, head turned slightly.

After a short pause, she threw her hands up and started walking toward Della.

"All right, let's just get this over with."

She held her hands out, palms up, ready for the books.

Destiny was focused as she sashayed along the path. Nevi gave one light tap to her forearm midway, guiding her elbows into a sharper angle.

"Y'all, that wasn't so bad." She shooed Olivia out of the seat with her hand. "Girl, get up, your feet are good and soaked now."

Olivia lingered, toes curling in the water, and cast a sidelong glance at Rae, testing her luck. Rae's answer came in the form of a firm little nod as she pressed a neatly rolled towel into Olivia's hands.

With a huff, Olivia began drying one foot at a time, the towel quickly darkening with streaks of soot. She tossed it into the wicker basket tucked beneath the table and eased out of the chair so Destiny could have a seat.

"I'll go next," Imani said, like she had something to prove now that she knew the rice walk wasn't as bad as she'd thought.

She stumbled a few times but managed to make it through without dropping a single book.

After Imani, the next girl followed, and so on.

Each walk was silent, save for the crunch of rice underfoot and the soft buzz of the city beyond the gate. The girls' shadows stretched long across the path, their silhouettes stark against the wood, posture perfect, heads lifted. Every now and then, Nevi's walking stick found a calf or brushed beneath the small of a back, coaxing them back into form.

Then it was Brielle's turn.

"This is harder than it looks," she mumbled to herself. "I have sensitive feet and these books are heavy!"

The books teetered. Her arms flailed slightly. She caught herself, only to feel a quick, stinging tap to the forearm from Nevi's silver-tipped walking stick.

"Lock your elbows!" Nevi barked.

Halfway through, her pace faltered.

Another tap, harder this time, landed between her shoulder blades.

"Straighten up," Nevi grumbled.

Brielle's shoulders twitched like she was fighting invisible hands. Her face flushed with effort, a tight, forced smile tugging at her lips before vanishing. Every step seemed heavier than the last.

"I can't do it." She dropped the books in the middle of the path. "Those books are too heavy. I can't hold them up and walk this thing!"

"Tsk, tsk, tsk," Della clicked her tongue. "Now you must start over."

"What?"

"Yes. You dropped the books. You need to return to the beginning of the path and do it again."

"Sorry, Madames," Brielle apologized. "I don't think I'll be able to finish this one."

"Oh, but you must!" Nevi stepped closer, the walking stick's tip resting just behind Brielle's calf. "The walk has to be completed."

Something in Nevi's tone told Brielle arguing would be pointless.

She bent down, picked up the books, and stepped off the path. She inhaled fast and shallow through her nose as she returned to the start. Her bracelet jingled faintly as her hand trembled.

The second time, Nevi was waiting. Every time Brielle's posture slackened, a tap to the elbow. Every time her chin dipped, the cold kiss of the walking stick's silver tip slid beneath it, startling her as it lifted her head back up.

She went slow, painfully slow, but she made it.

The girls applauded gently as she stumbled toward the chair to soak her feet. Rae took the books, slipped the blindfold off, and guided her into the seat. Brielle sagged into it, dunking her feet into the jasmine-slick water with a deep exhale. Rae passed her a towel, and Brielle dried her feet briskly before tossing it into the wicker basket beneath the table.

After Della reset the rice line, Alexis stepped up.

The rice bit at her feet. The warmth from the sun still clung to the path, but it wasn't unbearable.

She found her pace, balancing the books in her palms. Her arms burned, but she pressed on, and so did her thoughts.

Nevi paced the edge of the path, walking stick in hand, watching her with a small, approving smile. "Beautiful, Alexis, dear… steady… yes, just like that," she murmured, the silver tip tapping lightly against the ground in applause as Alexis passed.

Her arms trembled from the weight now, her shoulders screaming, but she held them steady, tightening every muscle just to keep from dropping the books.

Alexis couldn't shake the feeling that the whole ordeal was meant to shape more than just their posture.

"Lovely work," Nevi told Alexis as she reached the end of the path. "Not a single misstep."

Without a word, Rae took the books from her hands, guided her into the chair, and slipped away the blindfold.

Della reset the line again, the push broom gliding through the grains with a soft hiss, sweeping them flat and erasing every trace of what had come before.

When Alexis lowered her feet into the pan, the water was nearly black. Oil and ash drifted through it, swirling like ink around her toes.

Once everyone had completed the exercise and finished cleaning their feet, Nevi stepped forward, arms folded.

"And now… for our final exercise of the morning. The most important one."

The girls stood straighter, unsure what might come next.

She let the weight of her words settle before continuing.

"You've written what you believe is true. You've burned what you were told is true. You've offered your poise, your presence, your grace. But now… we look inward."

Her eyes swept across them like she was memorizing every face.

"This final offering is about what hides behind your shadow. What lives in the shadows when no one's watching. This is the offering through yourself."

Rae stepped forward and gestured with one hand.

"Let's return to the garden."

The girls rose slowly, retracing their steps across the lawn and back toward the circular bench that bordered the fire pit.

Alexis lingered, watching as Della stayed behind. She stood over the chair, carefully pouring the blackened water from the foot pan into a matte black ceramic vase.

Before Della could turn around, Alexis slipped away to catch up with the others.

Once they were seated, Rae gave a brief nod to Nevi, who addressed them again, her tone softer this time. "We'll call you one at a time. When it's your turn, Della will bring you to your destination."

The girls looked around, unsure whether to be scared or skeptical.

"Good Lord, this sun! I swear it's getting worse by the year…" Rae uttered, shading her face with her hand. Then she said to her sister in a voice just above a whisper, "Je ne pense pas que je vais tenir jusqu'à mardi."

"Tu dis ça à chaque fois, et pourtant tu tiens toujours le coup." In amusement, Nevi's lips curled before turning back to the girls. "We'll be just inside, having a spot of tea. The weather is a bit… persistent today, and my dear sister is terribly sensitive to it."

She offered them a graceful nod. "Take your time. Let everything settle."

Then, with a gentle touch to Rae's elbow, she guided her back into the house, the two of them disappearing through the double doors.

The second they were gone, the tension unspooled.

The bench creaked beneath them. Eyes began to move again.

Raven leaned in. "Okay. Now that the wicked witches of the south have dipped… what y'all think this is for real?"

"I mean, I think it's obvious what they're doing." She let the words hang, waiting for someone to bite. Nobody did. "Clearly, they're trying to open a portal."

Raven's eyes went wide, lips pursed. "Oh Lord! Next thing you know, we'll be chanting in Latin under a blood moon."

"Y'all are so extra!" Natalia exclaimed.

"You know, I find you to be very hypocritical sometimes," Destiny said to Natalia. "One minute you're crying about people not respecting your beliefs, and then you come for someone else's."

"Okay, okay, I get you. I'm not coming for your beliefs. I'm sorry. I mean it." Natalia lifted her palms slightly, a small gesture of surrender. "But… at least the first two exercises were okay, right?"

"The last one wasn't exactly what I'd expected, but yeah, I definitely really liked the first two," Olivia chimed in.

Natalia tucked a curl behind her ear. "Felt like a real release. Maybe this one's the same. Just some deep healing. Real alma work or whatever."

Raven playfully sucked her teeth. "Girl, shut up. You're always trying to be all positive and shit. Corny ass." She teased. "You are so boring."

"You shut up!" Natalia mushed Raven's shoulder playfully.

Then Brielle spoke up.

"I don't like it. Something about this doesn't sit right with me. My stomach is doing backflips!"

Alexis turned to her. "You think we should leave?"

Brielle jerked her chin. "I think we should've left last night."

Jade exhaled hard. "Well, it's a little too late for all that now, huh?"

Raven shook her head. "Nobody told you to come if you was gonna scare so easily."

Brielle didn't answer. She kept her eyes on her hands, fingers twitching in a pattern only she seemed to know. Her bracelet moved with the motion. Alexis noticed it. Noticed how constant it was.

She leaned in, "You good? I noticed you keep fidgeting with—"

Brielle cut in with a soft, slightly nervous titter.

"Oh. Yeah, this?" She lifted her wrist a little. "I don't know. It's just something I do when I'm nervous, I guess."

"My mama gave it to me. She said it'd keep me grounded. Or safe. Or… I don't know. She says all kinds of things." Her voice cracked a little, then steadied. "She's sick. Cancer. She's been talking about going on a cruise for the longest." Another shrug. "I came here hoping the prize money could help with that. Let her have that one good memory."

Alexis didn't push. She just gave her a soft nod.

Then the door flung open. Imani came flying out, wild-eyed and shaky. Raven nearly jumped out of her skin.

Destiny rushed over. "Are you okay?"

Imani didn't answer. She just collapsed into her friend's arms, silent. Still. Staring at nothing. Destiny rocked her gently. "Aww, what happened?"

Imani remained silent.

One at a time, they were called. Each girl went in without a word.

Then another.

Then another.

One came back pale.

One came back humming softly.

Natalia returned with her arms loose at her sides, a softness settling over her face that hadn't been there before. The tension was gone. Her movements calm, her body lighter.

Alexis watched each one. Studied them… how they moved before the exercise, and how they came back.

Then it was her turn.

"Alexis," Della called.

She stood. Swallowed.

The others turned to watch her walk away. Raven gave her a small nod.

Alexis hesitated a fraction too long, all the girls' attention pressing into her back. Then she moved.

The cool air inside smacked her in the face as she crossed the threshold.

Della led her through the dining room and kitchen, past the open sliding doors into the grand room. As they neared the archway, Alexis glanced around for Nevi and Rae, expecting to find them at the table, teacups in hand. But the room was empty.

Where the hell have they gone?

Della kept walking, and Alexis followed under the archway into the hall. They passed the bathroom and stopped at the coat closet just beyond. The door stood open.

Inside was a long mirror framed in oak, a wooden chair, and a candle on a shelf just above the mirror's edge, burning low.

Della turned to her.

"You'll be in here for seven minutes. Stare into the mirror. Don't speak. Don't turn away. Just… look."

Alexis nodded once.

Before she stepped back, Della added, "When your time is up, I'll come get you." She looked Alexis straight in the eyes. "And don't tell the others what you see. That part is yours."

Alexis stepped inside and sat in the chair, spine straight. Attentive.

The mirror met her eyes immediately. No fanfare. No trick of light.

Just her own face staring back at her, and it looked exhausted.

Her braids hung limp from the Louisiana heat. Her eyelids were slightly puffy, but she remained alert.

She didn't mean to start counting. But she did.

Three were missing when she took the case.

Two more after.

Jennifer. Gone. No leads. No signs.

Milan… confirmed. Ritualistic.

Now Kayla? Never showed up. No one asked.

Started with Seventeen.

Now, nine are left.

Her eyes clung to the glass.

Her mind kept reaching for the next thought, but the mirror took it. A twitch passed through her reflection. Then a shiver under its skin.

The cheekbones tilted higher. Unnatural.

The jawline stretched, tendons pulling like they'd been hooked from inside.

The corners of its mouth began to rip upward, like torn fabric.

Then the eyes.

A shudder crawled through the glass.

The right eye gave way with a wet pop, collapsing inward as though an unseen blade had been rammed deep into its center.

It struck again. And again. Each invisible thrust twisting the socket into pulp.

Alexis flinched with every jab, shoulders jerking like the blows were landing in her own skull. The pressure behind the eye. The bone giving way.

A stream of black bled down, clinging to the cheek before dropping out of sight.

The left followed. Harder.

The first blow caved it in. The second churned what was left into a wet hollow. The third scraped so deep it rattled her teeth, the sound vibrating in her jaw.

Her reflection's ruined eyes streamed black, the ooze dragging slow, fat lines down its face.

Its shoulders hitched with small, uneven jerks, each inhale shallow and each exhale leaving in a wet rattle. Black rivulets clung to the skin in thick ropes, pooling at the corners of that flat, too-wide mouth.

A thin, damp sound escaped through clenched teeth, faint at first. Then it grew louder, snagged deep in the throat, then tore free in jagged bursts and gurgles before spilling out.

The sobbing changed its tempo.

Its shoulders began to jerk in a quicker sequence, until the sound curved upward into something almost playful.

It bent in on itself. Cracked apart.

The mouth stayed stretched in that dead, too-wide line, but the noise it spilled was fractured between weeping and laughter.

Alexis's fingers dug into her knees hard enough to hurt. She wanted to blink. Wanted to turn away. But she couldn't. It was as if something unseen pressed her spine to the chair, holding her head steady, forcing her eyes open to make sure she bore witness to whatever was unfolding in the glass.

Her pulse throbbed in her ears.

She stayed there, rigid.

The candle beside her flared blue. Then died.

A knock on the door.

The lock clicked.

The door creaked open, the light from the hallway spilling in.

Alexis's hands stayed clamped to her knees until she could force them loose. She tried to push up from the chair, but her legs answered in tremors.

Della stood in the doorway, her expression unreadable.

She took one long look at Alexis. Her eyes moved across the slack in her frame, the hollow slope of her shoulders, stripped of whatever had once braced them.

Then she smiled.

"Looks like you've had a revelation."

Alexis didn't respond.

She looked at her only briefly before her attention jumped to the hallway.

Della didn't press. She stepped aside.

"Come on, then."

Alexis tried getting up again, this time successfully.

Her legs shook beneath her, but she moved out of the closet and past Della.

She wasn't sure if her legs were shaking from fear or from whatever the mirror had taken.

She stepped out into the sun.

But the warmth didn't touch her.

Everything looked the same.

But it all felt different.

The girls were still scattered along the circular bench, but no one spoke. No teasing. No side-eyes. No nervous laughter.

Alexis walked back to her seat, slow and stiff. Her legs moved without thinking. Her hands found her lap and folded there, tight. Her gaze stayed fixed on the ground, trying her best to keep it together.

Across from her, Brielle watched her closely.

Her expression changed slowly. Curiosity became concern. Concern slipped into unease. Then full-on fear.

She stood up too fast.

Della stepped back outside, pausing in the doorway.

"Brielle," Della called gently.

Brielle didn't move. "I'm not doing it. Whatever it is… I'm not doing it."

"Brielle," Della tried again, "You don't have to be afraid. Just—"

"I said I'm not doing it!" Brielle snapped, heat flooding through the crack in her voice. "I already put up with the last thing y'all had us doing, letting Nevi poke and prod me like I was some damn animal. But this?" She shook her head hard. "No! This is too much."

She stepped back, heel catching in the grass and twisting.

All eyes turned. But she wasn't looking at them.

She was staring straight at Alexis.

"Look at her," Brielle barked, voice splintering. "Whatever y'all did to her? No! I am not about to go in there and come out looking like that."

Her hand lifted. Shaky. Accusatory. Pointing at Alexis's face as if it held proof.

Alexis sat hunched forward, elbows braced on her knees, fingers slack and unmoving. Eyes half-lidded and unfocused, she looked past Brielle. Her lips parted slightly, drawing in slow, uneven pulls of air, each sound reaching her a moment too late.

From the back of the house, the double doors eased open. Nevi stepped through first, gliding in like she'd been waiting just out of sight. Rae followed a pace behind, giving Alexis one quick look before settling on Brielle.

"If you leave, you forfeit everything," Nevi warned.

Brielle turned fully now, her voice shaking as she faced them. "I don't care. I'm done. Forget the money. I'll figure something else out. But I'm done with these games. Y'all are not about to break me!"

Nevi pressed her lips into a line.

"As you wish, then… dear."

She turned toward the veranda, all grace and ice.

"Rae? Della? Would you two be so kind as to see our guest out?" She gave Brielle one last look. "Make sure she has everything she needs before she's no longer with us." Then she pivoted toward the others. "We'll stay out here. Give her a little space."

And with that, Rae and Della disappeared into the house with Brielle between them, the doors closing softly behind them.

No one else spoke.

Reluctantly, Alexis lifted from the ground.

The sounds of Mardi Gras thrummed around them, drums and horns swelling in the distance. Beneath it all, something else stirred.

Glass breaking.

From somewhere inside the house.

She froze, head tilting slightly, straining to catch it again.

Nothing.

Only the music of the city… and the uneasy thought that maybe she'd heard nothing at all.

CHAPTER 7

"Ease into your seat with intention. Don't just plop down!" Della stood at the head of the table, posture rigid.

Destiny pulled her shoulders back. Olivia pressed her knees together. Markeysha kept one hand on the chair, waiting.

From the kitchen, Rae called, "The same way you walked the rice path. Head high. Body steady."

One at a time, the girls lowered onto the velvet seats. Heels scraped. Skirts brushed wood.

Alexis sat down last. Just as poised as the others.

The table was covered in a cream lace cloth. In front of each girl sat a scatter of dishes and utensils.

"Listen up, Blue Hearts," Della commanded while moving to the head of the table. "You've been invited to a fine supper. Guests are arriving, and music is playing. You've taken your seat, and the first course of the night is…" She trailed off, blinking at the dishes, searching. "It is… um…"

From the kitchen, Rae's voice cut across the room. "Crawfish bisque."

Della's lips curved. "Yes. Crawfish bisque. Exactly. Now… your task is to set your place for that course. China, flatware, and glassware must all be where they belong. Let me see if you can manage order out of this pile in front of you."

Alexis looked at the jumble below. She knew the basics: charger first, then the plate, and the bowl on top. Simple enough.

She slid the gold-rimmed charger to the center, stacked the dinner plate, then eased the soup bowl into place. That much felt right.

The silverware was trickier. She knew the forks belonged on the left and the spoon on the right, but the two knives had her stuck. Her hand hovered over them, weighing one, then the other. Finally, she placed both on the right, the larger closest to the plate.

She picked up the heavy linen napkin, smoothing its loose corner and folding it into a clean rectangle like she'd seen in hotel dining rooms. It slid neatly beneath the forks.

The goblets glimmered at her elbow. She set the water glass above the knives and the wine glass just beside it, then sat back, steadying her face into calm.

Imani leaned in from her right. "Oh, wait! You've got your knife and soup spoon flipped. They should be on the other—"

Alexis glanced down, frowning slightly. "The left side of the bowl?"

"No, I mean… Here, let me help you."

Before Alexis could answer, Imani's hand darted in, sliding the utensils into a new order. "There. Perfect."

"Thanks, girl," Alexis told her.

"No problem." Imani settled back into her seat, with a sly grin.

Della moved to the first seat across from Alexis. "Nia…" She studied the placement before giving a crisp nod. "Correct."

Next came Olivia. Della's mouth twitched. "Perfect. As usual."

Olivia straightened in her chair, lips tugging into a small, pleased smile she tried and failed to smother.

After that, things moved smoothly. Every setting was near perfect. Then Della paused behind Natalia.

Without a word, she reached down, lifted a fork, and set it neatly on the other side of the plate. The faint clink of silver was the only sound. She gave a small nod.

Then she moved on.

By Markeysha, she stopped again. A slow correction

followed. The smaller plate centered, the bowl eased into place, the napkin unrolled and folded smoothly before being set beside the fork. Della stepped back. "Better." She continued down the line.

When she reached Imani, she paused again. Della's stare lingered.

"Your napkin," she finally spoke up. "It has a smudge."

Imani looked down, then back up. "Yes, Madame Della. I noticed that too, but it was already like that."

"Well, in that case, my apologies, dear. I'll get you a new one." She turned and walked off.

Alexis repositioned herself in her seat as she watched Della return to the table. After handing Imani a clean napkin, she stepped over to Alexis.

Della spared a quick glance at the arrangement, then leaned in, her hand landing on the knife and spoon. "These are in the wrong order." She placed them in their proper place with two quick motions. "Almost perfect, sweetheart."

Alexis knew something in the way Imani had moved was off. If she was willing to undercut her on something this small, what would she be willing to do when the stakes rose?

Alexis cut her a look. Imani caught it. For a flicker, her smile wavered, her hand still on the tablecloth, then she smoothed it back in place and lifted her chin like nothing had happened.

"Do we win anything for getting it right?" Imani asked Della.

Della let out a small laugh. "You win knowing you already knew how to set a table. Good job, girls." She clapped twice.

The sound had barely settled when the sliding door rasped open. Nevi filled the frame and, without a word, hooked her arm through Della's and tugged her into the grand room. Then the door slid shut.

The girls glanced at each other. No one spoke above a murmur.

Della returned a moment later, chuckling softly. "Rae, my darling baby sister, would you be so kind as to give these girls a brief lesson in the finer points of sautéing and seasoning?

It will serve them well, especially with tomorrow's activities ahead. Nevi requires my assistance with… a small matter."

Nevi lingered in the doorway behind Della, one hand resting against the frame.

Rae dipped her chin once in acknowledgment. Nevi reached for Della's arm, guiding her back through the sliding door and closing it behind them.

"Come along, Blue Hearts," Rae called from the kitchen.

Chairs scraped softly over the marble as the girls rose and filed toward the kitchen. She had already arranged her ingredients across the island. Slabs of duck were laid out beside bowls of finely chopped aromatics. Fresh okra. Crawfish tails nestled in porcelain dishes. Vibrant tomatoes. Thick slices of crusty bread.

"This," Rae gestured to the duck, "will cook low and slow until the meat slides from the bone."

The headless bird rested on a wooden board, its neck stump dark and ridged, a thin sheen of blood seeping into the grain before running onto the granite beneath.

Alexis's throat tightened. She forced her face still.

Jade saw the flicker cross her face and grinned. "Fix your face, chick," she teased. "Oh, you can eat it, but can't watch it being cooked?"

"It's not that… it just caught me off guard. And, girl, I don't even eat meat."

"She's pescatarian, boo," Raven chimed in right over Jade's shoulder.

"You three paying attention back there?" Rae's voice cut through.

"Yes, Madame Rae," they answered in unison.

"Good. Now, as I was saying…" Rae positioned herself at the head of the station, scanning the girls.

"Every tool has its purpose."

Laid flat across the granite were half a dozen knives of every shape and size, blades laid out like instruments in an operating room.

She lifted the most enormous blade, a heavy machete-shaped cleaver, and gestured toward Destiny.

"Come here, sweetheart. Show me how you'd hold this."

Destiny hesitated, then stepped forward. She wrapped her hand around the handle, awkward and tense, the blade oddly angled toward her chest.

Rae's brow twitched. "Lord, have mercy." She snatched the knife from Destiny's grip, holding it up between them. "You plan on gutting yourself first?"

A nervous laugh rippled through the girls, but Rae didn't smile.

"This is why every woman should know her way around a kitchen. The way you held that knife makes it obvious you can't cook. What man wants a wife who can't cook?!"

The words came out cold. Meaner than Rae ever sounded. Alexis made note of it.

Even Rae noticed.

Her shoulders dropped. "Forgive me." The harshness melted from her voice. "That was unkind. Fear makes fools of us all."

Rae set the cleaver down with a soft thud and reached for the smallest knife on the board.

"Alright, Destiny. Tell me what this one's for."

Destiny stared at it, silent. Her lips parted, then closed.

Olivia spoke up. "It's a paring knife. You use it for peeling and little cuts."

Rae's smile curved slowly. "Correct. Small. Precise. Designed for delicate work." She turned the blade between her fingers, the metal catching light. "Every household needs a woman who knows how to handle one of these."

She took a few steps toward Olivia. Destiny eased back, relief washing over her face as Rae extended the knife.

"Go on, dear. Dice me up one of those tomatoes over there." She pointed the knife toward the metal bowl of tomatoes on the counter.

Olivia reached for one, and Rae passed her the knife. The first cut came down too hard, crushing the flesh beneath the blade. She adjusted her grip, slowed her pace, and the next slice slid clean through the skin, each piece falling neat and even.

"Not bad," Rae murmured, retrieving the knife from Olivia. She grabbed another tomato to demonstrate. The blade glided through the flesh like silk. "The blade wants to cut. You're the one holding it back."

Then Rae returned to the board. She lifted her knife and, without hesitation, began slicing the tomatoes into flawless, tiny cubes.

Rae handled the knife with eerie precision.

Alexis swallowed, wondering if it was only food Rae had trained herself to carve up.

Rae set the knife aside and wiped her hands on a linen towel. "Now, let's start the roux for our bisque."

She crossed over to the stove and turned the knob. The burner gave a quick hiss, then the blue flame rose, steady and low. From the hanging rack above, she selected a copper-bottomed saucepan, old and polished to a mirror shine. Then she set it on the burner.

A small ceramic bowl of flour sat waiting beside the stove, neatly measured, untouched.

She looked toward Nia. "Would you hand me one of those sticks of butter right in front of you, darling?"

Nia passed it over, the paper wrapping softening under her fingers from the warmth of the room. Rae took it and dropped it into the pan.

Once the butter loosened and spread, Rae tipped the flour into the pan, stirring as the mixture thickened.

"The trick," she continued, stirring slow circles, "is patience. You don't rush a roux. I know most girls your age lack that sort of discipline. Luckily for you all, that's one of the very things Preparation instills within you."

The scent began to waft, buttery giving way to something deeper, warmer, almost sweet. "This is the base of everything worth tasting. Every good dish and every perfect presentation starts with preparation and time."

She smiled faintly at the girls, the spoon turning slowly in her hand. "You tend it. You watch. You never look away… until it's ready to be served."

Nevi reappeared without a sound. "Let's leave Rae to it." She brushed a speck of lint from her sleeve. "Della, be a dear and assist your sister with the final touches."

Then her tone cooled.

"Girls, come with me. Now."

What now?

Alexis waited for the rest of the group to start walking, then followed behind.

Nevi led the girls into the corridor of bedrooms.

Her steps struck harder now, her heels hitting the wood in a cadence that made backs straighten instinctively. She stopped at Imani's room and opened the door.

She moved out of the way and gestured for the girls to go inside. "Go on, have a look."

Alexis stepped in behind Imani and scanned the room. A silk robe hung halfway off one of the beds. Makeup sat open across the nightstand, powder dusting the surface in a fine gold haze. False lashes rested beside an uncapped lipstick. In the corner, Imani's suitcase sat wide open, some of its contents spilling onto the floor. The comforter of another bed was hanging off the edge.

"Come along!" Nevi called, and everyone followed her voice into Olivia and Nia's room.

On one side, a pile of clothes sat heaped across the bed in a wrinkled mound. On the floor beside it, the mesh wastebasket was overflowing with trash. On the other side, pillows rested on the floor next to the bed, and a damp towel lay sprawled across the bedspread. Candy wrappers and chip bags crowded the nightstand and spilled onto the floor beside it.

Nevi gave the room one last look, then swept into the next without a word. The girls were on her heels.

In this room, lip gloss tubes, perfume bottles, and jewelry were spread across the dresser. One of the nightstands had a half-full mug of what looked like green tea on it, crumbs scattered beside it, and a scarf draped over the lamp. None of the beds were made, the one in the middle nearly completely stripped, a corner of the mattress encasement exposed.

Alexis turned to Markeysha, Natalia and Destiny. Natalia's face was pinched with embarrassment. Markeysha looked irritated more than ashamed. Destiny stood there absorbing the scene.

"No dawdling!" Nevi didn't give them time to settle. They were already on to the next room.

Nevi opened the door, and the girls spilled in. Nevi stopped at the threshold.

On Raven's side there was a nightgown dangling from the

bedpost. On the floor in front of her bed was a neatly placed line of shoes. The dresser had both Jade's and Raven's clothes fighting to get out of the drawers, and there were makeup bags and supplies scattered messily atop it. Jade and Raven's beds were made, but the way the duvets were touching the floor made it clear there was minimal effort involved. Their pillows looked like they had been thrown against the headboards.

Nevi clicked her tongue once as she stepped in. She moved between their beds without hurry and stopped when she reached Alexis's bed.

The coverlet lay smooth and flat. Corners tucked. Pillows fluffed.

Nevi extended a hand and ran her palm slowly over the spread.

Then she reached into her pocket.

Metal flashed between her fingers.

The girls watched in silence as she flipped the quarter onto the center of Alexis's bed.

It struck the coverlet and sprang back up.

A faint hum of approval left Nevi's throat.

She turned, stepping back into the doorway so all of them could see her face.

"This," she said, looking at the girls one by one, "is how a bed is supposed to be made."

Nevi's approval barely registered. Alexis was staring at the suitcase under her bed.

It stuck out a little farther than before, turned slightly off-angle. She was almost certain she'd pushed it all the way under, flush against the wall.

Did Nevi or Della run into it by accident… or did they go through it?

"Strip the linens! Remake every bed until it looks like this one. I want them tight enough to make this quarter bounce." Nevi scolded. "Nothing should be under the beds, the floor should be clear of clutter, and all belongings must be stored away."

Then she shouted, "Ou dwe kenbe yon kay pwòp!"

Exasperated, she followed with the English translation.

"You must keep a clean house!"

The girls scattered.

Closet doors creaked open. Sheets flapped. Hangers rattled.

With all the bedroom doors open, the smell of floral lotion, stale perfume, and a faint tinge of mustiness mingled in the hall. A few girls murmured to themselves, shuffling faster now.

"This that army shit… she gon' come back with white gloves next," Raven huffed.

Alexis walked over to Raven's side of the room. "You need help?"

"Nah, I'm good," Raven said as she set her comforter in a chair on Alexis's side of the room.

"You good, too?" Alexis turned in Jade's direction.

Jade was already stacking her makeup bags by size, her movements neat and unhurried. "Mhm," she said, smoothing one hand over the dresser before tucking the last loose item into a drawer.

Alexis stole one last glance at the girls before crossing into Markeysha, Destiny, and Natalia's room. She met Destiny at the threshold, mug in hand, muttering curses under her breath as she headed to the kitchen to wash it. Alexis caught the faint herbal smell trailing after her as she passed. Inside, she heard Natalia talking to herself.

"My side ni siquiera está that messy." She was pulling the sheets halfway off her mattress, fighting with the fitted corner. "Qué quiere decir, ah? She wants to bounce a coin off the sheets? Please. Pa qué tanto show…"

Alexis stepped in to help her tuck it down tight. Once she was done, she glanced over and noticed Markeysha wiping the dresser.

"Markeysha, you good over there?"

"I got it. Thanks."

Alexis moved to the next room.

While Olivia picked up all the clutter, handling each garment like she hated seeing it wrinkled, Nia made their beds. Olivia kept her head down as she worked.

"Y'all need me to help with anything?" Alexis asked, standing in the doorway.

"We're almost done," Olivia informed her. "Thank you, though."

Alexis glanced from Olivia's careful hands to the pillows Nia had already squared at the headboard, taking in their room once more before stepping back out.

In the hallway, Alexis spotted Nevi standing sentinel, arms crossed, eyes tracking every motion.

Though Nevi said it was about tidiness, Alexis knew better.

This was about obedience. Domestication parading as discipline.

She crossed the hall toward Imani's room.

The room was almost in order now. The bed was the only thing left unfinished.

Alexis didn't bother asking Imani if she needed help. She stepped in and went straight for the mattress.

Alexis caught one side while Imani took the other. They pulled the sheet tight in one hard sweep, the fabric dragging across the mattress.

Imani moved to the head of the bed. "Thanks, Lexi… and about earlier—"

"Don't even worry about it, girl. We're good." Alexis tucked the corners clean beneath the edge and smoothed the spread with both palms, pressing out the last of the wrinkles.

Imani fluffed each pillow and lined them up against the headboard.

By the time Imani fluffed the last pillow, Nevi was stepping back inside.

The table looked almost exactly as they'd left it that afternoon. Same cream lace cloth. Same careful arrangement of plates and silverware. Only the lighting had changed. Candles now burned low along the center.

Without being told, the girls drifted back to their earlier spots, pausing behind their chairs. Olivia, Nia, and Destiny stood where they'd sat before, Natalia beside them. Alexis took her place at the end of the table across from Nia.

Raven stopped at the seat next to Alexis and rested her hand on the chair back.

Imani froze. "That's my seat," she whispered.

Raven didn't move. "Girl, if you don't go find another one…"

Imani stayed planted, arms crossed, waiting.

Alexis turned slightly, watching the stand-off.

"You think just standing there's gonna make me move?" Raven turned toward her. "Go on, maw. I am not Nia."

They stared each other down until Jade stepped in, sliding into her spot beside Raven.

"Y'all good?" Jade asked.

Raven gave a slow nod. "Girl, yeah, we good. Right, Imani?"

Imani sucked her teeth then crossed to the empty chair beside Natalia.

Alexis studied Imani a moment longer. She calculated, but not bold.

"Evening, Blue Hearts."

Alexis looked up to see Nevi entering the dining room. Her steps were unhurried as she moved to the other end of the table, away from Alexis.

Her presence alone was enough to still the room.

Nevi sat first. Then the girls followed suit.

Moments later, Rae strolled over in a sleek, fitted black dress and low heels. She was pushing a long, double-tiered cart, adorned with polished domes and bottles chilled in ice-filled buckets.

"Ladies," Rae began, "tonight's first course is crawfish bisque, finished with a chive oil drizzle and served with crostini. We've paired it with a White Burgundy, elegant, subtle, and perfectly balanced for the dish."

She and Della plated. Rae circled behind the girls, placing steaming bowls in front of each one while Della poured wine.

At Destiny's end of the table, Rae leaned in and murmured, "Use your soup spoon, not the teaspoon. Remember, outside in."

Destiny blushed, nodding.

When Rae reached Natalia, her hand brushed the untouched napkin. "On your lap the moment you sit, dear. Never on the table until you've risen."

Natalia lowered it quickly, cheeks hot.

As Rae completed the final pour, Nevi tapped her wine glass lightly with her fork.

"Before you eat, remember what you were taught. Posture. Utensil order. You do not lift a fork until every plate is served. And when you chew, do it as if eyes are on you… because they always are."

A cool draft stirred the room. The lace runners lifted at

the corners. Candle flames bent sideways, reaching for the girls.

The room settled again, like the house itself had corrected them.

Nevi smiled. "Good. You may begin."

The girls hesitated, then dug in. The bisque sat warm against the air, rich enough to tighten Alexis's stomach.

Rae and Della watched the girls.

Rae's gaze moved back to Natalia. "And when you've finished, place your fork and spoon parallel on the plate at four o'clock. That tells us you're done."

Nevi's eyes skimmed the line of bowls. "Slurping, Nia?! It's unbecoming."

Nia adjusted. Quickly.

Once the bowls were emptied and the room filled with the soft clink of silver and satisfied sighs, Della rose and cleared the plates.

Nevi watched from the head of the table.

Rae returned, this time trailing the rich aroma of roasted meats and spices.

"For the entrée, we have duck confit over dirty rice with smothered okra and heirloom tomatoes. The wine pairing for this dish is a Pinot Noir."

Della resumed her seat beside Nevi. Rae plated carefully.

When she reached Alexis, she paused.

"And for you," Rae lifted the dome, "blackened redfish meunière with crab butter sauce over caramelized fennel and celery root purée."

"Oh… wow. It smells amazing!"

"Figured you'd fancy this instead," Rae replied, pouring wine into Alexis's glass with a toothy grin.

Nevi stood and swept the table, taking in each girl before she lifted her glass.

"Tomorrow's event is what the Krewe of Lazuliè is all about.

"Since the beginning of time, a woman's power has been misunderstood. Her beauty reduced to vanity. Her allure treated as something sinful, rather than sacred.

"But we know better. A woman's presence can stir

desire, invite devotion, and leave an impression long after she has left the room. That is a gift.

"Sex is to magic, as the beauty of a woman is to spellcasting. Tomorrow, we shall use that gift to beguile our prey."

She drank. Della and Rae followed. Then, hesitantly, the girls.

Alexis raised her glass and sipped. The wine tasted like velvet wrapped around a copper nail. She didn't swallow right away. She held it on her tongue until it cooled, then let it go.

"Good!" Nevi exclaimed. "Now… let's eat."

Silverware lifted. Voices dipped. The girls turned to their plates like dancers waiting for a cue.

Raven leaned close.

"Bitch, what kind of voodoo shit did we just partake in?"

Jade slapped Raven's arm. "Girl, you know Nevi is extra!"

"Okay. But if somebody starts levitating, I'm leaving."

Alexis shook her head, lips twitching.

The fish was perfect. The wine was smooth.

Rae watched on. Nevi remained still.

Only the girls at the center whispered. The others remained quiet, locked in by nerves, obedience, or hunger.

Nevi dabbed her lips with a silk napkin. "Do finish your plates, girls. Rae has a sweet surprise for you." She turned slightly toward Rae. "Isn't that right, dear sister?"

"That's right." Rae set her glass down. "Dessert is bourbon bread pudding with brûléed bananas and warm vanilla cream."

A few girls brightened. Markeysha murmured. Olivia clapped.

Nevi gave a small hum of satisfaction.

Alexis didn't react. She stared at her plate. The wine. The toast. It all sat wrong.

"Sex is to magic as the beauty of a woman is to spellcasting."

"…we shall use our natural enchantment to beguile our prey."

Alexis ran the words back in her mind.

It wasn't so much what was spoken as what it provoked. Like she'd signed a contract she hadn't read all the way through.

CHAPTER 8

The salon door creaked open. It usually stayed locked and off-limits, but today it had been reborn.

Sunlight from the tall windows spilled across the room, catching on pearls, silks, tulle, and lace. Vintage couture unfurled in every corner. Pastel gowns draped over mannequins, folded like prayer hands.

One tall antique mirror leaned in the corner. Earlier, the girls hovered around it, giggling and shoving to check their outfits, reapplying gloss, and fussing with their hair. Natalia had practically climbed over Markeysha's back to snatch a quick look. Olivia had squinted into the glass, turning her head this way and that.

Moments ago, the mirror had been a battlefield, a beauty altar, a stage.

But now, the mood had changed.

The mirror sat serenely, absorbing all the nerves and vanity it had just reflected.

Barefoot and half-dressed, the girls sat in silence. The giggles and teasing had drained out of the room. No more lip gloss touch-ups. No more playful whining about corset lines or pinched toes.

They perched on worn benches and faded stools, needlepoint cushions flattened and frayed, their old floral patterns haunted the fabric underneath.

The gold fleur-de-lis wallpaper, once elegant, had turned unsettling. The flowers began to curl at their ends, wilting in real time.

The seconds dragged until time felt suspended.

At the far end of the room, Nevi worked her magic. She wore a long, slate-colored cotton dress, the sleeves rolled to her elbows. From her deep front pockets spilled folded scraps of silk, tailor's chalk, a pair of scissors, and a worn seam ripper. A measuring tape looped loosely around her neck. A row of red-tipped dressmaker's pins clung to the cuff of her sleeve.

She moved around Destiny, her fingers going to work, pinching the side seam and marking the fabric where it needed giving. Destiny stood stiff on the fitting platform with her arms raised. Her eyes stared past the mirror, unblinking.

"Tuck in your stomach, girl," Nevi muttered, pressing her hand flat against Destiny's side. "There's no grace in a gown that's fighting you."

Destiny exhaled through her nose. "It's just a little bloating…"

The corset dug in just beneath her ribs, locking them in place like a cage.

Nevi popped a pin between her teeth and gave her a look. "Bloating got hips, too?"

She crouched to tug at the hem, then frowned. Her fingers paused over a line of lace at the bottom seam. Threads had pulled, subtle as a bruise. She smoothed the fabric with her palm.

"Hmm. Didn't notice this one was torn, too. Might have to retire it as well."

"What did you say, Madame Nevi?" Destiny asked.

"Just talking to myself." Nevi continued to adjust the bodice. "Hold your arms still now. Let me finish."

The dress stopped fighting her shape, looking way more flattering now. Nevi tilted her head and stepped back with her hands on her hips. Her face softened just slightly.

"There. Much better. You've got a strong frame. Carries the fabric well."

Destiny cracked a smile, watching her reflection in the mirror across the room.

"Okayyy… I don't hate it."

Nevi gently brushed a wrinkle from the shoulder. "A proper stitch'll make anything look like it was meant to be."

She plucked the final pin into place, then inclined her head. "Alright. Step down, then ease out of it. I'll need to let it out more through the hips, then shape the waist and clean up the hem."

Destiny stepped carefully off the block and began shimmying out of the gown.

"Please be mindful not to bust any seams, dear." Nevi held the back steady as Destiny slipped her arms free. "Brocade's got a memory worse than an old man's grudge."

Nevi folded the dress over her arm, making a mental note of every correction as she turned to leave. "Good. I'll bring it back when it's ready."

Alexis caught her heading toward the door, the gown draped over one arm. Just before reaching it, Nevi stopped at the tall antique mirror in the far corner. Her free hand lifted, the tips of her fingers pressing lightly into her cheek. They slid upward to the fine lines near her eye, tracing them one at a time.

In the glass, her face seemed to lose its color.

From Alexis's vantage, Nevi's expression in the glass changed. What might have been concern gave way to something closer to disappointment… or sadness.

The moment was over as quickly as it began. Nevi's hand dropped, and she stepped out into the hall.

The door eased shut behind her.

The second they were sure Nevi was out of earshot, the chatter came alive.

"This weekend is turning into a damn debutante boot camp," Destiny muttered, twisting her lips and smoothing her tank top like she wanted a refund.

"For real, though." Raven crossed one leg over the other on the vanity bench. "They got us in here like we're pledging Delta Sigma Stepford." She pulled out concealer from her makeup bag, tapping it against her palm. "Shit, lowkey starting to feel like Brielle was on to something after all."

Nia leaned against the wall, arms folded. "I've been ready to leave since they took our phones. The only reason I haven't is because of the money. Ten thousand's hard to walk away from."

Raven laughed. "Who you telling? But, aye." She looked around the room. "If things pop off, who's getting active? Natty, baby, you gon' hit 'em with that Santa Maria or what?"

Natalia looked up. "You must mean Santería. And don't play with me." She folded her arms. "I'm not into brujería." She nodded toward Destiny. "Get your girl over there for that."

Destiny exhaled hard through her nose. "You see me with some tarot cards one time and swear I'm in a damn coven." Her eyes cut to Natalia, then away. "Santería isn't even witchcraft. Y'all love to judge anything that doesn't fit what *you all* believe." A short, humorless laugh slipped out as she leaned forward, her voice dropping to almost nothing. "Slow asses probably think voodoo's the devil too."

Tension briefly hushed the room. Alexis studied it and what it revealed about the girls.

Destiny sat with her arms crossed, chin tilted, irritation settling into her posture. Her shoulders stayed tight, her mouth drawn.

Natalia shifted on the narrow bench, spine straight but weary, head bowed. Her lips moved once, then again, the words too faint to hear. In a quick, practiced motion, her index finger brushed her forehead, the center of her chest, then each shoulder before her hand dropped to her lap.

Raven leaned forward on her knees, gaze bouncing between Natalia and Destiny, her mouth pressed in a thin line. She looked like she wanted to rewind the whole thing, realizing too late that she had fanned the flames of a fire she couldn't extinguish.

The rest of the girls stared ahead, faces blank but uneasy.

"Anyway," Markeysha spoke up. "I'm with you, Nia. Maybe we should've left with Brielle. I didn't know they would have us doing all this."

"I *love* it," Olivia gushed, spinning once in place. "I feel like I'm living in another era. The dresses, the frilly heeled slippers, the arm-length lace gloves; I'm obsessed!"

Markeysha gave her a look. "You're the only one trying to cosplay the damn 1800s."

Olivia didn't flinch. She twirled again, skirt swishing.

"This hoe is really crazy," Raven murmured. "Like, for real."

Alexis heard but didn't say anything.

A hush fell over the room again when Rae entered. Her arms were full of colorful wraps. Her eyes scanned the room before settling on her first subject.

"Olivia, you're first."

Olivia perked up immediately and stepped forward. She lowered herself onto the stool Rae motioned toward, her sandy brown hair tumbling down her back in soft waves.

Rae reached into her pocket and pulled out a soft-bristled boar brush, worn smooth at the handle. She gently brushed Olivia's hair back, sweeping it up with slow, even strokes. The curls caught the light with a warm, golden sheen, and Rae's hand lingered as she worked them into a loose, slightly messy bun at the crown of her head.

"This shade is perfect for your fair complexion," Rae murmured, selecting a tignon in soft copper and rose-gold threads.

Olivia beamed under the praise, practically glowing.

Across the room, Markeysha stood with her arms folded, eyes locked on Olivia. Then she glanced over at Raven, and they shot each other a look.

Rae began wrapping, twisting and folding the cloth. With one final motion, she pulled the headdress snug. Olivia blinked up at her, a little dazed.

"There. You look like you stepped out of one of Della's paintings," Rae said.

Olivia gave a quick nod and drifted back to her spot, one hand on the headdress like it needed support.

Then Rae turned her eyes toward Alexis.

"Your turn."

Alexis rose cautiously and sat on the same stool, facing forward as Rae approached in the tall mirror. Her braids were already pinned into a high bun, giving Rae enough shape to work with. She chose a wrap in deep emerald with thin gold stitching and folded, looped, and pulled it across Alexis's crown with delicate precision. Rae was close now, close enough for Alexis to feel her breath.

"Out of everybody… you're my favorite, you know that?" Rae told Alexis.

"Really? Why?"

"You came here bare of soul. That's rare." Her voice dipped to a whisper. "And honestly… I think you're our Crowned Heart."

A quick jab of pain struck the middle of Alexis's chest. She felt it deep, as if something unseen had reached inside and twisted. Her hand hovered near her heart, but she said nothing.

Della's voice reached through the moment, calling names for the photoshoot.

Rae finished tying the tignon around Alexis's head without another word, then slid over to the next girl.

One at a time, the girls were ushered into the photography room.

They sat and posed. She snapped and dismissed.

It felt coldly ceremonial. Like inventory being documented for future use.

When Alexis entered the photo room, she froze, noticing the tall mirror that stood in the corner next to the photo setup. She immediately turned away.

"Can we move that?" she asked Della.

Della just smiled and obliged.

Still, Alexis felt the need to explain. After letting out a nervous titter, she told her, "After that mirror exercise, I don't want to see another one for at least a week!"

Della smiled as she adjusted the camera.

"Oh, I understand. My sisters and I can't say we care much for the looking glass these days either."

She plucked a speck of dust from the velvet drape. "The creases, the puffiness, the way the skin sags where it used to hold taut… aging's a cruel thing." Her voice thinned slightly, but the smile held. "Mirrors don't lie. That's the damn problem." She turned to prepare the camera; a vintage model with a velvet cover and a bright flashbulb.

For half a second, Alexis considered saying something, some polite reassurance. Instead, she swallowed it down and cleared her throat. "Wow. I thought this camera was just a prop. Didn't think it actually worked."

Della chuckled softly. "Oh, it works. Vintage magic still has its place." She went on in a more serious tone. "Now, sit forward, turn your head slightly to the left… chin down… eyes here," Della instructed.

Pop.

The flashbulb exploded with a hiss.

The sudden burst startled Alexis. A halo of color lingered in her vision.

"Don't worry, your eyes will adjust by the third shot." Della removed the hot bulb with a gloved hand and replaced it. She opened the back of the camera, slid out the used film plate, and inserted a new one.

"Now lean back. Elbows in. No smile."

Pop.

Another burst of light. Smoke curled from the steel reflector.

Della stepped back again, replaced the bulb, swapped out the plate, and then re-focused the lens. Adjusted exposure. Reframed.

"Look down… Hold it there."

Alexis sat stiffly, her pulse ticking between each snap.

Pop.

Della frowned. "Shoot. That was the last good plate." She tapped the camera once, thinking. "Oh!" Her posture straightened. "I think I've got a few more in storage. Stay here, I'll be right back."

Alone now, Alexis glanced around.

Something above a dusty display case caught her attention.

Mounted on the wall was a vintage map of New Orleans, its parchment yellowed and curling at the ends. Seven black pins were stabbed into it. Her eyes tracked the curve the pins formed automatically, mind already tracing the pattern.

Her memory was good, unshakable even, but something told her memory wouldn't be enough.

"I'll come back later," she murmured.

Then she noticed a desk in the corner, cluttered with photo negatives and a textbook-sized photo album. Curious, she opened the book.

There were lavish balls held in high-ceilinged halls, women in corseted gowns twirling beneath chandeliers that dripped with crystal. The photos were all sepia-stained and slightly blurred.

Processions lit by gas lamps followed, slow and ceremonial, winding through streets lined with watchers holding paper fans.

Images of children in lace and collars filled the last few pages, their faces too still, too solemn.

She paused on one. A girl. Ten, maybe eleven. Hair parted clean. Big doe eyes. Her dress hung strangely, too big, like it had once belonged to someone else.

Alexis leaned in. Something about the child's expression caught her. There was something in those eyes. Something familiar.

She squinted closer. "Why does this little girl look just like…"

The voice hit her like static cracking open inside her skull.

Let it burn.

She recoiled.

The same tone stacked at different pitches, youthful and thin.

She looked up.

No one was there.

Back to the photo. The girl hadn't moved, but her mouth… had it been open before?

Then it came again.

Let 'em burn it.

Let 'em burn it.

The same sound repeating itself, higher, closer, crowding Alexis's ears.

Her whole body jolted. The album slipped from her hands and hit the floor with a slap of bent pages and brittle paper.

The sound dug in deeper.

Let it burn.

Let 'em burn it.

Let it burn.

Let 'em burn it down!

Her ears rang.

She cupped her ears and winced.

"Shit!" She doubled over. That same pain struck her chest, right through the center, like something had yanked a thread from the inside.

The silence that followed felt artificial. She could hear her own breathing. Shallow and uneven.

She forced herself to slow it down. Scooped the photo album off the floor. Returned it to its spot with careful fingers. Then sat back down, straight, still, as if nothing had happened.

What the fuck is going on with me?

"Alright, I've got the plates!" Della's voice floated into the room, stirring Alexis from her thoughts. She was cradling a box.

"Let's get that last shot in, shall we?"

CHAPTER 9

The kitchen swarmed. Pots clanged. Oven doors thudded. Knives kept pace with the shuffle of feet. Drawers slammed, flour fell in slow clouds, voices tangled in clipped bursts, all of them calling for spoons, for bowls, for space.

Some girls worked with quick hands. Others hesitated, colliding with one another as they tried to keep up.

Their elegant Edwardian gowns carried crisp, embroidered aprons cinched tight at the waist. Tignons stayed fixed as they'd been wrapped, unmoved despite the heat, while modest French-heeled slippers kept them lifted just high enough to ache.

It was domesticity performed.

Nevi had placed the fans out earlier, flimsy cardboard faces bound to broad wooden handles, and in the girls' hands, they felt more like props.

"Y'all, it's hot as hell in here," Raven muttered, blotting her temple with the end of her apron. "Alexis, can you hand me one of those fans, please?"

Alexis slid a fan across the counter. Raven snatched it up, fanning herself in short bursts before drifting back to her simmering pot.

Across the room, Olivia looked completely unbothered. She stood at the cutting board, smiling faintly as she sliced bell peppers into perfect, uniform strips. Her apron was spotless. The tune under her breath seemed less of a song than a spell to steady her hands, grazing the right notes but never quite hitting them.

Aside from Olivia's humming and the clatter of kitchenware, there was the persistent, grating buzz of a lone fly, circling in slow, hungry loops. Its wings whined just above ear-level, the sound rising and falling, too steady to ignore.

She tried to tune it out while tossing garlic butter over halved French bread. A sheet pan waited on the counter, meatballs rolled neat and even, slick with oil and flecked with herbs. She slid the pan into the oven, shut the door with her foot, and turned the dial without missing a beat.

Her spaghetti simmered nearby, marinara bubbling low in the pot, simple and steady. She wasn't here to show out; she just needed something quick to give her time to move.

At the far counter, Markeysha worked in silence, each motion calculated. The click of measuring spoons against ceramic kept time with her breathing. She didn't guess or eyeball. Every scoop was leveled, every pour exact. Butter slid into the pan by the spoonful. Pasta dropped into boiling water after a quiet count.

Jade leaned over her shoulder. "Damn, girl, you cooking or doing chemistry?"

Markeysha didn't look up. "It's my grandma's recipe. I've got it memorized down to the tablespoon."

In the middle of the room, Imani looked like she was about to faint.

Her pot had burned through. A smear of orange streaked her apron. She stirred with the look of someone bargaining. Half-prayer. Half-panic.

Alexis glanced over, bottom lip caught between her teeth. The poor girl had no business near a stove.

"You good, Imani?" She stepped closer to peer inside.

Smoke curled from Imani's pot in a sad little spiral. The smell coming from her station was acrid. Burnt beans and desperation. Still, Imani stirred… frantically.

"I don't know what I did," she muttered. "I tried to make the roux like Rae showed us, but… I don't know!"

Her composure unraveled before everyone. Sweat poured from beneath her headdress. Her flushed cheeks ballooned as she held a breath in her mouth, fighting to keep herself together.

Nia had been across the kitchen, wiping down her spotless station. She didn't have to help, and after their last blow-up, Alexis wouldn't have blamed her if she didn't. But something changed in Nia's face, a flash of grace, or maybe pity.

She walked over to Imani's side and leaned over the pot. "Smells like you scorched 'em. You might be able to make it work if you don't scrape the bottom."

"I should just start over, huh?" Imani sighed.

"Yep. You definitely should," Jade chimed in, not even looking up from her cutting board.

Alexis placed her hand on Imani's shoulder, bobbing her head in agreement.

Imani sucked her teeth but didn't argue. She yanked the pot off the burner and dumped the whole mess into the trash.

"Here." Nia slid in. "I'll handle the roux. You rinse the beans."

There was a pause, brief but heavy.

"Thanks," Imani said, just loud enough to be heard. The look on her face made it clear of how much she resented needing help, and surely she hated getting it from Nia of all people. Certainly, she took it because she wanted that Crowned Heart title more than she wanted to be proud right now.

Alexis watched the whole thing unfold, making note of the interaction.

Nia wanting to help made sense. She's a sweet girl, just more reserved than some of the others.

But Imani… she was the kind that kept you guessing. All that hard talk and quick temper, yet she'd swallowed her pride fast when it meant staying in the game.

She wanted that Crowned Heart title so bad it burned through her composure. Alexis couldn't tell if that made her ambitious or dangerous, but either way… she was someone to watch.

A hush settled as the kitchen eased back into rhythm. Pots simmered. Knives tapped. Flimsy fans fluttered lazily against flushed faces.

Then—

BZZZZZZ.

The fly had returned, circling with persistence.

It landed on the rim of Olivia's casserole dish.

"Oh no, you don't—" Olivia grabbed a dishrag and swung at it, missing.

The fly zipped over to the sink, then doubled back to the bread Alexis had just laid on a tray. She swatted it away, jaw tight.

"Hey y'all!" Natalia gathered the girls' attention. "Think they started yet?"

"Started what?" Markeysha asked without looking up.

"The ceremony. Out there."

Everyone went still.

Eyes shifted toward the back of the kitchen, toward the windows flanking the rear double doors.

The curtains were half-drawn, sunlight slivering through the center seam.

Natalia looked at Jade.

"Oh no, don't look at me," Jade replied quickly. "The Madames made it clear not to peep. You're not about to get me caught if they look up and see me."

"Ok, fine, I'll take a look." Alexis rolled her eyes, feigning annoyance as she stepped back, wiping her hands on her apron.

"I'll keep an eye on your sauce," Natalia told her. "Be careful."

Alexis moved to the far corner of the kitchen, just beside the door, where one of the long windows gave her a partial view of the backyard. She crouched slightly and eased her hand behind the curtain, careful not to pull it open too far.

The backyard had been transformed.

Rows of black wooden chairs lined the brick path. The men seated among them wore tailored suits in opulent colors. Satin pocket squares sprouted from breast pockets like exotic flowers. Several wore pendants on their lapels, though she couldn't quite make out the shapes.

"Lexi, tell us what you see," Nia demanded in an anxious squeal.

"Hold on, I'm looking!" Alexis waved her off with her free hand.

She leaned in again, careful not to let the curtain shift too much. Her forehead nearly touched the glass.

Nevi stood at the head of it all, back to the house. She was angled just enough for Alexis to see her mouth moving, fast, clipped, relentless. Alexis couldn't hear a word, but she could tell she was leading something. Commanding it.

That high, whining buzz returned. Closer this time. Louder.

Damn fly.

It looped around her head with a ragged hum that made her jaw clench.

Alexis flinched, her jaw tightening as she swatted near her ear. Her fingers hovered at her temple for a second, willing herself not to snap.

She inhaled slowly through her nose, blinked hard, and narrowed her eyes at the scene outside.

Della and Rae stood near Nevi, stationed behind a long table draped in heavy black fabric, and on it sat nine neat stacks of envelopes, each bound with a thin silk ribbon.

Nine stacks. Nine Blue Hearts.

A stack for each of us?

A moment later, they moved to opposite sides of the gathering, each carrying a silver tray holding half of a single stack of envelopes. Their movements mirrored one another.

Alexis examined the crowd again. Eighteen men. Some leaned back in their chairs. Others sat rigid, hands folded.

Among the cluster, she began to recognize faces. A big-time pastor with a face made for billboards and a congregation the size of a small town. A criminal court judge she had seen in headlines, always smiling for the cameras, shaking hands, and handing down life sentences like party favors.

Then she spotted a man she recognized from behind a podium once, surrounded by uniforms and yellow tape. A deputy chief from a neighboring parish. Just sitting there. Calm. Casual.

They were more than just wealthy men with influence. They were the ones who made the rules. The ones who knew where the bones were buried.

They accepted the envelopes in turn, eyes fixed forward

as Rae and Della handed them out.

Alexis caught flashes of the contents as they fished them out. A glossy photograph, a cream-colored card. She couldn't make out the details, but something about the way the men studied the items made her stomach tighten.

Then Nevi stepped forward. Her mouth moved, words spilling out toward the men, but Alexis couldn't make any of it out.

A moment later, a hand went up. Then another. In the men's hands were gold-colored cards, each marked with bold blue numbers.

From behind the table, Rae and Della now sat with notebooks in front of them. As each hand rose, one of them would write something down.

Alexis narrowed her eyes. "What the hell are they writing down?" she mumbled, but Raven still heard her.

"Oooh, let me see! I've got eyes like a hawk. Bet I can make out whatever they're writing." Raven stood, but Jade grabbed her wrist.

"You're going to get Alexis caught. Let her finish looking so she can tell us what's up."

Alexis didn't take her eyes off the scene.

She watched as the process repeated. Another stack. Another round.

Each time, more envelopes were handed out. More cards were lifted. More notes were taken.

And each time Nevi finished whatever she was saying, one or two men rose, unhurried, and walked toward the back gate.

The wrought iron opened for them. Closed behind them.

Alexis froze when her eyes landed on a man in the front row.

He was staring straight at her. A slow grin crept across his face. Then he winked.

Alexis quickly backed away from the window, letting the curtain fall back into place.

CLAP!

The sound cracked through the kitchen. Alexis jumped.

Behind her, Jade stood with both hands pressed

together, fly guts oozing between her fingers.

"Bitch, did you just kill that fly with your bare hands?" Raven hissed, face scrunched in complete disgust.

Jade shrugged and wiped her hand on the curtain. "It was getting in the way."

"You ain't have to do it right by my ear though," Alexis snapped, rubbing her temples.

"I know you better wash your damn hands," Raven castigated.

"Raven, don't play with me." Jade told her as she strutted to the sink. "I'm not nasty like that."

"What all did you see, Alexis?" Natalia asked as Alexis walked back over to eye her pot of simmering sauce.

"The ceremony has definitely started. There were eighteen men, but—"

Natalia blinked. "Eighteen? But there are only nine of us."

"Guess we'll be getting some two-for-one specials tonight!" Raven snorted.

"That's not funny," Olivia snapped.

Alexis continued, "Well… I saw some of them leaving. So maybe they're doing some kind of elimination process."

She hesitated, about to mention the familiar faces she recognized, forgetting for a second that she wasn't just one of the girls.

She caught herself. Maybe it was better to hold that part back, at least until the girls saw the men for themselves.

"What were you about to say?" Jade raised an eyebrow, just a little too slow.

"Oh!" Alexis said quickly. "I just meant they're all dressed up in suits. Bright, colorful ones."

"I'm extra nervous now," Nia muttered.

"Me too, girl," Markeysha echoed.

"Just calm down." Jade crossed her arms. "Y'all getting worked up off guesses and assumptions. Let's talk about something else 'til the Madames get us. Take your mind off it."

"Talk about what?" Imani asked.

Alexis heard them, catching the start of Jade's reply, but the words faded to background noise as her thoughts drifted elsewhere.

The way that man looked at her.

The wink…

Her thoughts wandered back to the photoshoot.

Maybe the pictures in those envelopes were the ones Della took of us…

She strained to remember. Tried to pull a clear image of what the men were holding. The glossy flash of photo paper. The shape of something familiar.

Then that map came back to her.

"I need to get a picture of it," she told herself.

"Alexis, what are you mumbling about, girl? You're always zoning out. I wonder what you be thinking!" Jade's voice made Alexis jump.

"Probably about how we get on her nerves," Raven joked.

She slipped out of the kitchen into the grand room, the noise and heat of the kitchen fading behind her. The space felt cooler, cavernous.

Alexis slowed, listening. Heels stilled. Her heart ticking fast.

Then she moved again, quick but careful, crossing the open stretch of the grand room and slipping into the hallway beyond. The hush deepened.

She passed the bath and two closed bedroom doors before reaching her own.

Inside, she dropped to her knees beside the bed. Her suitcase was already half-pulled out; she'd been ready for this. Glancing over her shoulder, she unzipped the hidden lining and reached inside.

Her work phone. Cold and unfamiliar in her palm.

It had been off since the day she arrived.

Her fingers trembled slightly as she powered it on. The screen lit up with missed calls, unread texts, and voicemails.

Tahir's name flooded the notifications.

She opened the thread and scrolled through.

Short messages.

Long ones.

And the last one:

At least let me know you're okay over there.

Her throat tightened as she tapped her thumbs across the screen.

She typed: *I think tonight might be the night.*

Whatever this is… it's way bigger than we thought.

Deputy Chief Gibbons is here.

Then paused.

This house… is starting to get to me. I wish you were—

She deleted the last line fast.

Heart thudding, she typed instead:

Brielle Robbins.

Kayla Evans.

Find out if they're alright for me.

Send.

In the hush, even the small whoosh of the sent message sounded too loud.

She slipped the phone into her bra before cracking the bedroom door to step back into the hall.

She crept forward slowly, this time toward the pale door tucked beneath the staircase.

She'd been itching to see what was behind it.

She took a glance down the hall as her hand hovered over the doorknob.

Her pulse ticked in her ears.

Fingers tightened around cool brass.

Then, she turned it slowly.

Click.

Locked.

"Damn it!" Alexis muttered.

She quickly scurried up the stairs and made a beeline for the photo room.

No hesitation this time.

She rushed straight to the map, yanked out her phone, snapped a quick photo, then stuffed the phone back into her bra just as fast.

But just as she turned to leave, something caught her eye.

A knob. Right where the mirror used to be, near the photo backdrop.

She moved toward it and reached out, fingers brushing the knob. She expected it to be locked like the other door.

But it turned. Smooth. No resistance.

With a gentle push, she slipped into the room.

Near the corner stood a single mannequin. Naked. Slightly askew. Beside it, a metal rack stretched from wall to wall, crowded with dresses hanging in clear plastic. They were the same style and cut as the dresses the girls had been fitted into. Corseted bodices. Layers of tulle and satin in varying hues.

Some were in pristine condition. Others were not. A hem coming loose. A shoulder strap fraying. A seam half-split and held together with a safety pin. It was as if they had been fitted too many times to too many bodies.

A sewing table stretched along the far wall, lined with bolts of fabric, ribbon spools, and lace trims curled like dried petals. A velvet chair sat beneath the table, its cushion visibly indented. Shelves above the machine held folded gloves, stacks of fabric, and small labeled boxes.

Alexis stepped deeper inside, trailing her fingers across the table's edge.

Then her eyes landed on it: a slim, brown leather volume, tucked neatly in a glass-front cabinet.

The spine was faded, but still legible.

The Ceremony of Plaçage.

She reached for it, the leather dry and cracked beneath her touch.

She opened it.

On the inside page, printed in delicate, formal script:

Written by Geneviève Meaux

Published 1910

She flipped past the title page and began scanning the first chapter, her lips moving in a soft, unconscious murmur.

"The Ceremony of Plaçage is a ritual social contract developed among Creole circles to maintain alliances, secure resources, and elevate Negro women into protected status under the guardianship of elite men."

Her eyes narrowed. She kept reading.

"What began as a private understanding between patrons and their chosen companions has extended the ceremony to all suitable candidates, regardless of origin. Its language speaks of legacy and refinement, but its structure teaches obedience. Each participant learning what it means to be desired and owned."

Owned.

The word crawled under her skin.

She shut the book with a dull thud. "Yeah, alright."

She slid it back into place and kept moving, sure there was something more useful hidden nearby.

Then she spotted the desk up against the side wall, slightly crooked, like someone had shoved it back into place in a hurry.

She crossed over and tested the drawer.

It stuck. Then gave.

Inside, nestled between folded pattern slips and a half-used measuring tape, was a notepad.

The cover was worn at its ends, stained by touch and time.

It looked just like the ones she'd seen Rae and Della scribbling in earlier.

She opened it.

At the top of the first page, written in neat block letters:

Krewes ki Konsakre Tèt yo bay Lwa yo

Beneath it, a list.

Krewe of Lazuliè

Krewe of Shadows

Krewe of Blades

Krewe of Masques

Krewe of Gatekeepers

Krewe of Serpents

Krewe of Sirens

She flipped to the next page.

The handwriting was different. Hasty. Tight.

Ink smudged in places, the strokes rushed.

She scanned each entry, logging patterns as fast as they formed.

Some offers were marked with small checkmarks. Others were slashed out violently.

Entire rows of initials lined the pages.

And in the margins notes spiraled down, the penmanship looping wild and fast.

She couldn't take the notepad.

Not without someone noticing.

But maybe…

She reached for her phone.

Hesitated.

A floorboard creaked behind her.

Alexis turned, shoulders tight.

"I thought I heard someone in here," Rae said from the doorway.

Alexis didn't bother making an excuse. Her eyes flicked to the drawer, then back to Rae, trying to play it cool.

She didn't say it, but Rae had noticed.

She gave a soft sigh, more tired than angry, and crossed to the counter. "You're late plating," Rae walked out of the room.

"I—yeah. Sorry." Alexis followed Rae closely, saying nothing else.

When they returned to the kitchen, the girls were already seated in the space between the dining and kitchen areas, backs straight, plates waiting beneath polished silver domes.

Rae stepped beside Alexis, wordless, and reached for two porcelain dishes from the overhead rack. She set them down and twirled the spaghetti noodles lifted straight from the pot high in the center of each, perfect nests that sat tall without spilling over.

Alexis followed, scooping generous ladles of the red sauce and letting it pool neatly in the center of both plates. Rae moved next. From the pan, she lifted the meatballs, setting them carefully atop one dish, spacing them just so. She spooned another veil of sauce over the meatballs, letting it cling and drip between them.

She added the final touch: a single basil leaf on each, the green vivid against the red.

Alexis took the plates, posture straight.

"Don't worry about the bread," Rae murmured. "I'll bring it."

Alexis paused. "Thank you."

Rae gave a slight nod and stepped back.

Alexis quickly untied her apron and slid it from around her neck, tossing it onto the chair in the corner with the others.

Then she gathered the two plates, adjusted her posture, and made her way to the table.

Rae's eyes swept over the room. "You girls truly look stunning."

"They do," came Nevi's voice from behind.

She was already in the dining room, standing just inside the space between the table and the back doors, like she'd been waiting for the right moment to speak.

"And now it's time to meet your suitors. Ready, my beautiful Blue Hearts?"

Nevi smiled and turned toward the back doors. "Let's not keep them waiting. Each of you, grab your plates. One in each hand."

They rose, brocade and taffeta rustling as they fell into a clean line in the narrow space between the kitchen and dining room. Nevi and Rae took their places at the open double doors.

Alexis slid into the flow beside Nevi, studying her carefully.

She wore a black veil pulled back over her head, revealing her hair for the first time: salt-and-pepper, pinned into a perfect French bun. Elbow-length lace gloves covered her arms.

Alexis took it all in, then fell back toward the end of the line.

Nevi stopped at the door. Rae came to stand with her, and that was when Alexis noticed the matching black attire, the gloves climbing her arms like Nevi's own. The only difference was the missing veil.

A chill slipped over her.

What is this, a funeral?

Nevi turned to face the girls, her tone light but her smile tight. "Alright, Blue Hearts. Tonight is about poise, charm, and presentation. Remember your posture, your table etiquette… and for God's sake, chew quietly." She paused, eyes locking on Nia. "And that includes no slurping."

A few girls stifled laughter. Nia blushed and looked down.

"Tonight is about elegance," Nevi declared. "Let them want to know your name… and your flavor."

She reached for one of the twin doors. Rae opened the other. Together, they stood just beyond the threshold, holding the doors open.

"Make us proud," Nevi added, just above a whisper.

The girls filed through the twin doors, guided by subtle touches, drifting into the glow beyond.

When it was Alexis's turn, Rae's hand found her shoulder, staying there just long enough to make Alexis feel uncomfortable.

And then they were through.

The backyard had been transformed again.

Where rows of chairs once were, now were round tables draped in ivory linen, spaced evenly across the yard. The men were already seated, one per table, bathed in the amber glow of hanging lights strung between the limbs of the old oak.

Nevi guided the girls to their seats one at a time. Alexis was the last to be seated.

Nevi's palm found the center of her back, gentle but directing. "Alexis, this fine young man here is Mason."

Alexis lifted her eyes and nearly forgot herself.

He rose slowly. That smile of his didn't hustle for attention. Nor did it boast.

Broad shoulders filled the cream suit striped in lavender, the tailoring fitting him perfectly.

His curls brushed his shoulders in thick, dark waves. Kept, but untamed.

Alexis tightened her grip on the plates and forced a polite smile.

Focus, Alexis. Focus.

Before she could speak, Mason gently took the plates from her hands.

"I've got it," he murmured.

Then, like it was nothing, he circled the table and set the plates down. He pulled her chair back with one hand and motioned her into it with the other, smooth as silk.

"Nice to meet you, Alexis," he said.

She offered her hand. Instead of shaking it, he took it in his hand, lowered his head, and brushed her knuckles with a kiss.

Her brows rose, but she kept her cool. "Nice to meet you, too, Mason."

"Well, I'll leave you two to it," Nevi murmured, already drifting away.

Just as she'd rehearsed yesterday, Alexis unfolded the white napkin and laid it across her lap.

Mason sat down across from her, straightening his jacket with one tug.

"You comfortable?"

"I am. Thanks for asking."

Their eyes met across the table. A flicker. A pull. Then Alexis looked down, smiling to herself.

Mason chuckled. "What was that?"

"What?"

"That little look just now."

She smirked. "I didn't give you a look." Leaning forward a little, she asked, "You're imagining things already?"

"You're gorgeous, you know that?"

Alexis smirked. "You're not so bad yourself."

"I'm serious. Your cheekbones… That jawline… You've got the type of features that deserve to be preserved on canvas and appreciated."

She hesitated, caught off guard by the directness. "Do you make a habit of analyzing people like this?" she questioned, creating space between them with a slight backward lean that contradicted the curiosity in her eyes. "Or is it just me?"

"Just you." He said it without a pause.

Her lips betrayed her, curving upward despite herself, and her body leaned into his orbit before her mind could pull back the reins.

He had a gravity to him, and she wasn't fighting the pull nearly as hard as she should have been.

Mason didn't notice.

"What can I say? I've got an eye for beautiful things."

A smirk tugged at his mouth, and the pull tightened.

She parted her lips, ready to lean in or pull away, she didn't even know, and then Rae appeared with the basket of garlic bread, cutting the moment clean.

"My apologies." Rae set the basket down. "I hope you

haven't started your meal yet."

"Thank you," Mason stated just a microsecond faster than Alexis. She was a bit thrown off.

Rae gave a polite nod and floated off.

Then Della was right behind them, a chilled bottle in one hand, white linen draped perfectly over her wrist. She stepped to Mason first, lifted his champagne flute from the table, tilted it, and poured the pale gold liquid in a perfect stream.

"Thank you," Mason said with a courteous smile.

Della clapped once. Then, without looking at Alexis, she shifted to her side.

She didn't pick up her glass. Instead, she leaned in from behind, reaching forward to pour. Her arm crossed just over Alexis's shoulder, close enough to whisper.

As the champagne streamed into the glass, Della dipped her head slightly. Just enough to speak into Alexis's ear.

"You wear your nerves like perfume," she murmured. "It sticks to you."

The whisper outlasted the pour. Then Della straightened and moved on.

Am I that readable?

"You gonna tell me what's under this dome, or am I supposed to guess?"

She blinked, caught off guard by how quickly the mood shifted.

"Oh. Right." She smiled, then gestured toward his plate. "Go ahead. You first."

Mason lifted the dome with a casual flourish, one hand practiced. The grin slipped from his face the second he saw what was underneath.

He blinked. Lips pressed.

"What? You don't like spaghetti?"

"No, no," he said quickly. "Just… wasn't expecting it."

Her brow lifted. "What were you expecting?"

Mason glanced at her, then back at the plate, hesitation written across his jaw. Finally, he muttered, "I mean, I just… don't usually eat red sauce from women I'm not kin to."

Alexis leaned in. "What? Why? Ohhh…" She shook her

head, the realization washing over her.

He shifted, almost sheepish. “It’s just… some things, us men gotta be cautious about.”

Her tone dropped flat. “I don’t even know you, Mason. Why would I put roots on you?”

That broke his mask, and he laughed, a genuine smile flashing. “It’s nothing personal. It’s just… my cousin got done like that once. Went crazy behind his baby’s mama. Still ain’t right to this day.”

“Well, you don’t have to worry about me doing anything disgusting like that. Trust me, just try it and tell me if it’s decent.”

He studied her face, then the plate, weighing odds. Finally, he twirled a forkful, lifted it slowly, and took a bite.

Then his eyes met hers.

“Mmm,” he grunted, already going back for another bite. “Simple, but it’s good. Really good. Got a little kick to it, too.”

“Here.” She grabbed a piece of garlic toast from the basket and handed it to him. “Try the garlic bread. Rae baked the loaf, but I’m the one who added the razzle dazzle.”

With a sauced-coated grin, he reached for the bread and took a big bite. He let out a soft groan before continuing his meal. “I haven’t had anything this good since I moved to New York,” he added, smiling now. “You sure you don’t do roots?”

“Boy, eat your damn food!” She rolled her eyes. Alexis took the lid off her own plate and began to dig in.

After a brief moment, the couple enjoyed their meal. Alexis seized the opportunity to dig a little. “You said you moved to New York?”

“Yeah. Been there a few years now,” he replied between bites.

“So what, you came back just for Mardi Gras?”

“Something like that. What about you? Are you from here?”

“Yep, born and raised. And the only place I’d rather be.”

“I used to say the same thing, before I really ventured out. Realized New Orleans isn’t all it’s cracked up to be.”

"Well, why'd you even come back?"

"Why not?"

"Touché." She lifted her glass for an air-toast, then let it hover near her lips.

Her eyes drifted across the backyard.

She saw Imani and her suitor first. They were deep in conversation, soft laughs and low murmurs passing between them, their plates untouched. He didn't take so much as one glance at the food. From where Alexis sat, it didn't look like that was what he'd come hungry for. To her, it seemed like he was hungry for Imani, and she was looking at him like she might let him starve just to see how long he could last.

Then she spotted Markeysha just sitting there, straight-faced, checking her guy out as he ate.

When her eyes landed on Olivia, she became a little uneasy. The girl was trying to eat, but her suitor kept reaching over to touch her. First her wrist. Then her hand. Each interruption seemed gentle enough to pass for affection if not for the way she stiffened every time, and he smiled the whole time. A slow prickle rose at the back of Alexis's neck.

Then it hit her. The men at the tables now… none of them were familiar.

She scanned the gathering again, slower this time. The judge. The pastor. The deputy chief. All of them gone.

Were all of them eliminated?

Even the guy who'd winked at her was nowhere in sight.

Back at her own table, Alexis turned to find Mason had been eyeing her.

"You good?" She tipped her head, eyes pulling together.

He ignored her sass. "The way that headwrap frames your face… I'd love to paint you sometime."

"Tignon, not headwrap," Alexis corrected automatically, her tone lightly mocking.

"Huh?" Mason looked at her, puzzled.

She let out a soft laugh, not realizing she'd said it aloud. "One of the Madames is always fussing at us about it. That's exactly how she says it, too." She slipped into a haughty imitation. "It's a *tignon*, not a headwrap."

They shared a brief laugh, then Alexis leaned back

slightly, letting her eyes drift from his face to the glowing candle centerpiece between them.

"So, you're an artist then?"

"Mhm. I specialize in oil. Mostly portraits. Color, form, light. It's all in the details."

"You've definitely got an eye for detail." She let those words hang, just long enough to land. "You sell your work, too?"

"Yeah. Commissions, gallery placements, and exhibits. That's the bread and butter."

He took a sip of champagne, then added, "And now and then, events like this open doors too. For networking and whatnot."

Alexis raised an eyebrow. "So this isn't your first one?"

Mason smiled. "First time with the Krewe of Lazuliè, yeah. But I've been to a few like this before."

"So how does it work? You pay to show up, or you bid on somebody?"

"Depends on the event."

"What about this one?"

He chuckled. "A bit of both. There are… guidelines."

"And what's in it for you?"

Mason didn't answer right away. He swirled his champagne like he was waiting for the bubbles to spell something out.

"Legacy," he spoke finally. "Access. Favor with the right people…."

Alexis observed him carefully. "So, it's about power."

"Isn't everything?"

She didn't answer. Didn't need to. That was the most honest thing he'd said all night.

She let a beat pass before leaning in. "You think you picked the right girl?"

Mason smiled again, shaking off whatever tension was building. "You tell me."

Alexis's head drifted a little to one side. "Alright then, tell me more about how this whole thing actually works. What, a bunch of y'all pick who you want, and if more than one of you picks the same girl, you bid on her? Loser walks?"

"That's how you think it went?" He laughed, raising his glass.

"I don't know." She let out a short laugh of her own. "That's why I'm asking."

"I don't think we're allowed to say." He took a long swig of his drink.

Her eyes dropped from his.

Not allowed? Who told them that? Why can't they talk about it?

She looked back up at Mason. He was watching her again.

"What?" Her face involuntarily twisted up.

"You got that faraway look."

"Oh!" Her face loosened. "I'm just… taking it all in."

"Are you always this analytical?"

"Only when it matters."

That made him pause, just a second too long. She filed it away.

He looked down at his glass. "You ever wonder if we're overthinking it all? Maybe this is just… nice."

Alexis gave a slight nod, but her eyes drifted again. Too many pieces were piling up, and none of them seemed to fit right anymore.

All this, just to find the next Crowned Heart…

Alexis knew what the prize was, but now she was wondering what they were giving up in exchange.

Mason leaned in again, his voice a little more personal. "My parrain met his wife at one of these. Told me she walked in, and he walked out with her on his arm. They've been together for about thirty years now."

Alexis raised a brow. "That sounds… romantic. And slightly terrifying."

He laughed. "Nah, back then it was different. Men knew what they wanted. Took pride in taking care of a woman. Not just showing up halfway and calling it love."

"I'm curious. Elaborate on that for me."

Mason grinned. "A woman should be taken care of. She holds down the heart, the home, the spirit. So, I handle the rest. That's just how I was raised."

She cocked her head. "Oh, so you're one of *those*."

Mason raised an eyebrow, smiling. "One of what?"

"You know the type…" She leaned back in her chair, letting the words roll slowly. "'I pay the bills, and when I get home, have my sandwich ready, house clean, and rub my feet'."

He let out a quick laugh, caught off guard. "Damn. That's how you see me?"

"Isn't that what you just said? If the shoe fits…"

He leaned in, slow and sure, reaching across the table. He reached, tipping her chin with two fingers. A featherlight touch, but it commanded her attention.

He licked his lips, eyes locked on hers. "I'm an old-school romantic," he shrugged. "I just want something real."

Alexis let him linger there. Then, slowly, she leaned back, slipping just out of his reach.

The longer he spoke, the more his beauty faded. His charm had soured, and something slow crawled beneath her skin.

His smile looked stretched now, carved too deeply. What had once held her slipped into something that unsettled her to the bone.

"I've got your angle now. Slide in real charming, talk old-school love, try to wife a girl in under twenty minutes." Her tone cooled a few degrees, but she didn't let up. "That's your plan?"

"If I said yes, would that be a bad thing?"

She met his gaze, feeling like she'd unknowingly entered a staring contest.

"Nah, I'm playing." I'm playing!" he laughed.

"You sure? Or just trying to save face?"

"Look at you," he chuckled. "Think you've got me all figured out." That sly smirk crept back across his face. "But for real though?" His laughter dimmed. "I just came for two things: make the right pick… and leave with the crown."

Alexis was still staring at him, searching his eyes for the truth. Mason had a good poker face. She wasn't sure if he was telling the truth now… or earlier.

CHAPTER 10

"Alexis…. Alexis, wake up."

A gentle shake to her shoulder. Then another, slightly rougher.

"Girl, come on!" Raven frowned. "Please, wake up!"

Alexis stirred with a groan, struggling to force her eyelids open.

Alexis tried to focus, but everything was blurry.

She rolled on her side and tried to push herself up. Her limbs felt foreign, unresponsive.

"What's wrong?" Alexis croaked once she was upright.

Raven pulled back just enough to wave her hands in that nervous, flustered way she seemed to do when she didn't know what to do. The strap of her silk nightgown slid off one shoulder.

"We're supposed to be packing our stuff right now. We've got to go, remember?" She exhaled hard, half-exasperated, half-concerned. "And you slept through the alarm and everything. I even let you sleep an extra thirty minutes. Looked like you needed it."

Raven hesitated, eyeing her closely. "Honestly? I almost got worried. You wasn't even moving for real. I kept checking, making sure you were still breathing."

Alexis pressed a hand to her forehead, fingers splayed like she could hold her thoughts in place.

What the hell happened last night?

She tried to think, piecing together how she'd ended up feeling like she'd been hit by a truck, but her memory stopped cold at dinner with Mason. Her mouth was dry.

"Wait." She blinked hard. "I don't even remember coming to bed."

Raven frowned. "Shit. Come to think of it… me either."

She turned toward Jade's bed. "You remember how we got in our room? Girl, when did we even come inside?"

Jade rubbed her forehead. "Shit, I don't know. Last thing I remember was that little wine tasting the Madames put together after dinner, and then…" She trailed off, blinked, then grinned slowly. "Guess we got a little too turnt up."

Raven hopped over to Jade's bed, laughing as she slapped her palm for a high five. "You already know!"

They laughed, but Alexis didn't join.

Something wasn't right.

Tap. Tap. Tap.

There was a gentle knock at the door.

The person on the other side didn't even wait for permission to enter. The knob turned fast, the door cracked open, and her face appeared in the gap, eyes wide and searching.

"I'm sorry, y'all." Destiny's voice came out thin and trembling. "Have y'all seen Olivia, Nia, and Imani?"

"Have you checked in their rooms?" Alexis sat up straighter, trying her hardest to shake off the dizzy spell.

"Yeah, and they're not in there," Destiny told her. "Their rooms are empty."

"What?" That jolted Alexis into motion.

On wobbly legs, she followed Destiny down the hall to Imani's room first.

Imani's bed was perfectly made. Her purse was gone. Her slippers too.

Alexis crossed the room and dropped to one knee beside the bed. She lifted the bed skirt and checked beneath it from one side to the other to find nothing but polished wood and dust.

She stood up and opened the nightstand drawer.

Empty.

She checked the dresser next, working through it fast. She pulled drawer after drawer. Just a few mothballs and rusty coins.

Then she crossed to the closet and slid the door back.

A few empty hangers. Bare floor.

Next, they rushed over to Olivia and Nia's room.

Same thing.

Beds made. Closets cleared. No luggage in sight.

"This doesn't make any sense," Alexis muttered after she finished combing through the room.

The rest of the girls met her in the hall. All of them asking the same thing.

"Where's Olivia?"

"Nobody seen Nia?"

"Wait… Imani gone, too?"

The echoing voices intensified the tension.

Then Rae appeared at the end of the corridor, looking ghostly in a white sleeveless dress that fell loosely to the middle of her calves.

"What's all the commotion about?"

"Imani, Nia, and Olivia are gone. Nobody's seen them. Their stuff is gone, too," Destiny informed her.

Rae's glare bounced from girl to girl.

Before she could answer, Nevi's voice floated from behind her.

"Ladies!"

All heads turned.

Nevi emerged in white as well, taking her place beside Rae. Her dress was long, with lace puffed sleeves that gathered at the wrists. The white tignon she adorned matched her dress perfectly.

"There's no need to panic. Last night, they decided to leave."

Murmurs rippled.

"Yes," she bobbed her head. "After such a successful evening with their suitors, they chose to leave early. Happens every time. Some girls just don't have the discipline it takes to be part of the Krewe. And some of those men… well. They can be very persuasive."

They left?

A sudden throb lanced through Alexis's chest.

"Mmm." She pressed her lips together, fists curling tight at her sides.

Nevi clapped her hands, making sure she had every girl's attention. "Now, Blue Hearts, let's focus on what's ahead." She let that hang for a little. "These past few days have been nothing short of remarkable. I'd say Preparation served its purpose well. And I know many of you have long drives, so we won't keep you too long." She gestured gently. "Check your closets. Dresses have been provided for tomorrow's ball. Perfectly tailored, if I do say so myself. We've also left a little something to help you prepare. It should be enough to cover everything else you'll need."

Then Rae added, "We'll be holding a brief service out back. You're all welcome to join, of course… but no pressure."

Alexis watched Nevi and Rae walk down the hall and through the grand room. A second later, the sliding door closed behind them.

Then Alexis and Jade retreated to their room, the door slamming shut behind them.

"I mean," Jade started, rubbing her temples, "Nia and Imani, maybe. They were in it for the money. But Olivia?"

"Right," Alexis agreed. "She loved all this stuff. And why would she leave before the ball?"

Jade shrugged. "Well… Now that I think about it, it does make sense. She wanted her little fairytale ending. Found her Prince Charming and dipped."

Raven burst in, rolling her eyes, hands thrown up.

"I need someone to explain this mess to me! Why my dude ain't offer to have me leave with him? I'm the main one down for whatever. Why ain't I get chose?"

"Maybe he saw through your act and just knew you were about to be too much," Jade remarked, half serious.

"That's cold," Raven shot back, snatching a pillow off her bed and hurling it at Jade with mock offense. "Please! Ain't like you gave Disney Princess either. I saw you with your dude, chewing all loud and talking with your mouth full!"

Alexis wasn't paying either of them any mind. She

plopped down on her bed, eyes fixed on nothing as her thoughts circled the same questions. It didn't make sense, none of it.

Plunk.

She jolted, snapping her head up. Jade had tossed a garment bag across the mattress. "Here y'all go." She dropped her own on her bed before sitting beside it.

Along the black bag was a strip of white tape with dainty script written on it.

Alexis.

Slowly, Alexis reached for the garment bag, fingers fumbling slightly as she unzipped it. The gown inside was champagne and royal blue, with soft gold embroidery dancing along the hem and neckline like delicate vines.

Then she noticed it, taped to the inside lining of the garment bag. Almost hidden.

It was an envelope, a thick one.

She peeled it free but didn't open it. Not yet.

Instead, she secured it in the front compartment of her suitcase.

Across the room, Raven zipped her own suitcase closed with a dramatic sigh.

"Okay, I've got everything packed. I hope."

She scooped up her garment bag and draped it over her arm, ready to carry it out with the rest of her things.

Jade was still half-dressed, slow-moving, tossing things into her tote with no sense of urgency.

Alexis stood, gathered her things, and laid her garment bag gently across her suitcase.

She didn't speak, just watched the girls finish up around her.

Once everyone was packed, they stepped into the hallway, where the shuffle of feet and the rumble of rolling luggage echoed softly.

Near the front double doors, a small basket perched on a short pedestal stand, the girls' phones scattered inside, waiting to be claimed.

"I barely recognized mine," Jade muttered, sifting through the pile before pulling hers out.

Alexis fished hers out next.

"I think I'm going to stay for the Madames' service," Alexis announced, turning to Jade.

"Okay, shit. Well, I'll stay for it too, then."

"It's Sunday, fool!" Raven slapped Jade's shoulder.

"Ough!" Jade yelped. "Bitch you hit me hard."

Raven smacked her arm again. "Stop cussing!"

"Hit me again and watch what I do." Jade stepped back, rubbing her shoulder. "You coming with us to this service or not?"

"Yeah, I guess I'll check it out with y'all," Raven said as she stepped up to retrieve her phone from the basket.

Raven and Jade carried on, chatting and laughing like it had all been just another long weekend. At least, that's how it seemed to Alexis.

She spotted Natalia making her way to the front door.

Jade turned. "Where you going in such a hurry, girl? You don't wanna stay for the Madames' little service? Me, Alexis and Raven are going."

Natalia shook her head, phone in one hand, keys in the other. "Oh, no! I go to Mass with *my family*. Every Sunday. That's our tradition, and the Madames are not about to make me break it." She gave a quick little wave. "Y'all be good."

And then she was gone.

"Well," Markeysha muttered, coming up to give the girls quick hugs one by one, "y'all enjoy yourselves. I'm getting the hell up out of here!"

Raven took a step back. "Wow! You just gon' leave us hanging like this?"

"Please." Markeysha rolled her eyes. "I'll see y'all tomorrow! Call me when y'all make it home."

Alexis watched her head out the door behind Natalia. Out of the corner of her eye, she caught Destiny making her way to the huddle.

"You coming with us to the service?" Alexis asked as Destiny approached the group.

"The only Sunday service I'm about to have is the one at my house. But I love that for y'all, though." She quickly hugged Raven and Jade.

When she made it to Alexis, she pulled her to the side and threw her arms around her in a firm, two-second grip, and pushed back just enough to meet her eyes.

"When you get home," Destiny whispered, "cleanse this house off you." Her voice was calm but serious. "The energy here is darker than I thought."

Then she pulled back and turned before Alexis could respond.

"Bye y'all. See y'all tomorrow!"

Alexis watched Destiny as she made her exit, unsure if she meant emotional darkness or something else.

Why didn't she say the same thing to the others?

Could she feel something on me?

Then, a distant chime pulled her from the thought.

Bong. Bong. Bong. Bong. Bong.

The sound rolled through the silence.

Sunday bells.

She recalled the old cathedral mid-block, just across the street.

Its bell tower rose above the neighboring rooftops, open-arched and unmistakable.

Alexis stood still a moment, the bells moving through the hall as the others wandered ahead. Then she turned to catch up with Jade and Raven at the mouth of the grand room.

"Watch we 'bout to be back there for hours," Raven muttered.

"Oh, uh-uh. Not me! I'll be the first one asking to be excused if they try to drag it," Jade said with a snicker.

"Shoot, I know that's right."

Alexis let out a quick chuckle, but her mind went back to last night.

She tried to force her way through the fog, but it was no use.

Something'll probably come to me once I make it outside.

As they crossed the grand room, Alexis rolled her suitcase beside the settee. Raven parked hers next to Alexis's and laid her garment bag across the arm of the settee. Jade dropped her tote beside the others and rested her garment bag on top of Raven's.

Alexis slid open the doors and cut through the dining room and kitchen, not bothering to wait for Jade and Raven.

At the back door, she reached for the handle and yanked it back.

"Damn it," she hissed, shaking off the sting.

"Mmm hmm. Static shock gotcha, huh?" Jade brushed past her to open the door.

"That's what you get for speeding off, trying to leave us behind," Raven said, following her out.

"Y'all play too much," Alexis muttered, stepping outside behind them.

Taken aback, she scanned the yard. All the tables and chairs had been removed. Even the string lights that were hanging from the trees were gone. It was like last night didn't even happen.

"Now, where's this service at?" Raven asked.

"There go Rae," Jade said, pointing toward the garden.

Rae stood with her back half-turned to them. One white-gloved hand held a small pair of shears. The other gathered clipped stems into a wicker basket looped over her arm.

"Excuse me, Madame Rae," Alexis called, walking toward her.

Rae turned just enough to look at her. Before Alexis could say anything else, she lifted her hand and pointed around the side of the house.

"Over there."

Then she turned back to the garden.

Alexis looked to Jade and Raven. "Come on."

They crossed the yard and rounded the side of the house.

A row of six chairs faced the veranda.

On the veranda, Nevi stood beside a round table draped in white. Two white taper candles burned in glass holders, one on each side of an empty silver dish with ruffled edges.

Alexis's gaze swept the veranda, then the rest of the yard.

"Go on and have a seat," Nevi said. "I'm glad you decided to join us."

Alexis took the first chair on the far right. Jade sat beside her. Raven dropped into the chair next to Jade.

Raven leaned toward Jade without taking her eyes off Nevi. "Dang. I'm feeling like maybe we should've changed."

"Don't the Bible say, 'Come as you are'? And if you had been paying attention, you would have *been* noticed the Madames were dressed in their Sunday's best," Jade murmured. "I know you peeped it, huh, Alexis."

Alexis shrugged.

"Yeah, but Alexis notices everything," Raven shot back.

"Hush now, girls, as we prepare for prayer," Nevi said.

"Will Della be joining us?" Alexis asked. She'd already searched the yard twice for her.

"Della is in the middle of making preparations. We'll be going on without her."

Nevi did not leave room for another question.

"A prayer more powerful when it is carried by more than one voice. So aren't we fortunate to have you three standing in. Some moments are better not left unattended."

Alexis listened.

Nevi went on. "There are times when something is interrupted before it finds its proper place. Times when what was meant to finish one way must be handled another. That is when order matters most."

Rae came around the corner then, the basket in the crook of her arm. She moved to Raven first. From the basket, she lifted a small bundle of flowers tied with thick twine and placed it in Raven's hand. Then Jade. Then Alexis.

Alexis looked down at the arrangement in her palm. A gardenia sat in the center with a smaller lily tucked beside it. A few sprigs of rosemary completed the tiny bouquet.

Rae stopped at the end of the row beside Alexis. She placed her hand in the middle of her chest.

Nevi looked at the flowers in the girls' hands before lifting her eyes again.

"What is gathered must be handled with care and what is disrupted must still be received."

"Some endings arrive before the thing itself has been fully understood. But grace does not require full understanding.

Only willing witness."

Raven and Jade held their bouquets in their laps, eyes fixed on Nevi.

Alexis looked past her to the table, then the candles, then the side of the house. The back gate sat closed beyond the edge of the yard.

"Repeat after me." Nevi reached toward the folded linen on the table, then let her hand settle. "What was disrupted—"

"What was disrupted," Jade, Raven, Alexis and Rae echoed.

If Rae hadn't been standing right beside her, Alexis would have only mouthed the words.

"Let it be received."

"Let it be received," Rae and the girls repeated Nevi's words.

"What did not finish—"

"What did not finish—"

"Let it find its place."

"Let it find its place."

Nevi held each of their gazes before giving the last line. "May nothing placed in willing hands be wasted."

"May nothing placed in willing hands be wasted," the rest said in unison.

"Now come up and place your flowers on the plate," Nevi ordered.

Alexis rose first. She crossed the short patch of grass, stopped at the veranda step, then climbed it. Nevi stood aside just enough to make room. Alexis leaned forward and laid her bouquet in the silver dish. Then she stood there, waiting for what was next to come.

Jade went next, quicker, one hand skimming her skirt as she mounted the step. She sat her bouquet down and stood next to Alexis.

Nevi lowered her chin As Raven placed her flowers atop the rest.

"Thank you for lending us your voices." Nevi rested one hand on the edge of the table.

"That is all. We appreciate your presence. We'll see each

of you tomorrow."

"See y'all tomorrow, Madames," Raven said as they quickly turned back toward the house.

Once they were inside the grand room, she looked between Alexis and Jade. "Okay, what kind of service was that?"

"Bitch, your guess is as good as mine," Jade scrunched her face up.

"You not gon' learn till I knock that shoulder off, huh?" Raven raised her hand like she was about to slap the living daylights out of Jade. "You better ask for forgiveness."

Jade pressed her palms together under her chin. "My bad, Lord."

"Need to stop playing 'fore you get struck down!"

Raven grabbed her suitcase and hooked her garment bag over her shoulder. "Matter-fact, gimme my hugs so I can get the fu— heck up out of here. I'm not trying to be nowhere near Jade while she's over here mocking God."

Jade laughed and stepped into her arms first. "I'm mocking *you*, idiot! Wanna act holier than thou on Sundays and a demon any other day, like God can only see you on one day."

"It's a respect thing, fool… something you obviously don't have." Raven moved her attention to Alexis. "Come here, girl, so I can go."

Alexis went in for the hug.

"See y'all tomorrow," Raven said, pulling back. Then she headed for the door.

Jade raised two fingers. "Be safe."

Alexis turned to her suitcase and saw the front compartment hanging slightly open. She bent, tucked the envelope deeper inside, and zipped it shut. By the time she straightened, Raven was already out on the porch.

Jade grabbed her tote and fell in beside her.

Alexis wrapped her hand around the suitcase handle and followed her to the front door.

Alexis stepped onto the wide front porch, suitcase in one hand and the sun hitting hard enough to make her squint.

Together, Alexis and Jade followed the brick path toward the gate.

Alexis took in the air as she walked. It smelled like wet concrete, car exhaust… and something burnt.

She paused a few feet from the gate. Her nose wrinkled as the stench caught her attention. She turned left, settling on one of the chimneys rising stark against the slate roof.

From it, faint threads of smoke drifted upward.

She sniffed again.

The smoke carried something meaty and bitter. It leaped straight into her nostrils, stinging until her eyes watered.

"That's probably part of their service." Jade nudged her, turning her nose up. "I think it's a Catholic thing. Don't they burn stuff during their ceremonies? Probably up in there burning them flowers and some more shi—stuff."

Alexis glanced at her, then back at the chimney. "Right." She shifted her bag and looked over at Jade again. "You need a ride?"

"Nah, I'm good," Jade stated, checking her phone. "My Uber's like a minute away."

"Okay, well, give me one more hug, and call me once you make it home." Alexis opened her arms.

Jade stepped in without hesitation. "You do the same."

They held on, long enough for Jade's nervous energy to transfer.

Then they let go.

Alexis gave her one last wave before heading to her car, her suitcase bumping over the brick path behind her.

A few steps from the curb, she stopped.

Pressure surged behind her eyes, a slow heat crawling up her spine until it settled at the base of her skull. Her skin flushed, damp and clammy.

She glanced back.

The smoke coiled in the sky, a gavotte of embers traced it upward.

She turned away and quickened her pace.

She needed to get to Tahir. Fast.

CHAPTER 11

Tahir's front door swung open before she could knock. "I figured that was you. Heard a car pull in the driveway." He was leaning against the frame with a mug in hand, the smell of chicory drifting out.

Alexis stepped in.

"I wasn't sure you'd want to meet here," he admitted as he walked toward the kitchen.

"I didn't want to meet anywhere else." She shrugged off her jacket as she followed, draping it over the back of a barstool before settling at the island.

From behind her, the low hum of the coffeemaker filled the quiet. Tahir looked over from the counter nook, the tiny space he'd turned into his caffeine corner. "You look like you've been through hell and back."

"Shit, feels like it." Alexis let out a small laugh that didn't go anywhere. She kept her elbows on the island, palms bracing her temples. "My head's been pounding since this morning."

"Could be exhaustion." He turned to lean against the counter. "Or maybe you got caught up in your college-girl act." A quick chuckle slipped out. "What kind of night did they talk you into?"

"No, nothing like that." She dropped her hands, eyes half-lidded. "Well… one of the girls, Jade, said there was a wine tasting. The crazy thing is…" She paused, shaking her head. "I don't even remember that."

"Well, that makes sense. Pounding headache, memory loss. Hangover."

"Tahir, I know what a hangover feels like. This ain't it."

She watched him weigh that, the way he does when he's about to offer a fix. "Might be worth letting Tox run a screen. Just to make sure."

"Already did. I stopped by Hugo first. Quick screen came back clean, but he said that doesn't mean much if it was off-panel or fast-clearing. He sent the rest out."

"Good." He walked around the island, pink mug in hand. "Till then, drink."

She lazily reached for it. The steam hit her first, and she wrapped both hands around the cup. She took a sip, tasting cinnamon, cream, and a hint of nutmeg, and felt her shoulders begin to ease.

"You still remember," she murmured.

"I don't forget important things."

Her mouth threatened a smile. She shut it down.

Alexis searched for words and found none. Then something familiar on the couch pulled her in.

"I've been looking for that blanket!"

He glanced over, the corner of his mouth lifting. "It's been here the whole time."

She stood and crossed to the couch. Careful not to spill her coffee, she eased down onto the cushions and, with her free hand, pulled the blanket into her lap, grounding herself in the worn softness of the fabric.

"I forgot how quiet it gets in here. Used to hate that."

"Back then was loud in a lot of ways."

She laughed dryly. "Yeah. Some of that noise was mine."

He let it sit. When he spoke again, his tone was careful. "I just want to know why—"

Simultaneously, she blurted out, "I don't want to mess this up." She winced. "Sorry. What were you going to say?"

"Ladies first."

She exhaled. "I keep thinking about how close it all came to going left. The girls. This case. Some of them are still unaccounted for. Olivia, Brielle, Nia, Imani… Kayla never even showed up."

"I called Kayla's school. Tried Brielle too. Nothing."

"Here. Let me send you what I've got for the others." She rested her mug on the coffee table before her.

They both bent to their phones, filling the room with the soft tap of screens. When Alexis finally set hers beside her mug, she pressed her palms to her forehead, elbows digging into her knees. She sat like that a moment too long.

Tahir leaned in. "What is it?"

She shook her head first, stalling. Then, softer: "I didn't want to tell you this but…"

"Go on," he tried to keep her talking.

Her hands dropped from her face, fingers knotting together. "I feel… lost. Like, let's be real for a second. I should be further along in this damn case, but it's just… every time I think I've found a viable lead, another girl goes missing or… some weird shit happens. I mean, half of it I don't even know how to put into words. Some of the stuff I saw in that house… I think I may be losing it."

She glanced at him. His posture changed, and heat rose in her throat. "Losing it might be too strong a choice of words." She cleared it up before he could. "I'm not crazy, Tahir. It's just… it's…"

He set his mug down with a soft click. "What *it* is is PTSD." When she tried to pull back, his hand stayed on hers. His voice remained even, his face composed. "I know you're strong, but I'm here. You don't have to carry it all alone."

"Yeah," was all she had for him.

He exhaled, his grip easing.

"We're not doing this again. Once this case wraps, you're getting more time and therapy. Mandatory. I'll make sure of it."

She didn't argue. The word therapy slid through her head and dissolved.

"So, let me just say this." His voice lowered. "I get you want to make things right… You see a problem, and immediately you jump to solve it." He snapped his fingers for emphasis.

"That's one of the things I love most about you… But if you keep running headfirst into burning buildings, you will not make it back out. You'll end up losing everything… Even the parts of you that were never yours to give."

She nodded, signaling she understood him, but her attention was truly elsewhere.

He shifted a few inches closer. She felt the couch dip and the warmth of him at her side. "So, you ready to tell me how your weekend retreat from hell went?"

She closed her eyes and gathered herself. Then she opened them. "Alright… Let's go."

"Walk me through it. From the top."

She pulled the throw tighter. "Day one, the girls traded rumors."

"About?"

"Nothing we ain't already heard."

She paused for Tahir to respond. He gestured for her to continue.

"They took our phones. Told us it was about being present at the house."

"Control tactic."

"Mmm." She leaned forward. "Next day, it got even weirder. They had us doing these strange exercises… Said it was to heal us or some bullshit like that."

He stayed quiet. She heard the coffeemaker click off behind them.

"I found a notepad in their photo room. The first page listed the seven krewes of the Voodoo Parade."

"You think that's worth something?"

"Not sure yet," she shrugged. "There was also a list of names. Some had tick marks by them, others were slashed through."

"Sounds like a ledger."

"More like a recruitment log… I think."

"Where is it?"

"Didn't take it. Didn't want to risk anyone catching me with it."

"Damn." She watched him drag a palm over his jaw.

She drew a breath. "Last night was this thing they called

the Plaçage Ceremony. The krewe heads had us tucked away in the kitchen cooking, but I was able to sneak a peek at what was going on before they let us outside."

"What did you see?"

"Several men. Eighteen, by my count. They were seated in rows. I saw Rae and Della pass out envelopes. Nevi stood in front, saying stuff… I couldn't make it out. Then the men raised cards, Rae and Della marked notes, and one of the guys would leave. They ran that sequence a few times. Until there were nine men left."

"What in the hell…"

"I think they were bidding… On us."

"Yeah." His fingers went still on the arm of the couch. "So, who got you?"

"Some dude named Mason. One of them sophisticated smooth-talking types. Told me his godfather attended one of those ceremonies back in the day."

"Sounds like this thing's been going on for generations…"

"I'll try to get more from him on that. I'll see him again at the ball."

His expression tightened, more calculation than concern. "Anything off about him?"

She hesitated. "As it stands right now… I don't think so. Just some idiot hoping to get lucky."

"And the others?"

"The guys?"

"Yeah."

"Didn't get a chance to ask the girls about them."

"You texted me Deputy Chief Gibbons was there."

"He was. I spotted him while snooping, but by the time we were placed, he was gone."

"Mmm."

"The pastor from that Gert Town megachurch showed. And Judge Beckerman. Both of them were gone before we were settled, too. They must've been among those who were… I guess… outbid. I mean, I'm not exactly sure of how it all works."

"I'll make some calls on all three. See what shakes

loose."

Alexis dipped her chin and kept going. "This morning is when I found out Imani, Olivia, and Nia were gone. Nevi said they left with their suitors, claiming it was a normal thing for girls to sometimes do."

"The fuck do *they* know about 'normal'?"

"Right. The heads of that organization know way more than they let on."

His fingers tapped the table once, then again, small and tight. "There's still a lot we don't know. But now we've got a pattern. That's something."

"There's a lot buried in there."

"Maybe. But unless you give me more, Cap's gonna say you spent four days with them and have nothing solid to show for it." He paused. "She brought Stewart in. Told her to start digging."

That news made Alexis's eyes roll to the back of her head. "I knew this was going to happen when she showed up on the scene of that thirty-C."

"Cap thinks you're too bogged down. You're too close."

"I *am* too close. That's the point. Those girls trust me… I think the Madames do too. Tiffany just wants to show me up." Alexis sucked her teeth. "That girl has never liked me. Not since we—" She stopped herself. Inhaled deeply, then exhaled slowly. "She doesn't like losing. Especially not to me."

He didn't press. The line of his mouth hinted he knew precisely what she was getting at.

"She's planning a press conference. Cap signed off on it already."

"She does that, and everything really will go to shit. We don't even know if the other girls are dead yet. What if they're being held somewhere? It'll just tip off whoever's behind this and give them time to cover their tracks."

"I told Cap we should hold off a little longer. But they're moving forward."

She dragged her hand down. "Jesus. They don't even…" Her voice broke off. "Oh!" She pushed herself up from the couch, leaving the blanket folded on the cushion.

Crossing to the counter stool where her jacket still hung, she dug into the pocket and came back with a thick envelope. "And look at this." She dropped it onto the table beside her mug before sitting back down. "They gave each of us one."

She watched him open the envelope and pull out a stack of cash. He thumbed through it. "Five grand."

"Told us to use it to get our hair and makeup done."

"Them ladies some generous, huh?" He fanned the mix of twenty and hundred-dollar bills out.

Alexis eased back down beside him. "Generous my ass! I think it's hush money, and a way to make sure the girls stay in the Krewe."

He squared the stack and slid it back into the envelope. "Anything else you remember?"

Alexis leaned into the couch, but her body wouldn't settle. "Not really. Nothing useful."

"You sure? Take a moment to think. I know a lot went down." He held the envelope out to her.

She hesitated, her mind slipped back to that house.

The sudden buzz against her chest shook her back to Tahir's living room.

Startled, she threw her hand to her shirt pocket. It was her other phone. The one she used for work.

Alexis slid her hand over the fabric and drew it out. The screen glowed in her hand.

No calls.

No texts.

She looked at it a second longer. Then it clicked.

"Actually." Her thumb hovered a moment before she tapped the photos icon. "There's one thing."

A few swipes, and she handed it to him.

He squinted at the screen. "What is this?"

"A map. It was hanging in the photo room. Look at the way the pins are stuck in it. There's a pattern. Has to mean something, right?"

He pinched to zoom in. "Wait. Bottom left corner. You see that?"

She focused on the spot he'd pointed to. "What is it?" She took the phone back and brought it closer to her face.

There, tucked near the edge. The words curved like a signature, handwritten in dark ink.

Seven moons, seven boons, seven gates, seven tombs.

"Shit. I didn't even notice that when I took the picture."

"Hold up." His chair scraped softly as he stood. He crossed the room and came back with his laptop. He set it beside her, and the hinge gave a small click. Their knees touched.

He angled the screen so she could see.

"Here." He tapped twice. The fan kicked on. "I checked the saying earlier." He tipped his chin at the page. "It ties back to something called the Seven Gates of Guinee."

She felt him watching her, so she kept her focus on the screen.

"Go on." She flipped her hand toward the laptop.

"There are supposed to be seven gates, each tied to a gravesite. You have to leave boons, offerings, at each site to open them."

"Open them for what?"

"To get into Guinee… Or let something out of it."

"What is Guinee?"

"That's what they call the realm of the ancestors, I believe."

The skepticism clawed its way out before she could tamp it down. "Hold on now." She gave a short, humorless laugh and gestured toward the screen. "So, you're trying to tell me the people who are kidnapping these girls are placing offerings across seven different cemeteries so they can go to the ancestral realm?"

Tahir bobbed his head. "Or bring something through it."

"Come on, Tahir. You're not telling me you think people can actually… what… open doors to the afterlife, right?"

"Of course, I don't believe that, but that's not the point, Alexis. The people behind this do. And that's what matters. Motive. If we understand how they think, we can understand how they'll move." He turned back to the keyboard.

Alexis nodded slowly. Her finger brushed the rim of her

mug, feeling the heat.

"They've got the St. Louis Cemeteries marked as gates."

"Milan… Her body was found at the one on Basin Street."

Tahir pulled up a map of the city and held his hand out. "Let me see that photo again."

Alexis placed her phone in his palm. He checked the phone, then the laptop, then the phone again.

"Fucking knew it."

"What?"

He angled the laptop again, his focus snapping tight. "Every pin on this map lines up."

He zoomed in on a black pin in her photo, matched it on the map, and clicked.

"St. Louis Cemetery Number One," he said. "Here's Number Two, and Number Three out on Esplanade."

Alexis watched the cursor flicker across the screen, pausing, correcting itself, then locking into place.

"Charity Hospital Cemetery." His hand moved with careful, small motions.

"Gates of Mercy. Saint Patrick Number One."

He paused on the last point. "And that one's the Masonic Temple Cemetery."

"That's seven…"

The laptop fan rose a notch.

"Yeah. Seven cemeteries." His voice had a scrape to it now. "Seven gates."

She stood, pulse pounding. "We need units out there. At every one of those cemeteries. Now."

"I'll make the call." He slid the laptop onto the coffee table and handed Alexis her phone.

"I'll loop in Cap and Stewart, too. You just bought yourself more time!"

"Okay, Sarge," she chuckled.

He leaned back, fingers laced loosely. A smile threatened but didn't show.

"You did good, Lex. We're finally getting somewhere."

She waved her hand dismissively. "It's not like I cracked the case. More like dumb luck and a photo I damn near forgot about."

He looked at her for a long second, then tipped his chin at the screen.

"You found solid evidence." His tone softened but stayed certain. "Don't play it down."

"Thank you." She avoided his eyes and reached for her mug.

He reached for his too, the two cups lifting almost in sync. "So, what's next?"

Still looking down, Alexis lifted her mug and took another sip. She expected the liquid to have cooled by now, but the heat lingered. At first it settled her, spreading slowly across her tongue and down her chest. Then it stayed, past the point of comfort.

She lowered the mug, its weight matching the weight in her chest, and let out a slow, uneven exhale.

"The ball."

CHAPTER 12

Alexis stopped cold at the entrance, the word slipping out before she could stop it. "Damn."

She knew the Madames had a flair for spectacle, but the sight before her was beyond that.

From the doorway, the ballroom spread wide, a theater of gold and marble. Chandeliers hovered overhead. Twin marble columns framed the stage ahead. Three lone mic stands waited at the center, their shadows stretching across a speaker in the far-right corner.

To the left, a jazz band grooved. The upright bass pulsed low while the drums held steady behind it. The saxophonist leaned in, slipping ad-libs between the notes. At the far right, a white-and-gold grand piano gleamed under the lights, its lid lifted in invitation.

The instant she stepped inside, something needled up her back.

Her attention dropped to the checkered floor beneath her heels, black-and-white tiles, ceremonial in their pattern. The marble warped her reflection, breaking her outline into fragments she didn't recognize.

When she looked up again, six velvet-draped tables sat roped off with gilded poles and cords the color of dried blood, each marked with a golden placard. Beyond them, she froze.

Masked faces stared back from across the floor, a whole sea of them hemmed in behind the ropes. Scaled masks in washed pastels. White masks hollowed at the eyes. Black masks crowned in crimson feathers. Some balanced on sticks, theater props suspended between gloved fingers. Others clung seamlessly to the skin. So many variations, none less unsettling.

She angled her body away from the room and pulled out her phone, thumbs moving fast as she typed a quick update to Tahir.

Made it. Was a little late, but it's—

"I've been waiting for you." Mason slid into view. His tux was immaculate, his posture practiced, his smile fixed in place like something carved.

Alexis shuddered at the sound of his voice. Without finishing the message, she tucked her phone into the cream quilted bag hanging off her shoulder. She hadn't even noticed him coming.

"Were you just… posted up with your eyes glued to the door, waiting for me or something?"

She let out a soft laugh, trying to play it off, though her heart was still catching up.

"Maybe," he smirked, then held out his hand. "Right this way, milady. Your *throne* awaits."

She played along, sliding her hand into his. The firmness of his grasp made her skin crawl. Her fingers twitched, ready to pull away, but she held on and kept walking.

Her eyes swept across the ballroom as they walked. Masked faces turned toward her one by one, heads turning as she passed.

She pulled her focus from the masked crowd and fixed it on something familiar… the girls. They were already seated with their suitors. Each pair wore matching sashes.

Raven looked calm but alert, fingers tracing the edge of her wine glass. Natalia was mid-laugh, leaning in close, her eyes jumping toward the stage between giggles. Destiny had one arm draped behind her chair, already deep in conversation like she'd known her date for years. Markeysha sat still, almost too still, her date whispering something in her ear that made her smile without showing teeth.

Where's Jade?

Once they made it to their designated table, Mason pulled out her chair with his nearly theatrical smoothness. Before she could sit, Rae appeared.

She floated up in a cream evening gown embroidered with delicate gold vines threaded from the hem upward, clawing their way to her delicate neck. Draped over her arm were two sashes.

Rae's gaze danced between the pair, then settled on Alexis.

"I hope you don't disappoint tonight." She tapped Alexis gently on her bare shoulder with the back of her fingers.

Then she turned to Mason, pausing on him before handing him both sashes.

"You have my blessing," she murmured, then turned and walked off, her heels lightly clicking against the checkered marble.

He has her blessing? The hell…

Alexis scrunched her face, the thought still souring in her head.

Mason's eyes followed Rae's sashay, then he turned back with a small shrug and that same exasperating charm.

"Shall I?" Mason lifted the twin sashes in an almost ceremonial presentation.

He didn't wait for her answer, draping the cream sash gently over her shoulder.

It brushed her collarbone, and something in her knotted. It crept higher in her chest, but she pushed it down and smoothed it flat.

"Thank you, Mason. You're such a gentleman." The corners of her mouth curled into a flirtatious smile. He didn't see her roll her eyes.

"Let me get a good look at you," he stated, towering over her as he lifted her hand overhead. He turned her slowly, his eyes raking each inch like he was cataloging rather than admiring.

The gown flared around her in a shimmering arc. Champagne silk laced with royal blue and gold, the fabric gleaming, eager to present her. No jewels adorned her slightly elongated neck. In fact, the only jewelry she wore was a pair of gold-plated raindrop pearl earrings.

Her braids were swept into a regal updo, high and coiled, a few strands wrapped in delicate gold string. The cream sash draped from her right shoulder. Couple Number One, stitched in blue. Dressed like royalty, paraded like possession.

She eased into the seat, smoothing her gown before setting her purse on the table.

"Showtime," she muttered, pulling her phone back out.

Mason slung the other sash over his shoulder and took a seat beside her. Beyond the velvet ropes, Alexis fixed on the far-right wall.

The buffet gleamed. Mini crawfish pies. Chargrilled shrimp shooters. Lavender-white chocolate mousse cups. Just a glimpse of what was laid out. And before the stage, a fully stocked open bar.

"It's top shelf only," Mason informed Alexis, noticing where she was looking. "Would you like me to get you a drink?"

"Oh, no." The refusal broke from her too quickly. She caught it and adjusted. "Not now, at least. I'm just… taking everything in." She set her phone down before continuing. "I didn't expect it to be such a grand event."

"Yeah." Mason tilted his head in agreement, sweeping the room with her. "Your krewe truly knows how to throw a royal affair."

Her gaze drifted, unwillingly, back to the masked crowd. Alexis let the moment drag before asking, "So, who are all those people?"

She tipped her chin toward the roped-off section.

"Members of other krewes," Mason shrugged.

"What, like affiliates or something?"

"Yeah, something like that. All of us are a part of the Voodoo Parade. Tonight's for us." He nodded, eyes moving from mask to mask. "Some heavy hitters in here. Real upper echelon. Good night to make connections."

"How do you know? It's not like you can see their faces."

"That's the nature of these events. Just trust me."

She studied the crowd a moment longer. "Why the masks?"

"Tradition."

"Then why aren't *we* wearing them?"

"The guests wear masks, but the entertainment doesn't get to hide."

Hide? Entertainment?

Those words flew through her mind and perched on her shoulders.

Then she noticed the pins. Fixed to tux lapels and fastened to the bodices of gowns, they gleamed in silver and gold, just like the ones from the Plaçage Ceremony.

Now she could see them more clearly.

Some held pendants shaped like snakes coiled around crooked staffs.

Others bore masks impaled on rods, fleur-de-lis flaring at each end.

A few displayed skulls with long crosses running beneath them.

"What's with the pendants?"

"They show which krewe they're with."

"And the colors? Some silver, some gold."

"Shows rank."

She looked at Mason's chest and then back at the crowd. "Where's yours?"

"I'm at the bottom. New, like you. We don't get pendants." He glanced at her and then back at the crowd. "After some time, or if you make a *substantial* contribution, you get a silver one. Krewe heads wear gold."

"So, what krewe are you with?"

"Gatekeepers. The ones who stand at the threshold."

"Gatekeepers, huh?" She pulled her focus from the crowd and leveled it at Mason. "What gates?"

"The kind you don't notice… until they're already open." He smiled, calm and casual. "And by then?" He tapped two fingers on the table. "It's already too late."

Still watching him, she paid close attention for a tell. "What's that supposed to mean?"

"I wonder that too," he said breezily. "It's the krewe's maxim."

Alexis leaned in, about to press further. But Mason was already pushing up from his seat.

"All these questions got me parched." He gave a quick smile, already turning. "You ready for that drink now?"

"No. I'm good." Her voice was even. "Thank you."

He nodded and slipped away toward the bar without uttering another word.

"Madames et Messieurs," came a voice, low, smooth, and indulgent.

Alexis turned.

Onstage stood a man in a raven-feathered mask, velvet coat, and white gloves. His tone floated above the crowd, smooth enough to lull the room into a slumber.

"Please welcome our musical mistresses of the evening, from the Krewe of Sirens, The Daughters of La Sirène."

Scattered applause followed. Neat. Restrained.

Then the singers appeared.

Three women stepped onto the stage. Their gowns were alive with sequins that changed from silver to teal to bruised rose. Silver fishtail pendants shimmered on the upper left side of their chests.

The woman in the center looked to the others as the piano began.

They swayed together. Arms looped. Steps matched. A seamless vocal trio. Rehearsed. Refined.

The singer took a half step forward, lips brushing the mic. She eased into a slow, dreamy version of "Fly Me to the Moon." Her voice unfurled, sultry and spellbound, wrapping the crowd in velvet.

The jazz flowed easily. Gold-lit and unhurried, it eased from the piano in gentle waves. The upright bass rolled beneath it. Brushes danced across the snare. A saxophone slipped through the center, curling around the room. The music spread through the ballroom, knowing exactly where to touch and when to hold.

The other two slid in beside her, their voices braiding into hers. Their harmony was lush and entrancing.

Alexis couldn't look away. The sound that came out of them felt alive, a language her body understood before her mind caught up.

"Hey girl!"

The voice snapped her out of it. Alexis blinked, pulse jumping, as the trance shattered and the room rushed back into focus. She turned toward the sound and exhaled when she saw Natalia approaching the table, with Raven, Destiny, and Markeysha close behind.

"Y'all look so good," Alexis exclaimed, standing to hug each of them in turn. "Destiny, your dress is everything."

"You see me, huh?" Destiny grinned, giving a slow twirl with her hands on her hips. The gown hugged every inch of her curves. "Royal blue is *definitely* my color."

"I'm glad mine's more cream than blue," Natalia glanced down at her gown. "Dark tones wash me out."

"I feel like your gown's the prettiest." Markeysha dipped her chin at Alexis in approval.

Raven folded her arms and rolled her eyes, feigning outrage. "Wow. So nobody's going to say a word about *my* li'l fit? That's crazy. I always knew y'all hoes were jealous of me."

Laughter bubbled throughout the huddle.

Breaking through the cackling, Alexis asked, "Jade's still not here?" Her gaze skimmed the room once before landing back on Destiny.

"Oh no, she's here. Crept her ass in a few minutes ago," Destiny let her know. "She had to hit the restroom to touch up her makeup."

Alexis nodded once.

"Where's your man at, Lexi? He's a no-show?" Raven wanted to know.

"First of all, he's not my man." Alexis caught herself and angled her chin toward the bar. "He's over there."

She gestured toward the bar, where Mason was still posted up, making small talk with another suitor.

"Oh yeah, I forgot how fine that man is!" That was Markeysha, eyes wide.

"He's alright," Alexis rolled her eyes. "Whose man is he talking to?"

"That's Destiny's dude," Raven replied. "Built like a linebacker, ain't he?"

"That's because he *is* a linebacker. Hmph!"

"That's right, Destiny, stand up for your man," Natalia teased.

"Wait, y'all, there goes my guy over there. Ryan," Natalia murmured, gesturing subtly toward a man just beyond the velvet rope, standing among the masked crowd. "He's the one talking to that man in the red-and-black feathered mask."

Raven followed her line of sight. "Hold on, *that's* your man?"

"Yep," Natalia beamed.

"Oh no, he gives me *'good evening, officer'* vibes! Like if you go missing, he'll be the first one volunteering to pass out flyers, meanwhile, he's got you chained up in the basement."

"Can you not?" Natalia laughed. "He's just… clean."

"Clean ain't the word, maw," Raven pouted.

Destiny was cracking up. "Not you saying that man's a serial killer!"

"I mean, he *does* look like one. Am I lying?" Raven grinned.

Destiny turned her head to get a better look at him. "He does have that little look about him, but did you peep the timepiece? Girl, that's a Patek."

"Oh, Ryan is definitely rico baby," Natalia confirmed. "Old money. Long money."

Alexis listened intently as the girls continued to talk.

Her attention shifted to the man they were discussing.

Ryan stood upright, posture perfect, blond hair combed back neatly without a strand out of place. His suit looked sharp enough to slice bread.

The man he was speaking to had swept-back salt-and-pepper hair, styled just as precisely. His suit was just as sharp. Maybe even sharper. Pinned to his lapel was a gold pendant in the shape of a mask pierced by a rod, fleur-de-lis blooming from either end.

"Did he say what he does for a living?" Alexis didn't take her eyes off him.

"He's a trust fund kid. His dad founded the original Creole Catch. And now they're planning to franchise outside the US. He said they're trying to be the McDonald's of seafood." She tipped her head toward the man Ryan was speaking with. "And he told me his dad is part of the same krewe he's in. He's supposed to be here tonight. Lowkey, that's probably his dad he's talking to now that I think about it."

Alexis kept her voice casual. "Oh, word? Did he mention which krewe he's with?"

Natalia paused. "You know… I didn't even think to ask."

"Hey hoes!" Jade slid into the circle, holding a rectangular tray lined with long wine glasses filled with champagne. "Y'all looked too dry over here. I'm trying to get the night going."

Jade set the tray in the middle of the table, then plucked the first two flutes from it. She kept one for herself and held the other out to Alexis.

"I'm good. Thanks, though." Alexis gently swatted the drink away.

"Oh, come on Lex! This is Dom Pérignon!"

"Dom P? Excuse me, girl." Raven shimmied past Jade to grab her a drink. The rest of the girls swooped in for their glasses.

"Lexi you better stop being stank, 'fore I take your glass." Raven took a swig of the chilled champagne.

"You can have it." Alexis shook her head.

Holding the flute back out, Jade said, "Girl, if you don't take this damn drink. You act like one little drink's gonna hurt."

"Just give me the drink, girl. Damn!" Alexis snatched the glass from Jade's hand, nearly spilling some. *She curled her fingers around the stem and* brought it to her nose. The faint jasmine-and-citrus scent danced up her nostrils immediately.

That's Dom Pérignon alright…

"Now, who were y'all gossiping about?" Jade took a sip from her flute.

"Natalia's man," Raven replied as she sat her empty glass back on the tray. "But girl, I'm done with Mr. Patrick Bateman."

"Well, where's your man at then?" Destiny asked, swirling her glass.

"Oh, my man?" Raven bit her fingertip, all fake coy. "He's right over there."

"Don't point," Natalia muttered, swatting her hand. "You're being obvious."

"And? What about it?" Raven grinned. "He fine, huh? That chiseled jawline? That dimple? Baby, he looks like he could be a model!"

"Well, that's my guy seated at the table like a lonely puppy," Jade announced, tipping her half-empty flute in the guy's direction. "Girl, he gets on my nerves."

With her free hand, she waved, lazily.

The guy saw it, his whole face lighting up as he waved back, then blew her a kiss.

Jade turned her head before it landed.

"Aw, why you do him like that? He seems like a sweetheart," Alexis asked.

Jade shrugged. "Yeah, he's very sweet. Complimented me all damn night. Pulled my chair out and everything."

"Okay, so what's the issue?"

"I mean, he's fine as hell… I'll give him that. Just comes off a little too gung-ho and clingy."

"Oh, yeah." Destiny sucked her teeth. "That's too much."

"Way too much!" Jade echoed the sentiment.

"Hey, ladies," Mason spoke, finally strolling back, martini glass in one hand and a rocks glass in the other. "Hope I'm not interrupting. Looks like y'all over here having a ball." He looked down at the empty champagne flutes scattered along the table.

"Oh no, you're good," Destiny told him.

"Yeah, you're *real* good," Markeysha muttered under her breath.

It was enough to make Mason smirk, but he didn't entertain it. He turned to Alexis instead. "I know you said you didn't want anything."

He handed her the martini glass. "I got you a martini, though. Just in case."

"Thanks," Alexis tossed a quick smile his way.

"Aw, and he's thoughtful too?" Raven grinned. "That's a good man, Alexis!"

"Tell her again!" Mason eased into his seat. "As a matter of fact, tell her to stop playing and give me a chance."

"Girl, please give this man a chance!" Raven pleaded, hand to chest.

"Yeah, give him a chance," Natalia echoed after polishing off her drink and setting the glass on the table.

Jade and Destiny cackled and joined the campaign. "Give that man a chance!"

"Shoot, if you don't want him…" Markeysha took a slow sip from her flute.

Alexis waved them off, half-laughing as she sank back into her seat, resting both drinks on the table.

"She has to tie up some loose ends first before she can give you anything," Jade uttered.

"Oh, so she is taken. I kind of figured that actually." Mason knocked back his whiskey with a straight face.

"Jade!" Alexis cut her eyes at her friend, then looked at Mason. "Like I told you last night. I am single, but just because I'm single doesn't mean I'm looking."

That smug look came back, but before he could say anything, a bell cut clean through the room.

The laughter quieted. Heads turned.

"Ladies and gentlemen," Nevi announced.

She stood at the mic, poised and glowing, her royal blue gown catching the light like midnight water.

"It's time for La Danse pour Trouver le Roi et la Reine!"

Alexis found herself staring at Nevi, the gold brooch sparkling on the left side of her chest.

The heart split clean down the middle, the long rod threading through it, fleur-de-lis sprouting at its ends, curlicues twisting from the heart like vines.

Her focus moved from Nevi to the crowd. The pendants glittered on chests and lapels, silver and gold winking in the low light.

Nearly every pendant had that same rod through it, piercing whatever symbol sat at the center, with fleur-de-lis coming out of each end.

Alexis held onto that detail.

"Blue Hearts!" Nevi called out. "Join your suitors on the floor."

She adjusted the mic with one gloved hand. Behind her, the trio hummed into their mics, a nameless tune that slithered under the skin.

"Tonight's waltz is more than tradition. It is legacy. The pair who carry it best will be crowned King and Queen of the Fifth Blue Hearts Inaugural Ball, held once every thirty years." She let the words settle. "May the best couple win."

The saxophonist, horn still in hand, stepped away from the band and toward the mic at the far left. The woman who had been standing there slipped aside at once, gliding across to join the singer on the opposite end.

He lifted the sax and let a slow, velvet-smooth melody rise from it. The lead singer watched him, smiling as his notes settled the room's pulse.

Only when he lowered the horn did she lean toward her own mic, her voice unfurling soft and spellbound.

"Your hands remember every vow you broke…"

The other girls rushed to the dance floor, their suitors close behind. Alexis stayed put, that knot tightening in her gut.

"You ready?" Mason asked, standing with his hand outstretched.

She shook off the nerves, downed the Dom Pérignon in one gulp, then grabbed her phone from beside the martini glass and tucked it into her bra.

"Now I am," she said with a grimace.

"Good." He pulled her to her feet.

Her heels tapped the floor at a careful pace, each step steadier than the last.

Mason's palm settled at the small of her back. Firm. Guiding.

Alexis glanced at the other girls, already gliding across the floor in slow, measured steps.

She looked back at Mason with a sly tilt of her head.

"I hope you're okay with losing," she assumed a low, teasing drawl.

"Why do you say that?"

"Slow dancing's not really my style, but give me something with a little bounce to it, and I'll eat it up."

He chuckled. "There's movement to it, trust me. Slower than what you're used to, but once you settle into it, it comes easy. Follow me. Start with your left foot. When I step forward, you go back."

She nodded once and stepped in.

His hand found the spot just beneath her shoulder blade. His other raised between them.

"Put your hand on my shoulder."

She did as she was told.

"In three… two…"

He moved first.

She mirrored, a beat off.

"You're doing fine," he murmured. "Just stay with me."

She tried. Still stiff. Her thoughts were half-present, posture too tight.

At the next turn of the melody, the saxophonist lifted the horn for one last gliding phrase, then lowered it and stepped in toward his mic. He let his voice glide into the room, warm and rough-edged, melting into the songstresses' harmonies as all four met the line together.

"If heaven calls, we'll slip away…"

The Daughters of La Sirène's voices drifted through the air, weaving around the baritone of the sax man.

The sound wrapped around Alexis. Smooth. Hypnotic.

Her feet started to follow. Her jaw unclenched.

"What comes next?" she asked.

"When I step forward, you step back on your left," Mason repeated, smiling. "You're getting it."

Their steps circled with the others. Alexis let her guard down just enough to fall into it.

"When dawn forgets where night begins… We'll dance until forever ends…"

The duet settled into the lyrics in unison, his roughened tone and her smoother one locking together. At the end of the stage, the other two singers swayed close, their subtle harmony coming together while the sax man's free hand rested lightly on the horn at his side.

The lullaby held the whole room in the performers' palms.

Even Alexis felt it. She drifted with it, suspended, almost forgetting herself.

"Would it be crazy," Mason murmured, just loud enough for her to hear, "if I said I could see myself doing this again with you?"

"Doing what? Dancing?" she posed, her feet finding the ground again.

"Just being here. With you. Caught in the moment… in each other."

"Mason, you barely know me." Her expression waned, patience stretched thin.

"That's the point, Alexis. I'm trying to get to know you." He looked down into her eyes. "Inside and out." She didn't answer. "Look, I'm trying to do this the right way instead of—"

A bell rang, cutting him off.

Nevi's voice buzzed through the speakers.

"Alright, Blue Hearts, switch partners!"

Mason's hand slipped from hers.

Without another word, cold as a brick of ice, he turned and stepped straight into Jade's arms. And just like that, the ice melted. His smile slipped back on, easy and warm as ever.

Alexis turned her head and noticed a guy bowing before her. Polite. Very handsome.

She caught sight of the "Couple Number Six" sash across his chest.

"You're Jade's guy, right?" she wanted to know.

"That's me." He rubbed the back of his neck. His nervous energy hovered around him. Strong. Anxious. "You must be Alexis."

"That's me," she parroted, keeping her tone flat.

"Yeah, she told me a little about you. Y'all are like really close, right?"

"Yep, that's my girl."

His hands were damp against hers as they fumbled through the steps. Alexis felt the jitter travel up his arm before he spoke. "Did she tell you I didn't pick her?"

She shook her head. "Wait, what?"

"Yeah. The Grand Master of my krewe picked her for me."

"Huh? Like, how does that even work?"

"He came with me to the ceremony. Placed the bid on my behalf."

"So, that's not considered cheating?"

He gave a helpless shrug. "I'm new to all of this. Still figuring things out."

Then he leaned in slightly. "But you wanna know what's weird?"

"Yeah, what?" She leaned in a fraction, grip tightening in his hand.

"As fine as Jade is… nobody else even bid on her."

She searched the floor, eyes tracking Jade's figure.

Before she could ask anything else, the bell rang again.

"Switch!" Nevi's voice followed the bell's chime.

Then Alexis twirled right into the arms of someone new.

Taller. Masked.

They danced.

"You move well," he told her. "Are you trained or self-taught?"

"I guess you can say self-taught." She forced a smile. Something about his aura felt off.

"You like it?" he asked.

"I'm sorry, like what exactly?"

"This whole shindig they've got going on."

"…It's beautiful."

"But?" The man's brow rose.

"No buts," she shook her head.

He chuckled. "I like that. A woman who doesn't complain… even when she wants to."

The comment slithered over her skin. Her tongue pressed against her teeth, a snarky reply itching to break loose, but she let it dissolve on her tongue.

Instead, she asked, "I notice you're not wearing a sash. Who's your—"

"I remember you." Alexis watched the masked man lick his bottom lip.

Her spine locked, shoulders freezing while the music carried on around them. "From where?"

"I saw you. Peeking through the window the other day. I know it was you." He tilted his head, eyes gleaming behind the mask. "Out of all of you lovely ladies, you're the only one with skin so chocolatey."

Chocolatey? Oh, I've got some chocolate for you, you bastard!

Alexis fought the urge to hike up her dress, pull out the Glock strapped to her thigh, and fire a warning shot at his feet. Just one. She bet *that* would change his tune.

Creeps like him made her trigger finger itch.

The gun was for emergencies only, for moments when she had real cause. She let him talk just long enough to see if he would give her one.

"Should've bid on you myself." He let his attention drift lower. "You'd have been worth every penny."

"Switch!"

The bell rang again. He was gone before she had the chance to register the last thing he said.

Alexis turned, searching for where that man had vanished, and was pulled into another's arms. She recognized him as Natalia's suitor, then a blur swept across her vision. She could still make out his mouth moving, but the words slipped past her. As they danced, she felt heavy and light all at once. She was keeping up, but barely.

Another bell. Another partner. His hand clammy, his laugh hollow. The sound leaked through her, already blending into the music.

The singers threaded their notes through the room, low and sweet, round and round. The floor swayed beneath her… or maybe she floated above it. Faces blurred, voices melted, hands trading too quickly to follow.

By the time the last note fell away, the saxophonist lifted his horn in a small parting gesture and stepped off the stage, slipping back toward the band. The singer he'd displaced drifted across to reclaim her mic, the trio settling into their original formation just as a quick surge of applause rippled through the room. Then everything stilled.

Alexis stood next to Mason, shoulder to shoulder with the rest, her pulse still ticking to a song that had ended moments ago.

Nevi's voice guided her out of the mist. "Please cast your votes. Couple One through Six. Choose wisely."

Rae and Della moved from table to table with wicker baskets to collect slips, the hems of their cream-and-gold dresses brushing softly around their ankles.

Once the final slips were counted, Della crossed the room to Nevi's side. She bent slightly, murmuring the chosen couple into her ear. Nevi's expression didn't change, not even a twitch.

"Couple Number Six!" Nevi shouted with glee.

A spotlight found Jade and her partner.

Applause rose.

"Crowned. Elevated."

"Jade… and Abram."

Abram.

From the crowd, a tall man in a black mask with white rings around the eyes stepped forward. Pinned to his chest was a gold fleur-de-lis with a grinning skull that had a top hat in the middle of it.

"For what you surrendered, for what you steadied, your place has opened." He lifted Jade's hand. "The ground beneath bows, the realm beyond receives, and you are raised among the chosen." He pressed something small and silver into her palm.

Jade's lips curved at the corners. Her posture stiffened as her fingers closed around the gift.

Rae and Della stood beside Nevi, each holding a crown atop a golden velvet pillow.

Nevi took one and placed it gently atop Jade's pinned locs, then pulled her into a brief hug. The first time Alexis had seen Nevi sentimental with someone who wasn't her sister.

Then came Abram's crown. Nevi placed it carefully.

"For the spring of your years, the force of your living, the depth of your marrow, we honor you as king."

The ballroom shivered with applause, cold enough that Alexis felt it crawl over her, raising goosebumps along her arms.

Nevi then threw her hand up and shouted like a war cry, "Danse pour Tous!"

The masked crowd surged forward, swallowing the dance floor in motion.

Alexis caught sight of Jade being led through the crowd, flanked on either side by two men in red masks and dark suits.

Her eyes moved over their broad shoulders and synchronized stride, catching on the silver pendants at their chests. Daggers fanned and fused at the hilt, gleaming where their blazers parted. The shine wavered, doubled, then steadied just long enough for her to take it in.

Jade wasn't resisting. But she wasn't smiling either. Her face was blank, her steps clean as they zigzagged deeper into the crowd.

Alexis followed, vision tunneling, her steps lagging just behind. The Daughters of La Sirène slid into their rendition of L-O-V-E. The tempo sagged and bent inward.

The lead singer stretched each letter into honeyed syllables, her voice warping until the notes sounded half underwater.

Bodies pressed on every side. She forced her way forward, her heartbeat knocking her vision out of focus.

Jade moved ahead, steady between the red-masked men. Alexis pushed after her, but her steps lagged, balance slipping, the floor tilting underfoot.

Hands struck her arms in passing. Grabbing. Urging. Repelling. Each touch a shock. The crowd coiled tighter, a spiral with no center, pulling her deeper the further she moved.

Then she saw her, a woman standing motionless within the spiral. Her dress was a mirror of Alexis's own. Champagne silk traced with royal blue and gold, the fabric catching every stray light until it glowed. She held a porcelain mask on a stick up to her face, painted with wide eyes, pink cheeks, and a red pout.

Fear pricked at Alexis as the mask lowered.

The woman's mouth had been carved open from corner to corner, lips split into a grotesque grin that reached her ears. Her eyes were mangled, stabbed until the tissue collapsed inward.

Still smiling, she began to weep. Thick black ooze poured in steady rivulets, trailing down her cheeks in glossy arcs.

The weeping fractured into laughter. Alexis couldn't pull her eyes free, no matter how much she wanted to. The sound swelled, spiraled, turned itself inside out.

It wasn't in the air anymore. It was the air. It was inside her.

She finally found the strength to look away. Now with every nerve lit, her chest buzzed in three quick jolts as her legs kicked into motion, flight outrunning fight.

She was back on the hunt for Jade.

As she worked her way through the crowd, the chandeliers dimmed. Shadows slinked along the walls. The floor buckled beneath her heels.

The song twisted lower, vowels melting into a slow croon, words blurring together.

The music distorted even more. Bent. Shuddered.

Her scalp tingled.

Then—

A hand on her shoulder.

"Are you okay? You look like you've seen a ghost." Natalia stepped from behind her.

Her voice grounded Alexis, and the room straightened itself. Now, the lights were steady, the crowd was composed, and the music smoothed over what she knew she'd seen. But she didn't have time to dwell. Not now.

"Shit," Alexis wheezed. She was sure she'd lost Jade now.

"Is everything okay?"

"Just a minute," she told her, breaking into motion toward the exit. If they'd left the ball, maybe she still had a chance to catch up.

But by the time she made it outside, there was no one in sight. Nothing looked out of the ordinary.

"Damn it!"

Bent over, huffing in the warm city air, she felt it again.

That sensation in her chest.

Three quick jolts. Pause. Three more.

"My phone!"

Buzz. Buzz. Buzz.

She dug it out of her bra. The screen lit.

Tahir.

"Hello?" Her voice scraped out, hoarse.

Static.

Then fractured.

"They…"

"What? I can't hear you. Hello?!"

She paced the sidewalk, angling for a signal.

The line crackled.

Then his voice. Sudden. Clear. "Can you hear me, Alexis?"

"Yeah. I can hear you now," she panted.

"They found her."

Her heart flipped.

"Who?"

"Jennifer."

CHAPTER 13

Alexis sat so stiff her back barely touched the seat. Her fingers moved without purpose, then froze. The engine buzzed beneath her feet, steady but useless against the crawl of tension up her spine. Words sat on the tip of her tongue, too strong to ignore, too risky to release.

Tahir's thumbs tapped the steering wheel at a steady pace. He glanced from her knees to her hands, then to her face.

With eyes back on the road, he told her, "Call came in around nineteen hundred hours. Signal Twenty-Four at Armstrong Park. Stewart notified me, confirming it was our girl. She was found half-dressed and disoriented. EMS got her stable, but she was in bad shape. Bruised up. Dehydrated."

"We know where she escaped from?" Alexis finally inquired, exhaling.

"Negative. She's been sedated on and off. EMS said she looked like she hadn't eaten or had anything to drink in days."

She didn't reply. Just turned toward the window, where the city blurred in long strokes of heat and color. Outside the car, the world kept moving, yet inside, everything felt still.

Alexis leaned forward, swiped sweat from her brow, and wiped it on her jeans. She adjusted her jacket, tugged at the sleeves, and flipped the visor mirror down to see if she looked as wrecked as she felt.

Tahir looked over at her. Then back at the road. Then

at her again.

She kept fidgeting, like her body needed somewhere to put the panic.

"Okay. So, run it back. And this time… just the details about Jade."

Alexis sat up, blinked twice. "She won. Queen of the ball."

Tahir glanced over. His brow twitched. "You mean *Crowned Heart*, right? Isn't that what they call them?"

"You're right." Alexis frowned. "I didn't even realize… so much was happening…" She started sifting through the details in her mind.

"Keep going," Tahir snapped her back.

"Right." She straightened. "After she and her partner, Abram, were announced as the winners, this man stepped out from the crowd. Black and white mask. Tall. Gave a little speech and then dropped something into her hand."

"What was it?"

"I'm not sure. Something small and silver. I couldn't really see it."

"And those guys you mentioned, the ones in red masks?"

"It was two men. Red masks… Both were fair-skinned, as far as I could tell. Black suits. They moved clean. Synchronized. I lost them in the crowd as they escorted her somewhere. She didn't fight it, but…"

She paused, voice soft. "She wasn't resisting… but she wasn't in control either. Like she let herself be taken."

Tahir's eyes stayed on the road. "Could've been security?"

"It's possible," Alexis responded. "She didn't look like she was in distress or anything, but I just wanted to talk to her and double check… just in case."

Tahir didn't rush her. Just let the silence stretch a few seconds before grounding them again.

"And the pendants?"

"Silver. Same design on both. Three daggers fanned out and bound at the handles. Kind of like a fleur-de-lis, but all knives."

Tahir's jaw flexed as he lowered his chin. "And you said silver means they've been with their krewe for a while?"

"Right. Or that they've made a substantial contribution. Mason's exact words."

She exhaled, the sound soft, like tension leaving her body.

Tahir gave a quick nod. "I went ahead and put a BOLO out on her and the two men. Gave them the exact description you gave me over the phone."

That pulled her eyes to him.

Tahir's mouth stretched and dragged down at the corners. He gave a subtle nod, one hand still on the wheel, the other dropping to her thigh without thought.

A gentle touch. Meant to reassure.

But her muscles tightened beneath his fingers.

He paused before sliding his hand back to the wheel. He opened his mouth, but whatever words he had for her died before making it out.

The engine's hum was the only sound pushing them forward as the quiet pressed in.

When he finally spoke, his voice was steady, all business again.

"We're still waiting to hear back on Jade's address."

Alexis exhaled. "Thank you. I know the facts don't warrant the urgency, but… if it was more than what met the eye…"

"Don't worry about all that," he told her. "You noticed something. I took it from there."

Alexis leaned her elbow against the window and watched the lights pass by.

"Any updates from the units canvassing those grave sites?" she finally spoke up.

"Nothing major yet. Just weird shit."

"Define weird."

"Random shit. A bundle of candles at one site. An urn full of burned index cards at another. One spot had a mirror, just leaning against a headstone."

Alexis frowned. "I wouldn't say that's nothing. Just don't know what it all means yet."

"Yeah, well… my guys didn't think much of it. Not until they noticed that at each grave was one of those wooden crosses. Same as the one we found on that girl."

"Milan."

Tahir glanced over, then back toward the road. "Right." Then he cleared his throat. "Anyway… I got screenshots if you wanna see."

"Yeah. Show me," she looked over at him.

"Bet. Just remind me when we get out."

"Will do."

Quiet filled the car again. Then—

"Her being alive… It gives me hope. I was starting to think all of them were…"

Tahir glanced at her but didn't speak.

"I just…" She exhaled, jaw tightening. "I need to find the motherfuckers behind this shit. Bring the rest of those girls home. Before it's too late."

She folded her hands in her lap and clenched them shut.

"Let me go in. Let me talk to her… by myself. Please."

"Come on now, Lex." His voice cut in low, a touch too stern. "You said you'd wait in the car. That's how we agreed to play it." He threw his head back and groaned, dragging his hand down before his shoulders finally sagged. "If I let you do that… it could blow the whole operation. You know that." He stared at her for a second longer, then shook his head as the realization clicked. "You never really planned on just sitting here, did you?"

Alexis ignored his question. "Just trust me. She'll be more open with a woman."

"Stewart already tried, and Jennifer barely said a word. Another female officer followed. Same result."

"That's exactly why you have to let *me* try. They're strangers to her. I'm not."

As they pulled into the hospital lot, Tahir told her, "I just don't want you walking in there thinking you're the one who can save her… then walking out crushed if you can't."

Alexis looked over at him. "I'll be okay. It's those girls we need to worry about."

He studied her face, the way she held her shoulders, the doggedness in her eyes. "Fifteen minutes. You get fifteen minutes. Then I'm coming in."

He looked at her again, deeper this time. "Not as your backup. As your damn shadow."

Alexis nodded. Reached for the door handle just as the engine shut off.

She drew in air through her nose. Held it. Let it go. Then stepped out.

The city met her ears with the soft whoosh of rooftop vents and the mechanical wheeze of ambulance bay doors.

Without haste, Tahir hopped out of the car, his door slamming closed behind him. Together, they crossed the lot into the hospital's main entrance. Their footsteps dull against the tile.

Inside, everything was washed in hospital white and chemical-clean air.

At the front desk, a young woman looked up from her monitor. The calm in her blue eyes wavered when she noticed Tahir's badge.

"We're here to see Jennifer Wright," he announced. "Sergeant Simmons, NOPD. The recovered missing person, we're here to speak with her."

She bobbed her head. "She's up on five. Room 517. Security'll take y'all."

In no time, a uniformed guard stepped from an alcove. He was lean and older, with a salt-and-pepper beard and keys and gear that clanked softly at his side.

"Y'all the detectives?" he asked, giving them a once-over.

"Yes, sir," Tahir flashed his badge.

The guard dipped his chin. "Her folks are already up there. The nurse told 'em law enforcement needed to speak with her, so they'll be expecting you."

"Understood."

The elevator crawled upward in silence.

As soon as the doors to the fifth floor opened, the whole floor felt different. The noise downstairs was gone, replaced by monitor beeps and that hospital hush that made every sound stand out.

She and Tahir followed the guard down the hall.

Then she saw them.

A man and a woman sat on a bench outside Room 517. The woman's eyes were red but alert. The man was hunched, unmoving. Jennifer's face sat somewhere between them. Her mother's mouth. Her father's eyes.

Alexis slowed.

The woman looked up at Alexis.

Alexis gave the woman a slight nod, then she looked at the man sitting next to her. "Hi, Mr. and Mrs. Wright. Y'all didn't have to step out. We could've talked to her with y'all in the room."

Mr. Wright spoke first. "No, ma'am. We're gonna wait out here. We think it's best."

Mrs. Wright added, "She might talk easier without us sitting over her."

Alexis nodded once. "Okay. I understand. Thank you."

Tahir stepped back. "I'll stay out here and talk with y'all."

Mr. Wright gave him a tired nod. "Appreciate that."

She reached for the door. Her palm was damp against the cool metal.

Behind her, Tahir's voice softened. "How's she been doing since they brought her up?" His voice trailed off behind her as she stepped into the room.

The hospital room was dim and sterile. The only sounds were the soft, rhythmic beeping of the heart monitor and the faint buzz of fluorescent lights overhead.

Jennifer lay propped on stiff white pillows, her skin washed out under the lighting. Bruises spattered her arms and collarbone like spilled ink. Her hair, once thick and styled in tight, glossy curls, now hung uneven and matted at the roots. She looked both impossibly young and far too old for nineteen.

An IV was taped to her hand, the bag above dripping saline into her veins. Her skin looked tight and drawn. Her lips were cracked. Faint marks circled her wrists, rope-burned and raw.

Alexis entered quietly, eyes locked on the fragile figure in the bed. The sight of Jennifer stopped her cold. For a second, all she could do was stare. Then she stepped forward.

Jennifer stirred, lids fluttering.

She squinted at the shape by the door, trying to make sense of it.

"…Hello?" The word rasped out, brittle.

Alexis moved closer.

Jennifer leaned forward just barely, eyes narrowing to a squint. "Wait… Alexis, is that you?"

Her voice cracked on the name.

Alexis's mouth twitched into a faint, nervous smile. "Hey, girl…" she said softly. "How you feeling?"

Jennifer tried to sit up too fast and winced, her body too weak to match her excitement. "Oh my God, Alexis! It *is* you!" She reached out, arms trembling. "I thought I'd never see you again."

Alexis stepped in, letting the hug ground them both. "How did you know I was here?" Jennifer wanted to know, voice muffled against her shoulder.

Still holding her, Alexis whispered, "There's something I need to let you know."

Jennifer's arms loosened slightly. She pulled back just enough to see Alexis's face. "What is it?"

"I—uh… I'm a detective, Jen. I joined the Krewe as part of an undercover detail."

"You're a cop?" Her expression twisted with disbelief.

Alexis stepped back fully, giving her space. "Girls were going missing, Jen. We didn't have any leads and had to move fast."

"So all that time we spent together… the stories we shared… that was just you doing your job?"

"No," Alexis said quickly. "Not all of it. Not even most of it, to be honest." She stepped forward again. "The bond we've built? That's real. That's why I begged my supervisor to let me come. Even if it meant blowing my cover. I had to see you with my own eyes."

"Really?" Her voice was soft, almost surprised.

Alexis swallowed. "Yeah. I'm sorry, Jen. I really am."

Jennifer looked down, lips curling into a tired, humorless smirk. "Now it makes sense… The way you're always analyzing things and watching people."

She wriggled in the bed, wincing as the IV tugged at her arm, then let her focus settle on the wall. "You're here to ask questions?"

Alexis shook her head. "Only what you're ready to share."

She dragged a metal chair closer, its vinyl cushion split at the seams, legs scraped raw. It creaked under her as she sat, elbows to knees, hands folded.

Her eyes never left Jennifer's face.

Jennifer looked down at her blanket. Her fingers trembled as they worked a loose thread.

"That day… after the second line. I was walking to my car…"

Her voice wavered. The following words slipped out raw, strangled by fear.

"I saw them. They were just… standing there."

Alexis didn't ask who. Not yet. She stayed quiet and let Jennifer keep going at her own pace.

Jennifer's voice dropped to a whisper.

"Two men. Waiting by my car like they owned it. One was leaning on the hood, arms crossed. The other just stared. I didn't even think. I asked if they needed something. Then one stepped forward as I was unlocking my door and said they'd been waiting for me."

Her eyes glazed, the scene playing behind them.

"The other one leaned in and pressed something sharp to my back. He said…" She paused, her jaw trembling. Tears slid free, hot and quiet, pooling at the corners of her mouth. "'Say one more word and…'"

"It's okay, Jen. Take your time."

Alexis placed a steady hand on her knee.

Jennifer sniffled, then went on. "He leaned in and said it, real low. 'Say one more word and I'll slice your fucking guts out.'"

Alexis grabbed the tissue box from the tray and handed her one gently.

"Do you remember what they looked like?" Her voice was even, careful not to press.

"Uh… I… can't." Jennifer dabbed her cheeks, the

tissue trembling in her hand. "I really can't."

The shame in her voice stung more than the tears.

"That's alright. You remembered plenty. Keep going."

Jennifer's hands curled into the blanket.

"I didn't say anything. Just lifted my arms. I was too scared to even move. They walked me to their van and shoved me inside. The one with the knife climbed in after me."

Alexis leaned in, gentle but focused.

"Do you remember the van? Make, model, color? Anything at all?"

"Big white cargo van. Tinted windows."

Her voice faded. Her eyes drifted, unfocused. Her hand rubbed at her wrist, tracing old pain. Her lips parted, then closed again. Her fingers brushed her collarbone.

"That's all I can remember, Lex. I'm sorry."

Alexis gave a small nod. She didn't rush to fill the silence.

"You did good," she affirmed. "That's more than enough for today. We can always—"

"No!" Jennifer cut in, her voice tight, strained. "We have to do this now. The other girls… they're still there."

"There were others? In the van?"

"No. Not the van. The room."

Jennifer's voice had gone flat. Distant.

"They took me somewhere. The drive wasn't long. Maybe… I don't know… five, ten minutes? Felt longer though." She swallowed and tried again. "The guy in the back blindfolded me. When the van stopped, they got out first, then came around and grabbed me on both sides. They walked—no, dragged me—into a house. Made me take off everything but my underwear. Then tied my hands behind my back."

Alexis watched her fingers claw at the blanket again.

"They threw me in a room," Jennifer murmured. "The floor was concrete and cold. I remember landing on someone and barely having room to move without bumping into anyone else. It was hard to breathe, too."

Alexis could see it.

A box of a room. No windows. No air. Thick with sweat and the sour stench of fear. Alexis's stomach tightened as the image became clearer. Girls stripped down to their underwear. Bound and blindfolded. Piled like discarded dolls. Breathing in each other's panic.

Jennifer leaned in, voice taut with urgency. "Kayla was there. I heard her voice. She was screaming. I know it was her."

Then it slipped under, muffled and waterlogged.

Hello?

Somebody?

Anybody?

Kayla.

Her voice cracked with terror, barely holding on. And then Alexis saw her. Kayla's mouth kept moving, her body bound and still, her lips pushing out words like they could rip her free.

Jen? Oh my God, Jen? Is that you? Are you tied up too? Where are we?

The monitor beeped faster.

"Then someone came in, big loud steps. They grabbed her. Dragged her like she was nothing." Jennifer froze. "She was right there," she whispered. "Right there."

Tears returned.

"Jen." Alexis kept her voice soft. "Are you okay to keep going?"

Jennifer didn't speak at first. Alexis waited.

"You're doing everything right," she told her. "But if you need a second, I'll take it with you."

"I'm okay. I promise."

Jennifer steadied herself.

"I worked the rope loose enough to slip one hand free. Then I did the other. Retied it, just tight enough to look like it had never been untied. Tucked my arms behind me again. And waited."

She paused, eyes searching the ceiling as if the memory lived there.

"They came back. Said I was being transferred. Like… I was cargo or something. When they picked me up, my blindfold slipped a little. And I saw him."

Alexis leaned in. "Describe him."

"Uh…" Jennifer rubbed the heel of her palm against her temple. "Um, he was tall and solid. Not fat or slim. Had on a black suit." She blinked hard. "Left side of his chest. He wore a brooch."

Alexis's back went rigid against the chair, fingers curling tight against her knee as that last part slammed into her. "What kind of brooch?"

"Um… it was gold. A little tarnished… Knives. Three of them. One pointed straight up like a sword. The other two here…" She lifted her hands slightly, searching for the shape.

"They looked fanned out? Coming together at the handles?"

"Yes! That's exactly how it looked."

Heat crept up Alexis's neck, but she nodded anyway. "Okay. That helps. Keep going."

Jennifer's voice dropped.

"When I tripped, he yanked me up and slapped me. Hard. Across the face. Then I heard one of the guys say…"

Alexis watched her lips move, but the sound was deeper, harsher, spilling out in voices that weren't hers. She shut her eyes and listened.

"Man, what the hell's wrong with you? Don't hit her in the face, dumbass."

Another voice cut in.

"She was tryna run, fool. What else am I supposed to do?"

The first snapped back, rougher now.

"Mess up her face, they dockin' all our shit. That man paid for a pretty wife, not one that's busted up."

Then Jennifer's voice bled back in, thin but steady, echoing through the dark behind Alexis's closed eyes.

"That was it. That was my shot. I took it. As soon as the door cracked open…"

Alexis lashes lifted.

Darkness split. Jennifer's words spilled forward, shaping into a scene before her.

The rope gave when she jerked her wrists, slipping loose just as she'd planned. The blindfold slid over her head.

Jennifer bolted, bare feet slapping pavement, skin slick, the night rushing wide around her.

Boots crashed after her. Shadows lunged close, spitting curses. The night swallowed it whole.

She cut hard into an alley. Pressed herself flat behind a

rusted dumpster.

She stayed still until the footsteps pounded past and faded into the distance.

She broke from cover again, faster this time.

In Alexis's mind, Jennifer's knees buckled in mid-stride. She staggered against a shuttered wall, her hand sliding down chipped paint slick with sweat. Exhausted, her body doubled over. Her hands landed on her knees as she tried to lift herself again, gasping for air as she struggled.

For a moment, it looked like she might give in.

Then, a white arch rose ahead of her through the blur.

Armstrong Park.

The sight pulled her upright. She pushed on.

Then nothing.

The picture collapsed.

Alexis sat with it, heart hammering, the phantom ache of running still burning in her legs.

She steadied herself, forced the image down, and spoke softly. "Their voices. Do you remember how they sounded?"

Jennifer nodded.

"The one in black sounded older. Down-by-the-bayou type accent. The other one? Younger. Black, I think. Real New Orleans."

"And the van you ran from. Was it the same white one?"

She shook her head.

"No. This one was longer. Boxy… like a Sprinter. Black. Same tint on the windows. Looked newer."

"And the house? What was it like?"

Jennifer thought for a long moment.

"Brick. Red… with black shutters. That's all I got. I know that ain't much."

Alexis laced her fingers, thoughtful.

"Anything else? Take your time."

Jennifer looked up at the ceiling, searching.

"I wish I had more."

Alexis reached over, resting her hand on Jennifer's.

"You gave plenty. What you remembered… it matters. And it helps."

Jennifer looked away. "I don't feel like I did anything except save my own ass." Her voice cracked. "Alexis… I can still hear those girls. Kayla's scream…"

Alexis squeezed her hand. "You did the right thing. You survived."

Jennifer wiped her eyes. "But I left them."

"If you hadn't, we'd still be blind. We'd have no clue where to look, no trail to follow. Now we have one, and we're moving on it. I swear to you, we're doing everything we can to bring them back."

Alexis looked at Jennifer and felt the words hit a bruise she wasn't ready to touch, but damn if they didn't echo.

She shifted, about to speak—

A soft knock at the door.

It cracked open, and Tahir stepped in.

"Miss Wright?" He kept his voice gentle. "I'm Sergeant Simmons."

He moved in just enough for her to see him fully, his voice lowering with calm reassurance.

"We're going to find out who did this. And they will be held accountable. You have my word."

Jennifer didn't speak, but her eyes lifted slightly and she gave a faint nod.

That was enough.

Tahir's attention turned to Alexis. "Did you get what we need?"

"Yeah," Alexis answered. "I got it."

She turned back to Jennifer, stepping in slowly. Careful of the bruises and the tubes.

She leaned in and wrapped her arms around her, light but full.

"You're safe now," she murmured, chin brushing Jennifer's temple.

When Alexis pulled away, Jennifer hadn't said a word.

Alexis did too.

Outside in the hallway, Tahir was already in motion.

"We've gotta move."

Alexis didn't respond. She fell in beside him, quiet.

After that conversation, everything sliced close to the

bone.

And she knew… tomorrow it would cut even deeper.

CHAPTER 14

The sun hung low, casting golden hour across the pavement like a blessing in reverse. The sky stretched cloudless and deep, its blue burnished with orange. A soft breeze stirred feathers, sequins, and curls. It was the kind of Fat Tuesday evening that shimmered with illusion, its calm no more than a veil.

Alexis leaned against the float's side rail, arms crossed. Her tutu sagged, wilted by heat. Perspiration bled through the glitter on her cheeks, making it gleam brighter against the stillness of her face. She didn't move, even as the rest of the girls filed in.

Markeysha and Destiny were already there. Raven and Natalia came shortly after. One was still missing. Alexis kept drifting to the street, waiting for Jade to appear at the last minute, the way she always did.

The back of the float had been divided clean down the middle by a tall partition, one side nothing like the other.

Markeysha and Destiny, laughter spilling out unsteadily, leaned over the rails on their side, tossing invisible beads to an imaginary crowd. Alexis shared her half with Raven and Natalia.

Music blared. Beads clinked. Laughter spiked, but all of it slid past Alexis like background noise.

"You good, girl?" Natalia peeked sideways. "You look tense over there."

Alexis gave a slight nod, her body present, her mind elsewhere. Jennifer's voice threaded back through her skull, dragging her again into that cramped, airless room.

All those girls pressed shoulder to shoulder… Who were they? That question gnawed at her. The subtle details Alexis gathered made it feel larger than the Krewe of Lazuliè. Like girls from all over had been swallowed into whatever this was, funneled into dark corners, stored like inventory.

Her thoughts snagged, veering to the others. Imani. Nia. Olivia… And Brielle. All were still unaccounted for. What if they were in a room just like that? Bound. Blindfolded. Stripped nearly bare.

Alexis scanned the crowd below, a tremor tightening in her gut. If they were keeping girls alive, why kill Milan? Why make her an offering and leave the others untouched? Or were there more like her, bodies waiting to be found? And Kayla. Her absence haunted Jennifer's story more than her presence. She said they'd taken her, but for what purpose? To be somebody's prize or another sacrifice?

She tried to shake it, but her hands gave her away, clamped tight around the worn leather corners of her clutch.

"You sure you're okay, Lexi?" Natalia wanted to know. She'd been watching Alexis the whole time. Clocking every twitch. That faraway stare.

"Yeah," she fibbed.

Then horns erupted, slow and sonorous, their notes marching through her body, seizing her thoughts and snapping her out of the spiral she'd been caught in.

She turned, curious, and leaned out just enough to glance behind them.

One float back.

She didn't even get a good look at the float before she saw it.

A black flag, fluttering high.

White emblem. Three blades fanned outward, gleaming against the black backdrop.

And underneath it, in bold white block letters, *Krewe of Blades.*

Alexis stilled, ironed into place.

That was the same emblem those men wore when they dragged Jade away at the ball.

The same symbol Jennifer described.

She strained to make out the rest of the float, but the partition hid whoever stood behind it.

That krewe had something to do with the missing girls; of that much Alexis was sure. But what she couldn't pin down yet was whether the Krewe of Lazuliè's members were just being hunted, or whether their leaders were in on the hunt.

Her fingers twitched near her clutch. She wanted to pull out her phone and snap a picture, but her gut told her to wait, and she obeyed.

"I'm hype." Natalia turned back, grinning. "Kinda sad though. Last day of Mardi Gras season. Won't see y'all again till next year."

"Next year?" Raven scoffed, sliding up behind her. "Girl, we'll be grandmas by the time they roll again."

"Oh damn, I forgot about that," Natalia laughed. "Why don't they parade every year like all the other krewes do?"

"That's what I'm saying." Markeysha strolled around the partition with Destiny. "It's like they only open this up once a generation, one set of girls at a time."

"Well, if I had to guess…" Destiny shifted her weight and lifted a white Styrofoam cup to her face. "It's probably because every thirty years Saturn swings back to the same spot it was in when this krewe became the House of Lazuliè." She bit her straw, eyes narrowing thoughtfully. "That kind of cycle's serious. Could mean renewal, realignment, or reckoning. I mean, there are *beaucoup* possibilities, for real.

And we already know Mardi Gras is when realms bleed into each other… the day of indulgence. Get all those desires out before Lent hits." She took a long sip, the straw gurgling.

"Now here she go with that hocus pocus shit," Raven rolled her eyes. "Yeah, alright, Miss Baby Badu."

"Believe what you want, boo. I'm not into convincing nobody. It is what it is," Destiny told her.

"Mmm-hmm. Anyways." Raven waved off the mystic talk. "How much time we got before we get this thing going?"

Markeysha shifted the Styrofoam cup to her right hand, then turned her left wrist. The smartwatch screen lit up on cue. "Forty-five minutes."

Alexis cleared her throat and nodded toward their cups. "What y'all drinking?" She didn't care about the answer, not really, but if she stayed quiet any longer, someone might notice. The mask she'd been wearing all this time, the wide-eyed college kid routine, threatened to slip, but she pinned it back in place. She hadn't uncovered enough to risk letting it fall just yet.

"Peach bellini daiquiris," they answered together.

"Of course," Natalia smirked.

"You want one?" Markeysha offered.

Alexis shook her head. "I'm good. Thank you, though."

"Shit, I do," Raven spoke up.

"Yeah, me too." That was Natalia.

"Let me go fix y'all a cup." Markeysha was already halfway on the other side.

The rest of the girls followed Markeysha to the other side of the float.

Alexis was the last in line. Her heartbeat stayed two steps ahead of her body. Something felt… off.

When they reached the other side, Alexis blinked. It was already fully set up.

Beads hung from rows of hooks drilled into the partition wall, bundled in clusters, and sorted by color: gold, green, purple, and blue. The boas and specialty beads also had their own rows. Some beads lit up, others had plastic medallions that blinked or played music, and a few were strung with oversized charms shaped like crowns, masks, or fleur-de-lis. They even had a row of cute little tote bags. Some of the stuffed animals had been arranged along the top of the partition like shelf décor, neatly spaced with their tags still on. A small drink station had been set up, too, with Styrofoam cups stacked beside a gallon jug of daiquiri, all neat and orderly on the ledge just before the built-in restroom.

"Damn, y'all's side looks so nice!" Natalia reached for one of the stuffed animals. "Y'all had to get here early to do all this, huh?"

"Only like an hour before y'all showed up," Destiny responded. "It really didn't take that long."

"Yeah, I dragged Destiny out a little ahead of schedule so we could fix ours up." Markeysha poured the frozen peach concoction into two cups.

"I should have known you were the one behind this. You're always so organized." Natalia took a Styrofoam cup from her.

"Where did y'all get those bags from?" Raven snatched up her own cup. "We didn't get any totes on our side."

"I brought those with me," Markeysha replied.

"Oh damn." Raven shook her head. "I didn't think to bring anything because the Madames said they would cover everything."

Destiny cut in before Markeysha could. "You know Markeysha is really into this shit. Her ass just had to go the extra mile."

"And did! This is a special occasion. This is my first float ride. I'm excited!" Markeysha wasn't ashamed to admit.

Alexis listened, trying to keep her mind from wandering, when her purse buzzed.

She muttered something about checking for more bottles of water in the cooler and excused herself, needing to answer her phone without the girls eavesdropping.

At her side of the float, Alexis dipped a hand into her clutch and pulled out her phone. Instead of a call, Tahir sent six text messages. She thumbed quickly through the thread, low-res shots but still clear enough to make out the details.

The first photo showed a low stone tomb, its face streaked with water stains. In front of it sat a bundle of candles lashed tight with thick twine. Bound against them was a wooden X, the same kind recovered at Milan's murder site. Its surface had been carved in deep, uneven strokes with that twisted chant.

She counted. Nine. Each candle a different color, a clash of hues. A few of the wicks leaned toward one another as if conspiring together, their tips blackened, split, and brittle from burning too long.

She scanned the background, searching for more, but the photo offered nothing else.

She swiped to the next photo, and it showed a different tomb.

It was taller than the last, its marble face darkened by rain and crowned with a stone cross that stabbed at the sky. Another wooden X rested at its base, identical to the first. Beside it sat an urn, wide-bodied and mottled gray, the rim blackened with soot. Inside, ashes curled around the charred remnants of paper. Ink had bled through the fibers, most of it burned away, but a few scorched words still clawed their way out.

…disposable.

…to be loved.

Alexis's jaw locked, teeth pressed until her molars ached. Her thumb hovered above the screen.

Then a sudden nudge knocked her off focus.

"Girl, I know you're not on that damn phone!" Destiny teased as she made her way around the partition.

Alexis let out a light laugh, brushing it off. "It's important. Just gimme a sec." She waved Destiny off gently, eyes already back on the screen.

Then Raven swooped in, grinning, and made a playful grab for Alexis's phone. "Uh-uh, no time for phones. We've got to get our side together like Destiny and Markeysha's."

Alexis leaned away just enough to dodge her. "Okay, just give me one minute." She angled her body toward the girls but kept the phone shielded in one palm, reluctant fingers hovering over the screen a moment longer.

"Alright, alright, I'm off my phone now." She held the phone out like evidence before tucking it into her clutch. "Now y'all gotta help me get this side together," she tossed the words out like a peace offering.

"We're a hot mess," Natalia laughed.

Markeysha cut in, eyes narrowing. "We? Natalia, girl, aren't you supposed to be with me and Destiny?"

"Ay, qué pena, niña. I was going to ask…"

Destiny waved her off. "Girl, if she wants to be over here, let her. Let them do them. Look a' that… they ain't even take the stuff out of the bags yet!"

"So that means, y'all aren't going to help us out?" Natalia posed, sipping her drink. "We left them bagged so you could sage them first for good luck." She giggled, then took another sip.

"Natty, don't nobody have time to play with you." Destiny rolled her eyes, already digging into a bag. "If you want me to help, then c'mon."

She started sorting. Markeysha joined in, hands moving on instinct.

The others followed. One by one, the throws dropped into place, their clatter thinning, laughter clipped, until the float seemed dressed in its own solemn choir. Then the door creaked open, a harsh slice through the hush.

"Hello, Blue Hearts," came Nevi's voice, smooth as velvet and just as rich. She stepped forward, Della and Rae closing in at her sides.

"I see you girls are still getting things situated." Della's tone was just short of scolding.

"Yeah, we lost track of time," Alexis replied, quick and polite. "Sorry, Madames."

"No need to apologize, sweetheart. Order always finds its way back, right?" Nevi's eyes swayed from Della to Rae.

"Right," Rae added with a soft lilt.

"Mmm-hmm," Della's agreement came low, unconvinced but letting it pass.

Natalia was still fussing with a stuffed bear, nudging it until it sat just right. Alexis caught the moment she looked up, her face softening and movements slowing, as the girls moved toward the door.

Natalia hurried to catch up with the others, who were clustering near the door, but sequins, feathers, and crowns slowed her steps.

"Madames!" Natalia beamed. "You three look stunning. Perfect!" Her eyes lingered on the porcelain masks edged in cobalt feathers, the gowns sheathed in sequins that shimmered like molten gold. Crowns glinted above each head. Della's sat high over soft, curled locs, their ends looping in delicate spirals. Nevi's rose above a bun wound tight and regal. Rae's rested atop a single braid wrapped around her head in a perfect halo.

Alexis found herself nodding along. Natalia was right, they did look perfect… too perfect. Almost artificial.

"No, dear," Rae corrected softly. "You girls are the stunning ones." Her attention moved across the corsets and tutus the way a collector might study their most prized possession. Satin cinched their waists. The tutus brushed their knees, flecked with glints of gold. Black leggings and gold ballet flats completed the look.

Every girl wore the same bold sweep of royal blue eyeshadow. Nude, glossy lips. Dewy skin with just enough highlighter to catch the light.

"Yes, you girls are beautiful." Nevi took in each of the girls, one at a time. "But I don't see our main girl." Her eyes swept the float. "Where is she?"

"Who?" Markeysha tilted her head. The drink had her floating a little, buzzy and grinning, not tracking the conversation at all.

Della cut her a look. "Jade!"

"She's not here yet, Madames," Raven spoke up. "But it's not a big deal. Y'all know that girl's always late."

"That's not good," Della snapped. "We've got under thirty minutes. We can't wait. She should have been here at least an hour ago."

Damn. Has an hour passed already?

That realization settled it for Alexis. The ground inside her seemed to give way. The hope she had held for Jade to show up collapsed with it. And in that moment, she added Jade's name to the list with the others. Another girl unaccounted for… on her watch.

"Well, someone will have to take her place," Alexis heard Nevi say, but her eyes stayed low.

Soft murmurs rippled through the group. Heads turned. Eyes darted.

"So… who?" Raven glanced around.

Rae didn't hesitate. "I think Alexis would be perfect."

Alexis blinked. Her shoulders tensed. "Wait… me?"

Rae stepped forward slightly, extending her hand like she was offering a benediction. "Don't act surprised. I've always said you should be the Crowned Heart. The grace. The strength. The space to be filled… you have all of it."

That last part snagged at Alexis. Wrong in a way the others didn't seem to hear. They nodded along, faces lit with easy agreement.

"Yeah, it should be Alexis, out of any of us," Natalia agreed.

"I—" Alexis started, but Della was already taking her arm, steering her forward.

"Come on, sweetheart. Let's get you in place."

The sudden hand on her arm jolted her forward, her balance breaking for a step before it caught again. They guided her past the float's partition, down a narrow corridor. Alexis ducked beneath the dip in the ceiling, slipping by the curtained bathroom until they stopped at a small arched door painted deep blue.

Della pressed her palm to it. It clicked open.

Inside was a short, winding stairwell. Velvet-wrapped rails. Wooden steps that creaked with each shift of weight. As Alexis climbed, the float's frame vibrated beneath her, pulsing with nerves and noise.

The stairwell led to a rounded hatch, just high enough to duck under. She slipped through sideways and stepped into the open air.

A velvet seat waited, royal blue and trimmed in gold. Two wide armrests rose and curled into cupped palms.

"That'll be your seat for the evening," Nevi told her. "Go on. Have a seat."

The Madames followed behind as Alexis moved to the throne. She eased into it, legs crossed.

"Comfy?" Rae asked.

"Mhm," Alexis forced out.

Then she felt something soft brush her head. Her fingers reached up, touched lace.

A veil.

Royal blue. Just like the papier-mâché bust of Lazuliè.

At the base of the seat sat a heavy, champagne colored tote. Della picked it up and placed it beside her with care.

"There are only so many of them. So give them out wisely. We'll be out here at least an hour and a half."

Then she stepped back, rejoining her sisters.

Rae moved forward next, holding a tall, gold crown shaped like cathedral spires, studded with blue stones. She lifted it gently and placed it on Alexis's head.

The crown was heavier than Alexis expected. Her neck pulled tight to hold it, shoulders squaring under the weight.

"We're moving!" Nevi called out as the float rumbled beneath them.

"So, it'll just be me up here… alone?" Alexis called after them, half-joking as she watched the Madames glide toward the door.

"We're just below. You'll be fine," Nevi called back as they disappeared down the stairwell, their heels clicking over the worn wooden steps, each hollow strike carrying down until the sound gave out.

Now alone, the applause and chatter faded into a blur. Alexis sat frozen, the crown pressing heavily, the veil fluttering at her shoulders. From this height, the world shrank.

She looked left, skimming the swelling crowd. Then forward.

Directly ahead, a float loomed, purple fringe dragging the street, faux tombs stacked high, lanterns flickering in shallow nooks. A crypt door painted across the rear gave way to a tangle of crosses and moss.

Her gaze climbed the paneling until the name revealed itself in gilt: *Krewe of Shadows.*

She studied it.

She turned.

Behind her?

Nothing.

The papier-mâché bust of Lazuliè blocked her view completely.

She seized the rare quiet, the sliver of privacy she figured she wouldn't get again.

She reached for her clutch, pulled out her phone, and picked up where she left off with the photos Tahir had sent.

She tried zooming in on the urn again, but the screen glitched and jumped ahead.

And landed on a new image.

A doll.

Propped up against the tomb.

Brown felt for skin. Blue overalls. A white shirt. Black yarn hair worked into waist-long braids, stitched down with uneven hands. A matte, red-tipped pin pierced its chest, holding a scrap of paper there, edges curled and burned, that damn rhyme scrawled across it.

What the fuck?!

She stared at it.

Dolls didn't usually scare her.

But this one?

Where the eyes should have been, the fabric gaped, torn unevenly. Threads curled back from the wounds, cotton exposed. The sight unsettled her.

Her hand dropped from the screen, and she quickly slid the phone back into her clutch.

The nausea came quietly, then deepened, spreading like dye in water.

She couldn't pin down what made her stomach turn, but something about it pressed against her. Half-memory. Half-mirror. She didn't know what it echoed, only that it did.

A gust of wind stirred suddenly, lifting the veil from her face just long enough to expose it to the crowd, then letting it fall again.

Alexis shook herself. The zydeco still played, gnawing on her nerves. Horns burst through it, bright, brash, and alive. The crowd's roar rose to meet them. The parade had begun.

She turned, catching the statue in her periphery. The paper-mâché Mistress rose high over the float, her body ending in a clean cut at the ribs. Her skin was painted matte onyx, dark enough to drink the light. Thick braids coiled tightly to her scalp, yet her face was erased beneath a royal blue veil, its folds sculpted into heavy, unnatural shapes, the edge trimmed in glinting gold. Across her bodice, the same blue stretched smooth. A single gold cuff bound her arm, gleaming cold against the calm she carried.

Set into the statue's torso was a small arched door, painted to match the float. Alexis knew what lay behind it: a stairwell that wound through the figure's hollow body, the passage she'd climbed to reach her seat. To ascend, she'd climbed through the figure's hollow chest.

Her arms reached forward with rigid intention, palms curved in presentation. The float extended its tribute to the city, an offering in royal blue: the Crowned Heart of Lazuliè, Alexis.

From her perch, Alexis hovered above it all. A doll on display. Fixed. Just out of reach.

And she alone would distribute the Krewe's most guarded gift, Lazuliè's Heart.

The Heart was a rare treasure, hand-carved from deep blue lapis lazuli, with veins speckled with gold. A polished wooden dagger, its handle studded with Swarovski crystals, pierced the middle, turning it from a trinket into a relic. Across the Heart, the words "Krewe of Lazuliè" were embossed in elegant gold script.

Collectors came from all corners of the city, hoping to catch one.

Now, all of them were in Alexis's possession.

She felt the weight of one in her hand as she looked through the crowd, landing on a little girl, perched high on her father's shoulders.

"This one's for you, sweetheart," Alexis called, leaning over to drop the Heart into the child's tiny, trembling hands.

The girl screamed in delight. Her father lifted her even higher, and the crowd around them erupted in cheers.

The float rolled forward.

Zydeco thundered from the speakers. Beads rained down like hail. Plush gators, feathered boas, sparkling cups, and trinkets of every kind poured from the float as hands reached from the mass below, clamoring for more. Around them, people moved with the music, sipping their drinks as they watched the show. The shine of celebration spilled down the street, festive spirit twinkling in every corner.

She stepped carefully from the statue's palm. Her body seized. The ache came again in the center of her chest, worrisome now for how often it returned.

Her hand closed on the Heart, that blue stone slick as river water, heavy with more than its own weight. The ache vanished as suddenly as it came, leaving her breathless in its wake.

She steadied, bent forward, and placed a Heart into the waiting hands of a man who had shadowed the float.

"Thank you, queen!" he shouted, voice rising above the music.

She straightened, easing herself back onto the throne.

Then the float jolted to a stop. Hard.

The crowd roared on, but nothing moved.

Seconds ticked. Silent. Still.

Then it lurched forward again in one quick jerk and slipped back into its smooth crawl.

Alexis pulled out her phone.

What the hell was that?

A second later, Raven texted back:

Idk. Prob just stopping floats so ppl can cross.

"I guess," Alexis muttered, sliding the phone back into her purse.

She lifted her chin, easing back into character. Smile. Wave. From left to right, she gave the crowd what they expected.

"Just gotta hang on for a few more blocks," she told herself as she swiveled.

Her cheeks ached from holding it, lips pulled too tight, jaw stiff with effort.

She tossed another Heart to a boy holding a wrinkled sign that read, "My mom was a Crowned Heart in 1996."

He caught it with both hands, his face lit with raw excitement.

The float rolled on, carrying the last calm of the crowd with it before slipping into its own shadow.

Golden hour rotted into evening.

Shadows stretched long over faces, catching glitter and sweat until everyone shimmered with the same fevered shine.

The parade fractured, becoming feral. The bass pounded loose, wild and uncontained. A woman screamed with laughter, baring her chest for a string of plastic-colored pearls. Close by, another dropped to her knees in the street, drink spilling on her blouse. Two men fought in the crowd, swinging wildly as loose feathers from boas fluttered around them.

Alexis had seen Mardi Gras chaos before… the drunks, the fights, the noise… but this was different. The crowd below pressed against the rails. The air had grown sour, smelling of beer, sweat, perfume, and the tang of metal. Voices blended into one endless cry of "Throw me one!" "Over here!" "Blue Heart!" until it became a single, raw, hungry sound. Hands shot up, clawing for her, for the Hearts, for anything that sparkled.

Alexis caught a glimpse of a man falling, the sea of bodies trampling him. His muffled cries went unheard as they kept moving, reaching for Alexis, drunk on the spirit of Carnival. She clutched the last Heart tightly. When she leaned forward to throw it, the crowd surged again, shouting and grabbing, a tangle of noise that didn't sound human anymore.

The float sailed through the chaos.

Their fury tangled with the sirens and horns until the noise became a single fever, swelling through the street.

And then, the beat stuttered to a halt. The crowd's roar dipped low, flattened, like the street had been swallowed whole.

She scanned the sea of faces, too many, too fast, each one open-mouthed, shouting, laughing, begging, but silent.

Then came a voice, low, static-laced, too close yet distant all at once.

A whisper in her right ear.

"Alexis."

She turned her head.

There she was.

Lazuliè.

She stood in the middle of the crowd, untouched by the frenzy. The chaos broke around her.

She looked like she'd walked straight out of Alexis's dream. That same deep blue lace dress stretched over skin the color of river clay. That veil lay flat against her eyes, hiding whatever waited underneath.

Blood dripped freely from her hands, her arms hanging limp at her sides. Her cheeks were streaked with thick black sludge that ran in endless streams. Her mouth curved faintly, holding the ghost of a smile that dared Alexis to keep looking.

Alexis couldn't make sense of what she saw. Her mind rejected it, tried to explain it away. A mask. Or maybe a trick of light.

She blinked, and the space she'd filled folded in on itself.

But she wasn't gone. Not yet.

"Alexis."

This time, Alexis heard her from the left.

She turned.

Now Lazuliè stood in the crowd on the other side of the street.

Then the image glitched.

Lazuliè bled through the crowd, face after face.

From one bystander to the next.

Each one momentarily became her.

Until she was right below the float, directly beneath Alexis, looking up.

Her mouth opened.

"Give in to me. Surrender your pain."

The voice fractured into seven tones.

Alexis shut her eyes. When she looked again, the Mistress was gone. Something stirred close, halting her as she turned. The bust above loomed larger than before. The veil quivered, folds drooping and swaying. The carved shoulders seemed to lift, then settle again. Alexis's thoughts scattered. Her mind tried to remind her that statues cannot move, but her eyes insisted this one just had.

Then—

Alexis glanced down. Her phone glowed in her lap. Raven had sent her a message: *Are the Madames up there with you?*

The Heart slipped from her fingers before she even registered dropping it. It struck the float deck with a hollow, wooden knock.

The last Heart of Lazuliè split clean through the center.

She stared down at it, her fingers twitching but refusing to bend.

She stood slowly, one hand gripping the statue's base to steady herself.

Her legs felt slow, light, too tight to trust.

She didn't want to move.

Didn't want to step through that door again.

But she had to.

She turned toward the entrance carved into the statue's chest, arched and dark, veiled in shadow.

The same door through which she came to ascend.

The same one that the Madames disappeared behind.

It looked different now. Something inside kept battering the frame, making the bust quake with each blow.

She moved anyway.

One step.

Then another.

The tambourines faded behind her.

She reached the threshold. Her hand brushed the frame.

It felt warm.

Then she crossed through.

Back through the body of Lazuliè.

Back to the girls.

Back to whatever was waiting.

Voices echoed ahead. Laughter.

Alexis stepped onto the lower deck.

Raven spotted her first.

She sat on a bench near the rail, chugging water, makeup smudged, one earring missing.

Phone in hand. Screen still lit.

"You good?" Raven watched Alexis rush toward her.

"Yeah," she huffed. "I'm good. Have you seen the Madames?"

Raven shook her head. "Nah. You?"

Alexis turned to the rest.

"Y'all seen them?"

The girls barely registered the question.

One of the girls giggled. Another burped.

They buzzed from the adrenaline and from the daiquiris, one too many. Laughter spilled easily. Limbs loose.

Raven sucked her teeth. "These hoes drunk. Can't hold liquor for shit. They not built like me."

She tapped her chest and grinned, then frowned again.

Alexis raised her voice, louder now, not to anyone in particular. "When's the last time anybody saw them?"

A few girls blinked. One shrugged.

Raven shrugged, too. "I don't know. After that big throw, maybe? Before the float paused?"

Almost on cue, the float came to another halt. Alexis looked outside to see that they'd finally made it to the end of the route.

The float barn was right ahead.

"What's happening?" Natalia slurred, trying to stand up.

"Ride's over, girls," Raven announced. "Get y'all shit together and get ready to get off."

"Okay." Natalia tried to walk over and tripped over one of the thick plastic bags that the beads had once been in.

"Come on now," Raven hollered, throwing her hands up. "Now I know good and damn well y'all hoes not that drunk off no damn daiquiris."

Just then, the float roared back to life, this time with a slow start.

It was the Krewe of Lazuliè float's turn to enter the barn.

Alexis left the girls. She was headed back upstairs to call Tahir.

The Madames were missing. At some point, they must've slipped off the float.

She needed to let Tahir know to have all units on alert after seeing those photos herself. She was now sure they were at least accomplices in whatever the hell was going on.

As she made it to the front of the float just past the makeshift restroom, she felt her phone buzz. It was still in her hand. She turned it over to look at the name on the screen and instantly felt the blood pumping through her veins run ice cold.

It was Jade.

Her heart sank to her stomach.

She swiped to answer. "Jade?" She wasn't sure if the voice that'd reply would be hers… or someone else's.

What came first was breath. Fast. Ragged. Unsteady.

Then the voice, splintered with panic.

"Alexis, listen to me. You have to come. Now."

"Wait, what's going on?"

"I don't have time to explain! Just come. Come now!"

"Where are you?"

"The manor. Please, just come. Hurry!"

The call ended, leaving Alexis staring at her own reflection in the dark glass.

Then she lifted her head.

Around her, the warehouse pulsed with leftover energy. Prop carts rolled. Riders laughed. Voices crooned, horns blared, drums rattled, all of it crashing together at once. Yet none of it touched her.

She turned toward the exit. Her veil fluttered behind her.

"Alexis!"

Destiny's slightly slurred voice chased her across the floor.

"You're not waiting for the shuttle? It's on the way!"

"I can't—I have to go. It's urgent."

"Wait, what? Girl—"

She was already gone, ballet flats smacking the pavement.

She pulled out her phone. Called Tahir.

It rang.

Once.

Twice.

Three times…

Voicemail.

Her heart hit harder. She didn't hesitate.

"Hey, it's me. Jade just called. She's at the House of Lazuliè. Sounded scared, but she wouldn't say what was wrong."

She paused beneath a warehouse floodlight.

The shadows made her skin look off. Uneven.

"Nevi, Della, and Rae aren't on the float. I think they slipped out during the route. They might be at the manor, too. Could be holding her."

She started walking again. Fast.

"I'm heading there now. Meet me as soon as you get this. But hold off on backup. Let's get a clean look first… just you and me."

She stopped only long enough to hang up, then tore the crown from her head, the veil with it, and flung them down. They landed in a heap. She never looked back.

Her pace broke into a run, lungs burning, urgency driving her across the lot toward her car and whatever waited in the dark halls of the House of Lazuliè.

CHAPTER 15

The house crouched across the street, its columns pale as bone. The windows stared back at her, black sockets rimmed in lamplight, glass swollen. The iron fence curved inward, bars bent like teeth waiting to close.

Alexis gripped the wheel tighter. The longer she stared, the more the house seemed to press forward.

Then she spotted the car parked crooked at the curb. Trunk yawning wide. A mouth mid-scream.

Jade's?

The question snapped her loose.

Her body jolted into motion, a reflex after too much stillness. She killed the engine and slid her hand into the center console, closing on cold steel. She stepped out with the gun already in her grip. Layers of tulle snagged against the doorframe; she tore it free in one quick motion, the rip cracking through the night. She dropped the tutu onto the driver's seat and slammed the door, the sound sealing softness away.

She crossed the asphalt in measured strides, the weight in her hand steady. Behind her, a streetcar rattled by, wheels shrieking against the rails before fading into the distance. Farther off, carnival music drifted, brass and drums pulsing steady beneath the night. She looked left, then right, scanning the row of porches and parked cars as she advanced. With every step, the sound thinned, the Mardi Gras madness fading one block at a time.

She moved toward the car at the curb, weapon raised, her steps cautious. Crouching down, she peeked inside.

Empty.

She moved closer to it and placed her free hand on the hood. It was still hot. She glanced behind her briefly then moved forward.

At the brick walkway, she swept the fence line, corners checked as she advanced. The pavers shifted beneath her gold ballet flats, uneven stone grating underfoot. The wrought-iron gate sighed open just enough for her to slip through, its hinge groaning faintly against the night.

She climbed the front steps. Every motion was strained by the boning of her corset biting into her sides.

Ahead, the manor's front door stood ajar, black panel outlined in glass, the brass hardware catching stray light in a dull glow.

She faltered at the threshold. She was supposed to stake out from the street and wait for Tahir. But the open door dragged at her, logic fraying with every inch of its gape.

She knew something was off. Whatever it was wanted her to notice. She gave it what it wanted and went in.

Gun raised, Alexis eased through the threshold. Darkness flexed around her, walls swelling then sinking.

As she neared the door, her voice cracked clean through the quiet.

"Police! Hands up where I can see!"

Finger resting along the trigger guard. Eyes slicing through every inch of shadow.

She moved down the hall, each step measured, gun close but low.

She worked the hall room by room, clearing each bedroom and bathroom as she went.

She kept moving, following the corridor as it opened toward the grand room. She paused at the entrance, breath catching when she noticed the sliding doors shivering in their frame. Slowly, they pulled apart. Amber light spilled out, framing a figure as it slipped through.

Jade.

Relief surged through Alexis, cracking something open inside her. She lowered the gun.

"Jade!" The name tore out on a ragged breath.

She moved toward her, quick steps she barely registered. She was so flooded with relief she could've wrapped Jade in her arms.

"They have Abram."

The words cut through her warmth, clean and merciless. Alexis froze, the relief collapsing into something cold.

"The Madames?"

"Yes! They're downstairs." Jade jabbed a finger toward the foyer stairs. "The crematorium. You need to hurry."

A chill gripped her neck, and instinct took over. Measured steps. Steady aim. Breath held to the count.

"Get behind me."

She led Jade down the hall in a low crouch, knees bent and gun raised, her breath steady until the hidden door to the crematorium came into view. Alexis reached for the knob. This time, it opened. A drumbeat thumped from below. Faint, but constant.

She signaled Jade to stay close. They descended the staircase, shadows rising around them as they sank deeper into the house's belly. Candlelight shivered over the walls. The steps glistened like wet teeth.

"Get down," she whispered to Jade as they made it to the last few steps. Crouched just high enough to see over the wrought-iron railing, Alexis took in the sight before her.

Candles burned in a ring around a throne of bark, roots clawing up through the floor.

A bed sat in the corner.

Abram writhed, limbs bound to each post, ball gag wedged between his teeth, forehead glistening with sweat. His muffled scream barely rose above the drums that pounded through the walls.

The Madames stood barefoot in their undergarments, skin slick beneath the light. Nevi towered with arms raised while Della and Rae knelt by the circle of flames.

Then she saw Della parting from her sisters and heading toward Abram. She stopped in front of a nearby table, reaching for something Alexis couldn't see. Alexis shifted her stance, gun angled low, ready.

Alexis's jaw locked, a bitter taste rising in her mouth. She wasn't sure if it was fear or fury. Maybe both.

Jade stayed beside her, silent.

Her pulse slowed, every sound narrowing. The drums. The shallow breathing beside her. The sound of her own heartbeat counting down.

She sank deeper into the lair.

"Police!" she yelled, aiming her weapon at Nevi's back. "Don't move!"

The Madames turned.

Hands lifted, palms exposed.

Nevi glanced at Alexis's weapon, then at her stance. The faintest strain entered her voice.

"An officer of the law." She was amused. "Well now… that explains so much."

Rae's lips parted in a grin. "Told you there was something special about this one."

Nevi didn't respond right away. The stillness around her broke only in the twitch of her jaw.

"And here I thought I'd read every kind of woman that crossed my path." She tilted her head, studying Alexis as if searching for the oversight. "Should've seen it from the start… This changes things."

Della moved first. Calm. Certain. She placed a hand on Nevi's arm, her smile all faith and teeth.

"It won't," she murmured. "You worry too easily. Mistress Lazuliè has walked us out of tighter corners than this." Her hand fell away as she stepped forward, slow and low.

Alexis leveled the gun at Della's chest. "Stay the fuck back. I promise you I won't think twice about pulling this trigger."

Della stopped, though the smirk on her face stayed in motion.

Nobody rushed her. For a second, that felt like control.

She took another step into the room.

"Somebody tell me what the fuck is going on."

No answer from Rae. Only that lazy simper.

Then Nevi spoke, light and warm: "Nyoka, darling?"

Alexis stiffened. "Who's—"

Cutting her off, the girl beside her responded. "Yes, Madame Nevi?"

Her tone changed. High. Lilting. Almost sing-song, dancing where Jade's voice had never danced.

Nevi nodded. "Now, sweetheart."

Now?

The word snagged, but it was too late.

The needle struck her neck before her mind caught up. The room spun instantly.

Jade… Nyoka… stood there, syringe in hand, steady as if she'd done this several times before.

Alexis's stomach clenched, and each tender moment with the girl fell apart inside her. Faith. Loyalty. Trust. Each one eroded before the truth came out. It had all been a lie.

She tried to bring the gun up, but the world tilted instantly, candlelight smearing into dizzy spirals. Her knees wavered, each step a battle to stay upright. She managed one stagger forward before the haze closed in.

The gun slipped from Alexis's hand.

She fell hard. The ground didn't catch her so much as it claimed her. Cold shot through her side.

The last thing she saw was Della smiling as she bent low, fingers curling around the weapon Alexis could no longer hold.

Heat prickled along her limbs, then nothing. She could feel herself shutting down, piece by piece. Her mind screamed orders her body ignored.

Blackness. Void. An infinite abyss.

Alexis floated there in the dark, numb to everything but sight and sound.

Then faint and distant, like voices behind glass, the words drifted through.

"Nou twa nou bay."

—We three have given. —

Pssshhht.

A match strike.

Blue flames flared across the void, carving a heart into the dark.

The heart pulsed, glowing blue.

Every word struck, dissonant and unresolved. Yet, it was beautiful in its wrongness, vibrating with a pull that demanded Alexis to lean in.

"Souf ak doulè, chak baryè nou louvri."

— Breath and sorrow at each gate, risen. —

Pssshhht.

Another spark.

The rod appeared, piercing the heart from crown to base. The dark hissed as the rod held.

"Nan zo ak sann, dèt nou siyen."

—In bone and ash, our debt is sealed. —

Pssshhht.

Third strike.

From the rod's tips, fleur-de-lis bloomed in fire. Silent flowers curling open.

Something old inside Alexis lit up, an ache she'd buried beneath steel and duty.

"Baron Samedi, fè chemen an parèt."

—Baron Samedi, let the path be revealed.—

Pssshhht.

Fourth strike.

Spirals expanded from the heart, thin as frost on glass.

The pull was in her marrow now, reaching for her grief, for the scars beneath the ones people could see.

"Papa Legba, soti nan fèmen ak lapriyè…"

—Papa Legba, from lock and plea…—

Pssshhht.

Fifth match.

More curlicues, winding faster, dancing from the divided heart.

They twisted outward in spirals, doubling over themselves, a glowing root system etching through shadow.

Through them, you could see what lay on the other side of the darkness.

Not all at once. Just glimpses. Slits between the spirals.

First, the sky.

Or something like it.

A ceiling of storm clouds hung low and swollen, charcoal gray streaked with electric blue.

Lightning flashed inside it, its branching forks firing as synapses in the mind of a deity.

Behind them was a cobalt haze.

It pulsed and stretched, veiling everything in a deep ocean glow.

"pa manda san,"

—By blood's decree, —

Pssshhht.

Sixth flame.

The fire deepened.

The spirals' outward surge continued.

The blue light ate through what remained of the dark.

The cobalt haze expanded.

It soaked the air, curling into everything.

"Lage Lazuliè lib!"

—Set Lazuliè free! —

Pssshhht.

Final strike.

The veve erupted in lacework, burning open until the dark was completely effaced, giving way to a crack in the pressure.

Wind howled through the realm, whipping from every direction before suddenly falling silent.

Then Nevi's voice rained down.

"Maitrès Lazuliè… Tanpri sòti vin ranmase ofrann ou yo…"

—Mistress Lazuliè… Please come out to collect your offerings…—

The haze began to clear in shuddering waves.

The cobalt thinned into a blackness so deep it felt like the void had returned.

Below it was an ocean. Blackened. Endless.

Formed of centuries of tears.

The water didn't ripple. It *lamented*, bleeding upward in slow motion.

Then the wind fell silent.

And she began to ascend, her head emerging first.

Her dark blue lace dress shimmered with sorrow.

She no longer wore a veil.

Where her eyes should've been was only ruin.

Deep, weeping hollows, blackness spilling toward her chin.

Her mouth was void of expression, but the corners had been cut, slashes curling upward, making her look locked in an emotion she no longer felt.

The sound in the haze thinned to a low drone.

It was as if the entire land of the ancestors waited for her to speak.

For it was at that moment she would call… and expect an answer.

"Surrender to me."

Against Alexis's will, her body responded.

Her chest unfurled, ribs blooming outward.

She leaned into the moment.

No pain.

No shame.

No doubt.

Everything burned away.

She was ready to say yes.

Yet, in that stillness, something crept through.

A warmth slipping under the door of her mind.

A voice she knew before she knew language.

You've always had a big heart.

The echo wrapped around her, threading through the pull, through the pressure.

This city needs that heart.

The words landed deep within Alexis, in a place where memory and longing blurred.

Something inside her reached toward it without thinking.

A scream split through that place.

The Mistress's cry shook the void in every register of grief, seduction, rage, jealousy, vengeance, longing, and despair. The echoes tore through her mind, through the floor, through the foundation. Each note pierced a separate wound.

Instead of resisting, Alexis went limp.

The void folded into an amber glow. Heat pressed back into her skin. She could feel again.

Rope bit her wrists. Bark dug through her clothes.

Her fingers twitched, then her jaw. Her legs were free, but she didn't move. She waited, coiled between stillness and spring.

She opened her eyes just a sliver. Dim light seeped in, shapes edging into focus. The chair beneath her rose from the floor like something grown, not built. Her spine stayed rigid, head tilted forward, chin slightly lifted.

From that angle, she saw them.

Rae. Nevi. Della. Abram.

All were there… except the girl she had known as Jade.

The corner where Jade had stood before was empty now.

Alexis scanned the rest of the room, but she was nowhere to be found. Then she looked for her gun and didn't see it anywhere.

She forced herself to stay limp, to let her pulse slow, her chest lifting and falling with the shallow rhythm of someone not yet awake.

Rae stepped forward with a golden tray held in both hands, arms stiff with ceremony. A dagger rested on top, its blade curved.

She knelt and lifted the tray.

Nevi approached, took the dagger without looking at Alexis. With one slow motion, she dragged the edge across the rope. The fibers split. The binding slipped down.

Still, Alexis didn't move.

Nevi returned the dagger to the tray. The metal kissed the gold with a dull clink. The tray stayed level in Rae's grip, but her hands trembled almost imperceptibly, a minor fracture in the performance of grace.

Della stepped forward next, kneeling on the stone. She held a shallow ceramic bowl; its rim etched with faint markings. When she tipped it, a coarse powdery substance fell in a slow trail, beginning to take shape across the floor.

The pour was meant to be smooth, but her hands shook. The powder spattered like spilled bone. She clutched the bowl tighter.

That's when Alexis saw it.

A glint caught Alexis's eye. Wedged in the powder near the bowl's rim, lay a bracelet, half-buried and warped by heat. The metal was blackened but intact, its charms clinging stubbornly to the band. Stars… maybe a moon.

She closed her eyes and drew one careful breath, steadying the tremor in her hands.

Then the door slammed open.

"Alexis! ALEXIS!"

Tahir burst through the door, weapon raised, every muscle wired tight. His eyes swept the dimly lit space, searching for her.

Della moved first. The bowl left her hand in a flash, spinning wildly. It missed his head by inches and shattered against the wall. Ash drifted down like bone dust.

Rae recoiled, eyes widening. "Della!" she hissed, but Della was already reaching for another weapon that wasn't there.

Tahir stepped forward, one arm braced, the other steady on the trigger. His boots crunched over glass.

Rae snatched a champagne bottle from the altar and hurled it. It hit the floor at his feet, bursting into foam. He staggered back, arm jerking up to shield his face from the spray.

That was all Nevi needed. She pulled a small vial from her pocket, tapped powder into her palm, and blew it hard into Tahir's face.

Tahir winced. His pupils widened, his step faltering as the powder took hold. He blinked hard, once, twice, then staggered. His vision blurred. He tried to lift his arm again but veered sideways, striking the doorframe with his shoulder. A cough tore out of him, dry and ragged.

Alexis knew this was her moment. Her focus tightened, every muscle bracing for what came next.

Time to move.

She drove forward and grabbed the dagger from the tray.

The Madames froze at first.

Then Nevi stepped forward. She tried to keep her composure, but the slight tremble in her voice gave her away. "Please, dear. Midnight's almost here. Don't make this any uglier than it needs to be."

Behind her, the twin-bell clock ticked. Loud.

Rae's tone turned syrupy. "It's not forever, Alexis. She just needs a moment. That's all. Just let her in for a little while."

Alexis stared.

"You reckless little strumpet!" Della spat. "You should've been the one whose throat I slit!"

With fury driving her forward, she lunged.

"Just knock her out again so Lazuliè can finish!" Nevi pleaded.

Della's hands clawed for Alexis's face with the single-minded desperation of a zealot trying to restore divine order.

Fingers grazed skin.

A gasp caught between them.

Then Alexis slashed. The blade met flesh, tearing a clean line across Della's cheek.

From the cut, fine creases spread. The flesh around it slackened, tugging downward as the hidden years worked their way through. Alexis's eyes locked on the change, but she had no time to process it. She kept moving.

Nevi and Rae stumbled back, horror bleeding onto their faces as they took in what Alexis had done to their sister… what the blade had revealed.

Alexis turned. Abram lay slumped but alert, one hand twitching toward the edge of the bed.

"Can you run?" she asked as she cut his bindings.

He nodded.

"Then go. Now!"

He didn't hesitate. Once free, he bolted for the stairwell, shirtless and barefoot in nothing but boxers.

A sound tore through the chamber. It was long and low. Mournful.

It surged, rattling every stone.

Alexis's spine arched, a tremor rattling through her skull.

The walls shook. The altar groaned.

Then she looked—

The clock.

Its twin bells vibrating, arms frozen at midnight.

Playing a dirge made of metal and memory.

The floor cracked beneath the veve, right at the rod, splitting the heart clean in two.

Nevi clutched her face.

Skin peeled back in glistening, wet curls. Beneath it, her features buckled and sagged, the exposed layers red and raw.

A wet gasp slipped out of her, bubbling through what had once been lips.

Rae staggered.

Both hands cradled her stomach like it held something trying to escape.

She doubled over, spine jerking in unnatural pulses.

Blood foamed at the corners of her mouth, followed by a wet, choking retch.

Della's face warped to a smear, one eye drooping, the other bulging wide.

She reached for the altar.

There was still pride in her posture, even as her body crumbled into ruin.

Her fingers knocked the base of a candle.

Flame met fabric.

The fire grew.

She leaned in, welcoming the burn. It was the only mercy left.

Nevi and Rae turned toward her, faces breaking open with acceptance, and allowed the fire to take them too.

It spread unnaturally fast.

The tree-throne groaned low, then collapsed inward.

The altar cracked.

Across the crematorium wall, the mirror flickered with a strange blue light.

The glow blinked out, leaving a churning void that devoured all reflection.

The atmosphere became brittle and charged.

The house was dying around them.

Flames feasted on the walls as they climbed.

"Alexis? Shit!" Tahir rasped, coughing hard. "We gotta do something."

He lurched forward, burying his nose and mouth into the crook of his elbow. His other hand swept out ahead of him, searching, until his palm struck brick slick with heat. A wet, choking sound ripped from his throat.

Alexis started toward the fire, eyes cutting over the blaze for something to use. Then she stopped. Went still for half a beat. When she moved again, it was toward Tahir.

Alexis caught his outstretched hand before he could stumble farther.

"C'mon. I've got you."

He staggered with her, teeth clenched, muttering a curse as the fire roared closer, but he didn't fight her grip.

Alexis hauled Tahir through the chamber, step by step, dragging him toward the stairwell. His legs buckled more than moved, his body half-limp against her side. The climb was brutal. Each step dragged pain up her thighs, but she didn't stop until they reached the main level. She pressed him against the wall, her body tense and unsteady.

"I have to grab the evidence."

Tahir snapped his head toward her. "Alexis, we don't have time!"

"I'll be right back!" She was already moving. "I know where it is."

She took the stairs two at a time. Smoke smeared the upstairs hallway as she slammed into the photo room, eyes already cutting to the corner. The album sat where she'd left it. There. She snatched it up and kept moving.

Without slowing, she veered to the door beside the backdrop and shoved it open.

Inside, the alterations room was thick with smoke. She coughed, swallowing heat as she pushed forward.

She yanked open the drawer where she'd found it before. The notepad was gone.

She blinked hard, leaning closer, her mind refusing the truth her eyes had already delivered.

Desperation surged through her as she tore the room apart.

Bins crashed to the floor, fabric ripped from hangers, silk ribbons unspooled like guts. Lace scattered like shed skin.

Smoke crawled up the walls as she emptied the final drawer.

No notepad.

A raw scream tore from her chest, shaking the room.

She stumbled back into the hall, coughing, eyes streaming. She thrust the photo album into Tahir's hands.

"Take this. I'll be right back."

"Where the hell are you going?" Tahir hollered as Alexis started back toward the staircase.

"I need to get that notepad. I think it's in one of their rooms," she rasped. "Just stay here. I'll make it quick."

"You are so damn stubborn," he barked, fumes burning his throat. Tahir squared himself, pain written across his face. "We. Don't. Have. Time."

Down the hallway, smoke punched through the crematorium doors.

She looked, calculation flashing behind her eyes. Alone, she might've risked it, but not with Tahir.... not in the state he was in.

She grabbed his hand and ran.

The fire moved with purpose now. Floorboards curled. Plaster buckled. A chandelier in the foyer let out one final screech before crashing in a shower of sparks. The walls bent, groaning deep and slow.

The front door sagged as they shoved it open. Flames snapped at their heels, chasing them out before the house could swallow itself whole.

Behind them, the House of Lazuliè released a long, shuddering moan and collapsed, dragging every ember and memory down in its ruin.

On the sidewalk, Alexis bent forward, one hand resting on her thigh. Next to her, Tahir was dragging his forearm across his mouth, his shoulders shaking.

He stooped before his own body had settled, reached for her, and missed at first. Then he caught her arm and guided her upright with a gentle pull. His hand rested on her shoulder for a moment before sliding to her cheek. His thumb brushed her skin, smearing ash.

"You okay?" he asked, breath still rough.

She hesitated, but her eyes stayed on his.

Then she nodded. "Ye—yeah. I'm good… You?"

A small smile pulled at his mouth. He lowered his chin.

He dropped his hand from her face, then removed his radio from his belt, thumb hitting the orange button first, then the side button.

"Dispatch, what's my updated ETA on fire and EMS? You got any additional units started this way yet?"

A staticky voice came through the speaker, "10-4. Two units en route, along with Fire and EMS… All available units, start that way."

Tahir turned toward the House of Lazuliè.

Alexis turned too. Where the manor had stood, only ash and ruin remained.

CHAPTER 16

Alexis stood still as the sun pressed against her skin, the heat settling over her with a stubborn, unwelcome hold. Sweat gathered at her temples and slid down the side of her face. She smoothed her palms down the front of her slacks.

A hand brushed the small of her back.

She looked left. Tahir stood beside her, tall enough that his shadow cut clean across her shoulder. His sleeves were rolled just above his elbows, forearms streaked with sweat and sun.

"Breathe," he told her. "You're good."

She nodded once. "Yeah."

A faint breeze moved behind them, followed by the low whir of the doors parting.

Captain Landry stepped out first, her posture straight as ever, and beside her came a man in a pressed white shirt that gleamed against honey-brown skin. The brass at his collar found the sun, throwing off a brief gleam before he adjusted his navy cap. Even from where Alexis stood, she could feel the weight of command around him.

Alexis and Tahir shifted aside as the two approached.

"Sergeant. Detective." The man's voice carried without effort as he turned to offer Tahir his hand.

Tahir met it with a firm shake.

"Great job on the case," he told him.

"Yes, sir."

Then he turned toward Alexis and extended his hand to her. "Both of you."

"Thank you, sir," she managed.

"Two of our best," Captain Landry added, turning with a nod before facing the crowd.

That was the moment Alexis truly felt the room turn toward them: the eyes on them, the cameras, the waiting faces, the microphones sprouting like metal weeds from the podium ahead. She'd seen it all from the start, but now every flash and murmur landed harder. It was time.

She looked out over the developing crowd. Behind the barricade, reporters clustered together, some talking to their cameramen, others flipping through notepads, pens ready.

Beyond them stood the families, clustered shoulder to shoulder, hands locked around wrists and elbows.

She noticed a man in a light-blue ball cap rocking gently on the balls of his feet, wiping his face with his sleeve, eyes fixed on the pavement.

As she kept scanning the crowd, something else caught her off guard. A girl stood near the front in a faded T-shirt printed with Kayla's face, the words *Have You Seen Me?* stretched thin across the cotton. A sting rose at the bridge of her nose, and her eyes watered before she could stop them. She looked down, gathered herself, and willed the tremor out of her throat.

When she lifted her head again, Superintendent Deveraux was already stepping to the microphone.

"Good afternoon. I'm Superintendent Walter Deveraux of the New Orleans Police Department. Thank you for being here. Today, we're releasing what we can confirm at this stage regarding the Krewe of Lazuliè and the recent fire at their headquarters. Captain Marlene Landry from Homicide will lead the briefing, joined by key members of our investigative team. We'll take a few questions afterward, time permitting."

He stepped back, and Captain Landry moved to the mic.

Her white uniform shirt caught the glare of the cameras, the fabric stiff with starch. The gold bars at her shoulders flashed each time she moved. She looked composed, but Alexis could see fatigue just beneath the surface. Her jaw stayed tight, her hand flexing once at her side before settling again.

When she spoke, her voice came blunt but measured. "At approximately twelve fifteen Wednesday morning, a structure fire was reported in the sixteen-hundred block of Saint Charles Avenue, at the property historically known as the House of Lazuliè," Landry said. "The cause of the fire is still under investigation. Human remains were recovered at the scene and are pending official identification."

Click. Flash. Murmurs.

"Based on early forensic analysis and evidence recovered so far, we believe the deceased to be Geneviève, Désirée, and Adelaide Meaux, direct descendants of the family that originally founded the Krewe of Lazuliè. The exact cause of death remains under investigation. We are working closely with the Fire Marshal and the Coroner's Office to determine the sequence of events leading up to the blaze."

A low wave of murmurs moved through the crowd; Alexis caught fragments she couldn't make out.

"A photo album was recovered at the scene," Landry continued, eyes steady on the press. "The contents are under review. We are working to determine whether the individuals pictured have any connection to ongoing or historical missing-persons cases."

A reporter near the front raised his hand halfway, then spoke over the hush. "Have any of the women in the album been confirmed missing?"

Superintendent Deveraux stepped forward at once, tone clipped. "We'll take questions after the full briefing."

Landry didn't move. "We're not prepared to comment on that at this time. The review process is ongoing."

More flashes. Reporters leaned forward. She tapped the corner of her notepad once, then lifted her eyes to the cameras.

"This investigation was already underway before Wednesday's events," Landry continued. "We believe it may be connected to a broader pattern involving several individuals and locations. We are working with our federal partners to process evidence and pursue all viable leads." She paused, then glanced toward Alexis. "And now we'll hear from Detective Gabrielle Rochon."

The name hit her the same way it always did. A little too formal. It still carried the weight that came with being in trouble. She shook off the wince and stepped forward, squaring her shoulders. The crowd waiting beyond the podium didn't feel much different; she could already sense the judgment, the questions, the heat.

"I'm Detective Rochon," she began. "I want to start by saying this case means a lot to me… and to the department as a whole."

Her fingers brushed her waistband, and she cleared her throat to steady herself. When she spoke again, her tone had changed. Now it was firmer and cooler, the detective stepping forward.

"We are investigating ten cases originally reported as missing persons in connection with this matter. One of those cases, Milan Richardson, was confirmed deceased. Her remains were recovered on February eleventh."

Alexis wiped a line of sweat from her brow and shifted her stance, a small but restless movement. She wanted to say more, to name what the badge wouldn't let her, but she caught herself and drew a steady breath instead.

"Another of those cases, Jennifer Wright, was located alive. She remains in serious condition and is receiving care at an undisclosed facility."

A ripple moved through the crowd. Alexis scanned the faces watching her. Some were hollowed by grief. Others showed anger, straining to stay contained. Pens moved, cameras clicked, the restless shuffle of bodies filling the quiet.

"We're seeking information on a woman currently known as Jade Green," Alexis stated. "She is considered a person of interest and may have played a role in the operation."

Tahir stepped in beside her, dark suit, eyes like stone. He didn't wait for the crowd to settle. "We believe 'Jade Green' is an alias."

Alexis added, voice calm and controlled. "She may also be using the name Nyoka. At this stage, we can't confirm if that's another alias or not."

Tahir pressed on. "If anyone recognizes this individual or has information on her whereabouts, we urge you to contact the tip line immediately."

He lifted the blown-up photo that was hiding behind the podium. Jade's face filled the frame. Her hair pulled back, mouth set, eyes distant. Even cropped from context, the unease showed through.

Cameras snapped in succession. Reporters adjusted their footing, eyes locked, hands twitching with the urge to speak.

Beside Tahir, Alexis added, "These young women were targeted and exploited." She drew a slow breath through her nose, pressing her lips together until the surge behind them stilled. "They are daughters. Sisters. Friends. Loved ones."

Then she turned toward the cameras. "We intend not only to find every last one of them, but to bring everyone responsible to justice. Fully. Without mercy."

She stepped back. Tahir followed.

From the corner of her eye, Alexis felt it. Landry's stare. A cut of cold steel, sharp enough to nick through her composure.

Captain Landry stepped in again, steady and composed, reclaiming the room. "We'll now be taking a few questions."

That's when the crowd erupted, echoing the rumors already spreading through the city.

Before a single microphone could rise, a voice broke through from behind the barricade. "That's it?"

The front row rippled with movement. Necks craned. A few people stepped aside just enough to let her through.

The woman stepped forward. Mid-forties, maybe a tad bit older, with tear tracks dried dull on her cheeks and a purse clutched so tight the straps bit into her hand. Her voice was steady but rising. "Y'all stood up there and talked about fire and evidence, but not one of you said our babies' names."

Then a man stepped beside her. Beer belly beneath a faded contractor tee, steel-toes worn to the sole. His voice came low and gravel-thick. "My girl's name is Imani Pierre. She's twenty-three. One of the toughest girls I know."

His mouth twitched. Grief tried to settle, but pride held firm. He gave a small shake of his head, the memory stinging and steadying him at the same time.

"That's my baby girl," he sniffled. "I watched her mama push her out. Watched her grow into the outstanding, overachieving young woman she is."

He looked up.

Eyes locked on Alexis's. Bloodshot. Wet at the corners. She couldn't look away.

"With all due respect." He was still holding her stare. "Don't talk to us about no damn patterns and timelines. Talk to us about action. Talk to us about resolution."

His words pinned her where she stood.

A voice from the crowd cut through. "Y'all keep patrols stacked three deep on Bourbon, but somehow no one's out here looking for these girls!"

Another followed. "How many more have to disappear before y'all start taking this seriously?"

That set off a ripple of overlapping voices, the noise rising from low chatter to a swelling wave as a woman near the barricade broke into sobs and someone else cursed under their breath.

From the podium, Superintendent Deveraux lifted a hand. "Please. Let's keep order."

But it was the next voice that brought the quiet back.

"My daughter is still out there," the woman said. "And I have cancer. I don't know how much time I've got left," she said, gripping onto the barricade, nearly leaning over the barricade.

Alexis's gaze caught on the scarf wrapped around the woman's head, the bare smoothness showing at the hairline, then dropped to the hand clenched around the barricade, knuckles whitened. She looked light enough for a hard wind to take. Beside her, a little girl no older than ten clung to her blouse with both fists.

Her voice wavered briefly. "I just need to see her again. I need to know if she's okay."

She looked at the line of officials.

"Please don't let me die not knowing where my child is."

Alexis's jaw locked and, for a moment, she couldn't feel her hands.

Then the woman who had started the commotion found her voice again. "Y'all say y'all are doing everything to find our girls, but where's the news coverage? Where are the search parties?"

A rumble spread through the crowd. Voices rose in scattered agreement.

Remorse moved her Alexis's feet. She started toward the mic, but Tahir stepped forward first.

"We're cross-referencing every girl's last known location with cellphone pings, bank activity, and social media accounts," he stated. "We're working with the state fusion center to share profiles with agencies across the Gulf region. We're checking bus depots, train stations, hospitals, and combing through surveillance footage."

Alexis steadied herself beside him, swallowing down what she couldn't say. Tahir finished. "We're exhausting every lead and following every tip."

Alexis looked at him once, then at the crowd. Her hands stayed at her sides. Fingers twitched once, then stilled. The grief she'd been hauling all week pressed through her expression, mirrored in the faces before her, each one hollowed by the same ache.

Then a voice called out, "What about Deputy Chief Gibbons?"

Captain Landry stepped back in, giving Alexis a little nudge to give her some room. "We cannot comment on that at this time."

Another reporter cut in, louder, "There are rumors those women, the Meaux sisters, were priestesses performing voodoo rituals on the girls at that manor. Can you speak to that?"

Alexis drew a breath, but Captain Landry took the mic. "There are always rumors. Voodoo, hoodoo… witchcraft. Whatever makes it easier to believe evil only looks one way." Her voice hardened. "We're focused on facts. And the facts are still under review."

"There's been speculation that the disappearances may be linked to an organized trafficking network. Is that angle being pursued?"

Landry didn't waste time with her response, "We are actively exploring several lines of inquiry, including the possibility of coordinated exploitation. But at this time, we are not in a position to confirm any specific motive or operation. The investigation is ongoing."

The murmurs flared again.

"Captain Landry, what about Abram Wallace?" a reporter called out. "His story about what happened that night has gone viral on several social media platforms. He says he was nearly sacrificed by the Meaux sisters when their house burned down. He also claims the Krewe of Blades and the Krewe of Shadows were involved, and that the woman known as 'Jade' is tied to the Krewe of Shadows. Are those krewes part of your investigation?"

Alexis's teeth pressed together. Of course, it was him. She'd saved that boy's life, and now he was out here turning trauma into headlines.

Captain Landry returned to the mic. "As we've stated," her voice flat now, "we cannot comment on any active or ongoing aspects of the case."

"So, you are investigating them?" the reporter pressed. "Are the Krewe of Shadows or the Krewe of Blades currently operating in the city? Was Mr. Wallace questioned by your department or federal partners?"

Another hand lifted. "Can you confirm whether any of the other women were also affiliated with those groups?"

But the podium mic fell silent.

Superintendent Deveraux stepped in, hand raised to settle the room. "That concludes today's press conference. Updates will be provided through official channels. If you have tips or leads, please get in touch with our Special Investigations Division or our tip line."

The reporters erupted again. Hands flying. Questions shouted. But the podium was already clearing.

Superintendent Deveraux closed his folder, Captain Landry at his side. They exited through the glass doors, their security detail falling in behind them. Tahir and Alexis trailed, slower.

At the metal barriers, Alexis paused. Tahir lingered beside her, eyes tracking the crowd. Near the front, an older woman stood with her face twisted up in disbelief, chin lifted, eyes hot with fury. "Whole press conference just to not say shit worth a damn. Waste of time!"

Tahir let out a breath and turned away. He followed the others, blending into the procession until he disappeared back inside.

Alexis stayed.

Around her, the crowd thinned. Reporters collapsed tripods, their eyes dulled now that the frenzy had passed. Families drifted back in clusters.

The space that had boiled with urgency minutes before now felt drained.

Alexis glanced once toward the stone obelisk rising over the precinct steps and the benches beside it, then turned to go. But the plaza behind her remained alive, absorbing what little energy remained.

New Orleans doesn't forget easily.

It remembers not only through headlines, but through its music, its architecture, and its burial grounds that rise like cities of their own.

Where the living come to sit with the dead, pay their last respects… or make an offering.

EPILOGUE

The chair held Alexis without comfort. She sat there quietly, feeling a pull in her shoulders that hadn't eased in weeks. The muscles kept their argument. She let them.

A faint scent of lemon polish and something green lingered close, too clean for how her mind felt, cluttered, crowded, circling the same corners. The noise of her thoughts pressed until her temples ached. She rested one elbow on the armrest and cupped her head in her palm, eyes unfocused.

"You look like you've got a lot on your mind," the woman told her.

It pulled her back.

Only then did she realize she was sitting in a different kind of room. Lamps spilled gold across a patterned rug. The glow climbed the wall, brushed a framed print, then settled on a plant in the corner. A cream sofa stretched along one side, its cushions shaped by use. Across from it sat a deep-blue chair. In it, a woman with salt-and-pepper hair, wide-framed glasses, and a warm smile watched her quietly.

"Um, I—yeah, sorry." Alexis straightened fast, tugging at the seam of her jeans, a faint warmth creeping into her cheeks.

"No need to apologize," Dr. Celestine Brooks said. "I'm glad you decided to give this another go."

"Well, I don't really have much of a choice," Alexis muttered, eyes dropping to her hands.

Dr. Brooks heard her but let it pass. "So, how's life outside of work?"

Alexis pulled her mouth into something practiced. "It's fine… just been enjoying my little 'vacation'."

Dr. Brooks noted the undertone of irritation in her voice but didn't press. "Okay. That's good. Can you tell me more?"

Alexis's gaze drifted past her, fixing on the painting hanging behind the therapist's shoulder. The colors blurred together, pulling at her thoughts, tangling them. So much she could say. So much she didn't want to say. The last thing she felt like doing was stepping into the emotional fallout the conversation would drag up.

So, she reached for something harmless. Safe. True enough.

"Finally moved back in with Tahir. Got tired of him begging." She tried to make it a joke. Dr. Brooks didn't bite, letting her sit in that uncomfortable silence. A second passed before she gave in. "He proposed. Again." Her hand lifted just enough to flash the ring, more proof than pride.

"Oh, wow. Congratulations, Alexis." Dr. Brooks offered a small, reassuring smile. Then her expression softened into focus. "I imagine that could get complicated… with him being your superior."

Alexis's eyes cut toward Dr. Brooks, for a moment before she pulled them back. Her shoulder pressed into the cushion, her body angling away just slightly. "Well, I'm not under his command anymore… I've been transferred to the Special Victims Section."

"Fitting," she replied, the slightest hint of a nod.

"Yeah. I'm a sergeant now."

"Congrats again! I knew you were holding back on me." Her voice carried a trace of wryness. "A proposal *and* a promotion… that's a lot of change, Alexis. Do you feel ready for all of it?"

"I think I am, but if Tahir were here, he'd argue otherwise."

Dr. Brooks adjusted in her chair, her voice calm. "That must stir some tension."

"Among other things," Alexis exhaled harshly. "But I know he means well. He's protective. Always has been."

Dr. Brooks let that hang for a beat. "And do you let him be? Protective, I mean. Do you trust him to handle things… handle you?"

A low sound slipped from Alexis's throat, half laugh, half scoff. "You sound just like him."

Dr. Brooks inclined her head slightly. "How does it feel hearing it from me?"

"I don't know… Like maybe he's right? Maybe he does know what's best for me, even more than I know for myself sometimes. It's like I—I act like I can handle everything on my own. But that's just out of habit. Maybe I mix up being strong with being closed off. Shit, and it probably makes him think I don't trust him… when really it's me I don't trust. I always figure I can let myself breathe after the 'danger' is over. But in the middle of it? That's when I mess up."

"Mistakes?"

Her chin dipped once in answer. "So, I just… don't breathe."

Dr. Brooks's tone stayed even. "Is that what happened at the bank robbery? Did you stop breathing then too?"

The muscles in Alexis's jaw pulled tight. She uncrossed her legs, crossed them again. "I didn't know we were going there today."

"You mentioned it last session."

"…You read the file."

"I did," Dr. Brooks confirmed. "But I'd rather hear it from you."

Her chin dipped in a faint refusal, her eyes fixed low. She inhaled once. "I put myself out there. Gambled with someone else's life because I thought I could save us all. I thought he was just misguided. But he wasn't. He was just evil." Her hand dragged across her mouth as if to press the words back, but they kept coming. "He was scared. I saw it in his eyes. He was unraveling. Kept tightening and loosening his grip on the gun, like even he didn't know what he wanted.

"I don't know… it's just—being who I am in this job? It's never simple.

Half the time, I feel like I'm proving myself to everybody. Folks in the community think I sold out. Folks at work act shocked I can actually do my job, some of them."

She rubbed her thumb across her palm, avoiding the therapist's eyes.

"I feel like… if people like me aren't in those rooms, then who's speaking for us? But that day…"

Her breath dipped.

"I saw him and thought… that could've been my cousin. My brother. Somebody I grew up with. And I hesitated. I thought I could talk him down."

Her throat worked as she swallowed. "I was wrong. I saw likeness and called it humanity. I should have judged him by his actions."

Dr. Brooks stayed quiet, letting the words settle.

Alexis's eyes dropped. "I can still see it … everything replays so damn clearly. He yells something… I can't even make it out… and then he moves fast. Knees bending. Elbow up. I don't have time to think before it's happening, and then he shoots her."

She stiffened, throat tight.

"I don't think. I just pull. We fire at the same time. His bullet hits my vest, knocks the wind clean out of me, sends me back. Mine hits him right between the eyes."

Her jaw trembled.

"And I hate saying this… but for a second? I felt something. Like relief. Or satisfaction. I don't even know. Just… something ugly."

Her voice faltered. Tears spilled, warm against her cheeks.

"Then my eyes drift a few feet over… and that feeling disappears the moment I see her."

Dr. Brooks slid a box of tissues from the end table next to her.

"Thank you." Alexis took a few from the box to dab the corners of her eyes. "You know… she didn't even scream. Isn't that a little weird?" Her voice cracked. "Pamela… that was her name. I remember the necklace. Big and bright gold lettering, like they used to wear back in the day. I saw the light strike it right before she hit the floor." Her hand pressed against her chest. "If I'd taken the shot sooner, she might still be alive. But I had to play negotiator. Had to believe in people."

Dr. Brooks let the silence stretch, giving it room to fall.

When Alexis's shoulders dipped, she spoke. "That's a heavy memory to carry." She leaned in slightly.

"What makes it worse is this last case spilling in. The faces keep changing, from Pamela to Milan, then the other girls. It's like… like my brain can't decide which one I failed first."

"When memories return this strongly, it's often trauma resurfacing. The mind fills the gaps, repeats the details, tries to stitch together what felt too much to process in the moment."

"You make it sound clinical, but there's nothing clinical about it. It's not my mind repeating… I'm reliving it. Over and over. Like it's stitched into me."

Dr. Brooks kept her tone steady. "Then let's stay with that. You've said the older case blends into the most recent one. When that happens, what comes forward from that case? What triggered you most?"

"The women who ran the Krewe of Lazuliè made us do these… I don't even know what to call them. Rituals, I guess. One was with a mirror. They'd lock us in a closet, one at a time. Alone. Just staring at ourselves. It felt like forever, even though it was only a few minutes. And I started seeing things… things I can't explain."

Dr. Brooks spoke softly. "When people are forced into isolation, it's common to start seeing or hearing things. It doesn't mean you're losing touch; it means your brain was under strain."

Alexis let out a faint sound, not quite in agreement. "Yeah… well, it wasn't just that. There were several times in that house where I saw things. Heard things… I hated staying at that place, the House of Lazuliè. Shadows looked like they were moving even when nobody was there. No matter the temperature, it always felt muggy. And the voices… the walls were leaking them. It got to the point where I didn't trust my own eyes and ears." She shook her head. "But like you said, trauma distorts things. It's just… it felt real."

"That conflict is common. You can know something isn't real and still feel it in your body as if it were. Both truths can sit side by side. Outside of here, have you told anyone about what you saw?"

"Well, Tahir, of course. And I ran the whole thing down to my sister. My grandmother overheard too. But when I told them, I made sure they knew I was clear that it was just hallucinations."

"How did they respond?"

"The typical way. Tahir brushed it off, said I'd been under too much pressure and needed to rest. Toni just stared at me, then told me to quit scaring her with that kind of talk. But my grandma? She's convinced that what I saw was real… and fussed at me about not trusting my own eyes." Alexis let out a short chuckle at that last part.

Dr. Brooks briefly shared in the laughter. "I understand that. My people are from Mississippi. I heard plenty growing up. Didn't believe it then, and I still don't now. But belief, especially when it's generational, carries weight. Once someone's set on something, it's near impossible to convince them otherwise." Her eyes stayed on Alexis. "Healing means grounding yourself in what feels true to you. If you push the unexplainable aside, it has a way of circling back."

She leaned forward slightly. "I'm not encouraging superstition. I'm saying the unresolved needs somewhere to land, or it keeps holding on." Dr. Brooks let the words settle before adding, "Ask yourself what your mind reached for in that moment. Why that picture? And if you're still not sure," she paused. "Sometimes… proof is the only way to quiet a question."

Alexis didn't respond. But something moved behind her eyes.

Dr. Brooks studied her a moment longer, then softened. "Well." She glanced at the clock. "That's all the time we have today. I think we made a lot of progress. Same time next week?"

Alexis nodded. "That works."

"I'll send it through the portal. And I'll upload a little homework for you. Nothing heavy. Just something to get you thinking before our next session." She smiled. "You did very well today. And congratulations again. On the promotion. And your engagement."

Alexis returned her smile as she stood, smoothed her pants, and slung her purse over her shoulder. At the door, her steps slowed in front of the mirror on the wall. She hadn't looked at one in weeks.

She lifted her eyes, braced for the glass to ripple or split, for her reflection's face to warp.

What looked back was only her.

Her mouth curved into a faint smirk as she tucked a braid behind her ear, then she dropped her gaze and pushed through the door.

Outside, she slid into her Impala. The sun had fallen low, streaking the windshield in red. Her phone buzzed in the cupholder. A text preview lit the screen. She didn't open it. Instead, she picked up the phone and called Tahir.

He answered quickly. "Hey. You good?"

"Yeah." She hesitated, then added, "Just… thank you. For pushing me to do this. For not letting up. I needed it more than I wanted to admit."

The line was quiet, then his voice returned, lower. "You sure?"

She swallowed. "Yeah. I'm sure."

"I love you."

Her lips curved faintly. "I love you too. And I'm making your favorite tonight: steak, potatoes… a little asparagus."

"Ooh, alright then." His smile carried through the line. "Somebody's in a good mood." That pulled a chuckle out of her. "Oh, sweetheart! Can you send me a pic of that paint you wanted for the accent wall? You told me to get mauve, but I don't know colors like that, and I'm not trying to get cursed out for coming home with the wrong shade."

Her laugh loosened this time. "You definitely would walk in with neon pink. I'ma send it right now, babe."

She ended the call and thumbed open her gallery. Images slid past beneath her finger. She stopped on one. Tahir, mid-laugh, head tipped back, mouth wide, eyes nearly shut. Her thumb hovered there, the corners of her own mouth tugging upward before she swiped again.

The following image opened, daylight spilling over Alexis, Raven, and Jennifer's faces, drawn close to fit the frame. She swiped, and another surfaced, Raven at her shoulder again, Jade leaning in from the edge.

Her thumb lingered a moment longer over Jade's face before she swiped hard, tension creeping up her neck. She kept going.

A gravesite filled the screen.

The mirror lay flat in front of it, waiting, its glass holding the sky. Along the wooden frame, the chant had been scrawled across every side.

She scrolled again.

Then came a shot of the blue vase brimming with blackened water.

She stopped when she reached the doll.

A pressure rose in her chest, tugging hard at something she'd kept buried. She pressed her hand there, trying to ease it.

In that stillness, a thought uncoiled, and she had to see it for herself. In person.

Alexis hit the doors, slipped through like a riptide cutting into the chorus of voices, phones, and boots scuffing tile. The front desk loomed ahead, but she was already angling right, card in hand.

The reader's light glowed red. She pressed her card against it, and the green light lit up; the lock clicked, and the door opened. She stepped through, briefly shivering as a chill brushed her skin.

She kept her stride down the hall, eyes forward, until a door opened a few doors in on the right.

Detectives filled the room, some seated, others propped against desks in loose clusters. At the front, Detective Stewart led the lineup, posture crisp. She caught sight of Alexis the moment she stepped through the door.

"Rochon!" Stewart's voice lifted, bright, almost sing-song, too friendly for the woman saying it. "Didn't expect to see you back for months."

Alexis kept her line. Past the desks. Past the stares. Past Stewart.

"Bitch!" Stewart muttered.

The hallway opened again, chatter thinning behind her until it broke into the sealed hush of the Evidence Room.

The chemical bite hit fast, a stench she never got used to. She pinched the sting off and pressed on, eyes locking on the mark she'd come for.

Box 47B.

She pulled it from the shelf and carried it to the steel table ahead. A box of gloves waited there. She slipped a pair on, latex snapping tight, then dragged the box closer.

Inside was a clipboard, a ballpoint pen dangling from a short ball-chain. She picked it up, ready to sign… until something stopped her.

Her name capped the log, letters pressed hard into the page.

This doesn't make sense. I haven't been to Evidence since I went undercover.

She shoved the clipboard aside and left the pen where it hung.

Shoulders tight, muscles drawn in, she reached back into the box.

She pushed aside evidence sleeves and numbered tags, rummaging without care for neatness. Her hand stopped on a clear bag filled with navy wax-sealed envelopes. She slid one free and broke the seal, the paper tearing under her thumb.

Inside was a single index card.

The handwriting caught her at once, letters pressed hard into the page, every curve and line familiar.

I am enough.

She remembered the heaviness of the pen, how she had carved the words into the card, forcing them steady while her hand trembled. The feeling threatened to surface, but she shoved it back where it came from.

She slid the card into its envelope and set it aside, reaching deeper into the box.

And then she saw it.

This time, not through a screen.

She reached in and picked it up. The weight startled her. Her thumb grazed the pin buried deep in its fabric, the red bead, fresh-blood bright.

She turned it over before her eyes could settle on the paper the pin kept fixed on the doll. That riddle. She had grown tired of seeing it.

No stitches across the back, only brown cloth unevenly patched.

Her finger traced one braid down to the end before she flipped it upside down.

That's when she spotted it.

The seam at its bottom gaped slightly, thread pulled thin and frayed. She pressed her finger into the opening and felt something tucked inside.

Curiosity nipped at her as she worked the object free.

It was a thick piece of paper folded once into a square, its edges softened from being handled too many times. The fold line had nearly worn through, a pale scar dividing the paper in two.

As she worked it open, something slipped free and dropped to the floor.

She pinned the paper to the back of the doll with her thumb and bent to pick it up.

It was a hot pink hair tie.

She brought it to her nose. Peppermint. Tea tree. Unmistakable.

She bit her bottom lip and tucked the hair tie into her pocket, then looked back at the paper still pinned against the doll.

Red strokes bled through, puckering the back.

She stared at the letters.

ALEXIS

Her knees dipped. She shoved the paper back into the seam, fumbling, as if hiding it might erase what she'd read.

Then she turned the doll over one last time.

Seven moons. Seven Boons. Seven gates. Seven tombs.

The chant caught her first, but something else pulled harder.

That pin. Still there, lodged deep.

Her fingers tightened. She hesitated.

What if that pin was the only thread keeping her together… or worse, fastening something else to her?

She fixed on the holes ripped into the doll's face. The hollows seemed to sink deeper, shadows pooling inward.

Then the fabric darkened, cotton soaking until the pits shone wet. It swelled. Black rising slow, thick, and tar-slick until it spilled down her fingers.

"The fuck?"

Her hands jerked into view. The goo smeared her skin, slick to the touch.

Her pulse rattled as the black crept lower, past the cuffs of her gloves, dragging toward her wrists.

She flung the doll to the floor and scrubbed her palms hard against her jeans. Looked again.

The black gook was gone. Not a single trace of it remained.

She blinked hard, staring at her hands, at the floor, at the doll.

"Did I…?" Her mind was trying to knit the moment into something that made sense, but nothing did.

On the floor, the doll waited, hollows stuffed with clean cotton, that tiny curved red line of a mouth unmoved.

Still shaken, she reached down. Fingers closed around the limp body as she picked it back up.

The pin remained, its red tip bright against the brown felt, stubborn as a thorn.

She gripped the ball of the pin between thumb and finger and braced.

For a jolt. For pain. For release. Maybe nothing at all.

She held it a moment longer.

Then pulled.

Sometimes… proof is the only way to quiet a question.

ACKNOWLEDGMENTS

For everyone who held a light while I built this world, thank you.

The support of early readers and new believers of *The Krewe* played a meaningful role in bringing this project to life. Your encouragement motivated me to keep writing when moments became too overwhelming.

I'd like to acknowledge a few people whose contributions stood out in specific ways.

Thank you, Marchelle Davis, for being my very first beta reader and for helping me see the Blue Hearts as fully realized characters rather than background figures. Your insight, care, and long-standing friendship mean more to me than I can fully put into words.

Another person who showed up early and often for this book is Bronwyn Ware. Your engagement, feedback, and encouragement helped move this story forward, and I thank you for that.

Kevia Dauphiney, you deserve special thanks for your unwavering attention to detail. Your ability to catch cultural nuance, character consistency, and continuity errors helped to strengthen this story so much.

Kylee McCumber, your encouragement and general support throughout this process meant more than I can easily say. The way you showed up for this book made the journey feel far less solitary.

Thank you, Quaniqua Epps-Brown, for the care, intention, and professionalism you bring to everything you do. The thoughtfulness behind your content is evident, and I appreciate the way you show up for writers like myself.

CLASSIC XVII PUBLISHING
READER CIRCLE COMPANION

The Krewe
House of Lazuliè

A Novel
E. Lane Redmond

This Reader Circle Companion was created to help spark reflection and conversation after reading *The Krewe – House of Lazuliè.*

Inside are discussion questions and pathways for deeper exploration that touch on the real histories, rituals, and beliefs that shaped the story.

Whether you are meeting in a book club or reading alone with a candle burning low, may these pages guide you further into the heart of the House.

FOR DISCUSSION

1. What does the House of Lazuliè come to represent by the end of the novel?

2. How does Alexis's belief in logic and evidence change over the course of the story?

3. How do Nevi, Rae, and Della use ritual, control, and sisterhood to hold power?

4. How does the novel connect modern exploitation to the history of plaçage and enslavement?

5. How does the novel make the reader question what Alexis is truly experiencing?

6. How do race, gender, duty, and justice shape Alexis's choices?

7. How is grief shown in different characters throughout the novel?

8. What truth does Alexis carry with her after the fire?

9. What ideas or emotions stay with the reader most strongly by the end of the novel?

10. What question would you ask Alexis after finishing the book?

AUTHOR'S REFLECTION

I wanted to write about the ghosts we carry with us: the ones in our families and the ones buried beneath the streets of New Orleans. This book explores what happens when beauty becomes a form of currency, and when survival demands its own kind of faith.

I was also drawn to the subtle war between generations, how youth and age often stand on opposite sides of the same mirror. The old guard clings to its prime, desperate to hold onto power even when the world is asking it to change. Meanwhile, the young overlook their elders, forgetting that wisdom is not always loud, soft, or easy to recognize. Both sides hold truth, and both suffer when they refuse to meet each other halfway.

And then there's Mardi Gras, my city's crown and disguise. It's joy and spectacle, but it's also chaotic and claustrophobic. I wanted to write about that duality, to explore what happens when celebration turns into excess, when beauty becomes bait, and when a city built on ritual and rhythm begins to dance too close to sin.

New Orleans is a place of history and horror. *The Krewe - House of Lazuliè* taps into both.

ABOUT THE AUTHOR

E. Lane Redmond is a Southern Gothic novelist whose stories delve into inheritance and the generational traumas that shape womanhood.

Her debut in The Krewe series, The Krewe – House of Lazuliè, reimagines her 2020 novella The Krewe of Heaux. Originally intended as a simple anniversary expansion, the project evolved into something entirely new. It became a full-length novel pulsing with darker mystery, richer lore, and deeper emotional resonance. What started as a return to familiar ground revealed a far more layered world than the author ever expected.

Writing has always been her sacred space. A self-proclaimed shy soul, she found her voice through vivid storytelling. Her work invites readers into places where beauty, horror, and healing walk hand in hand.

CONNECT WITH THE AUTHOR

For updates on upcoming releases, events, book boxes, appearances, and future entries in *The Krewe* series, visit:

elaneredmond.com

Facebook: **Author E. Lane Redmond**
Instagram: **e.laneredmond**
TikTok: **e.laneredmond**

JOIN THE KREWE

CHARACTER EVOLUTION

The Madames of Lazuliè

The earliest visual concepts for the Madames were sketched by my father in 2020, when the first version of this story existed under a different name. As the world of Lazuliè deepened and transformed, so did the Madames themselves. These updated renderings reflect their final forms in The Krewe - House of Lazuliè; mythic, modern, and fully stepped into their power.

This section preserves the lineage of their evolution.

Original concept sketch of Madame Nevi – 2020.

Official rendering of Madame Nevi – 2025

Nevi's Evolution:

Nevi has always held the heart of the House. The original sketch captured her elegance and authority, but her final form deepens those elements: her face serene yet unreadable, her beauty sharpened by devotion and danger. This rendering embodies the Nevi who keeps the House breathing.

Original concept sketch of Madame Della – 2020

Official rendering of Madame Della – 2025.

Della's Evolution:
Her earliest design emphasized severity and ritual strength. As the House evolved, Della's appearance sharpened. Her locs lengthened, her posture became more regal, and the quiet fury beneath her spirit took shape. This final rendering reflects the Della who rules through silence, discipline, and an unbreakable spine.

Original concept sketch of Madame Rae – 2020

Official rendering of Madame Rae – 2025.

Rae's Evolution:
Rae's first design showed her raw intensity with a high tangle of locs and bone accents that marked her quiet menace. As her character sharpened, so did her look. The loc bun transformed into sculpted finger waves, a style that reflects her precision and controlled power. This final rendering captures the Rae who moves with calm authority, holding the House's deepest secrets.

The House of Lazuliè
Alexis's Sketches

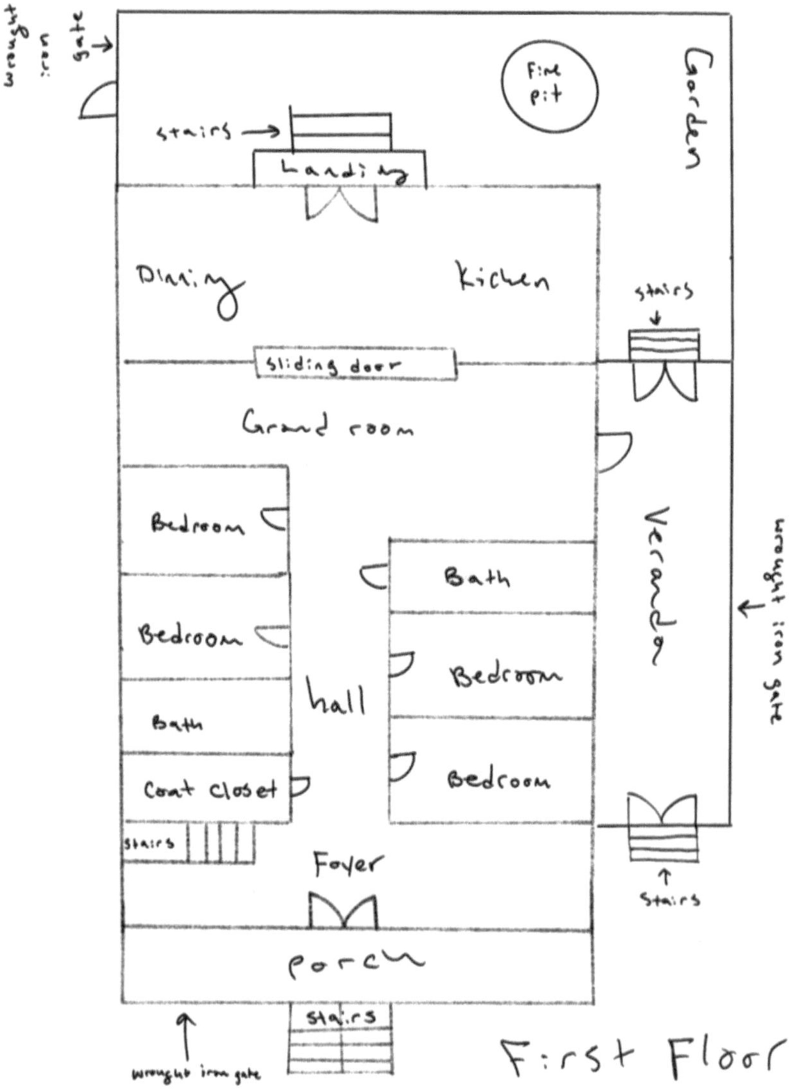
wrought iron gate
Fire pit
Garden
stairs
Landing
Dining
Kitchen
stairs
sliding door
Grand room
Bedroom
Bedroom
Bath
Coat closet
stairs
hall
Bath
Bedroom
Bedroom
Veranda
wrought iron gate
Foyer
stairs
porch
stairs
wrought iron gate
First Floor

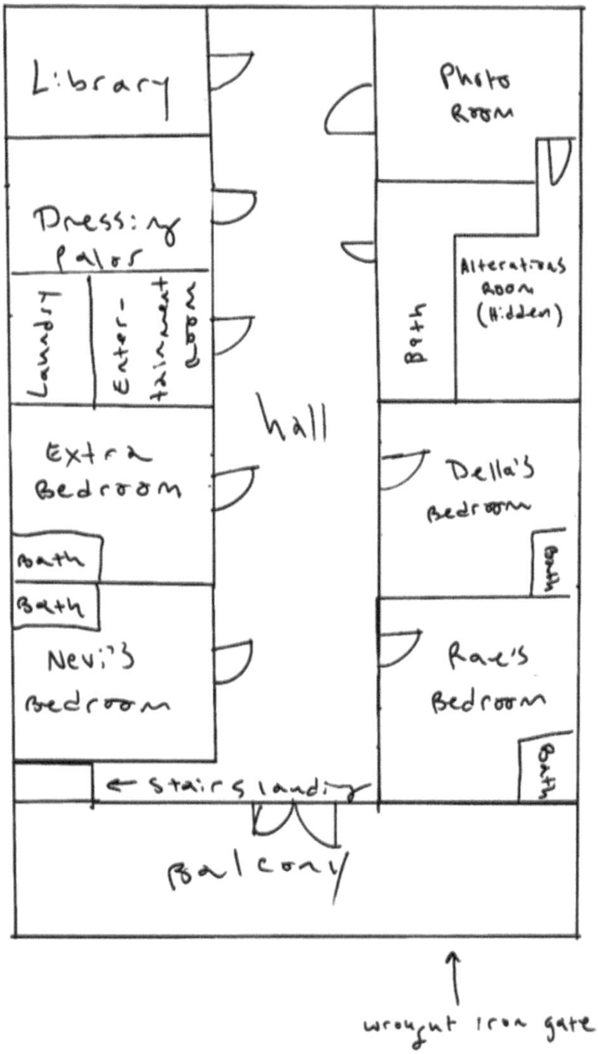

Second Floor